PENGUIN TWEN[...]

THE [...]

AND [...]

David Herbert Lawrence w[...]
shire, in 1885, fourth of t[...]
middle-class wife. He atter[...]gn ocnool and
Nottingham University College. His first novel, *The White Pea-cock*, was published in 1911, just a few weeks after the death of his mother to whom he had been abnormally close. At this time he finally ended his relationship with Jessie Chambers (the Miriam of *Sons and Lovers*) and became engaged to Louie Burrows. His career as a schoolteacher was ended in 1911 by the illness which was ultimately diagnosed as tuberculosis.

In 1912 Lawrence eloped to Germany with Frieda Weekley, the German wife of his former modern languages tutor. They were married on their return to England in 1914. Lawrence was now living, precariously, by his writing. His greatest novels, *The Rainbow* and *Women in Love*, were completed in 1915 and 1916. The former was suppressed, and he could not find a publisher for the latter.

After the war Lawrence began his 'savage pilgrimage' in search of a more fulfilling mode of life than industrial Western civilization could offer. This took him to Sicily, Ceylon, Australia and, finally, New Mexico. The Lawrences returned to Europe in 1925. Lawrence's last novel, *Lady Chatterley's Lover*, was banned in 1928, and his paintings confiscated in 1919. He died in Vence in 1930 at the age of 44.

Lawrence spent most of his short life living. Nevertheless he produced an amazing quantity of work – novels, stories, poems, plays, essays, travel books, translations and letters . . . After his death Frieda wrote: 'What he had seen and felt and known he gave in his writing to his fellow men, the splendour of living, the hope of more and more life . . . a heroic and immeasurable gift.'

THE MORTAL COIL

AND OTHER STORIES

... was born at Eastwood, Nottingham-
... the five children of a miner and his
... (1898), attended Nottingham High School ...

D. H. LAWRENCE

The Mortal Coil
AND OTHER STORIES

Edited by Keith Sagar

PENGUIN BOOKS
in association with William Heinemann Ltd

PENGUIN BOOKS

Published by the Penguin Group
Penguin Books Ltd, 27 Wrights Lane, London w8 5tz, England
Viking Penguin, a division of Penguin Books USA Inc.
375 Hudson Street, New York, New York 10014, USA
Penguin Books Australia Ltd, Ringwood, Victoria, Australia
Penguin Books Canada Ltd, 2801 John Street, Markham, Ontario, Canada l3r 1b4
Penguin Books (NZ) Ltd, 182–190 Wairau Road, Auckland 10, New Zealand

Penguin Books Ltd, Registered Offices: Harmondsworth, Middlesex, England

'A Prelude' was first published in the *Nottinghamshire Guardian* 7 December 1907;
'The Miner at Home' in the *Nation* 16 March 1912;
'The Fly in the Ointment' in the *New Statesman* 16 August 1913;
'Her Turn' in the *Saturday Westminster Gazette* 6 September 1913;
'The Thimble' in *Seven Arts* March 1917;
'The Mortal Coil' in *Seven Arts* July 1917;
'Adolf' in *The Dial* September 1920; 'Rex' in *The Dial* February 1921;
'A Chapel and a Hay Hut Among the Mountains' and 'Once' in *Love Among the Haystacks*
(Nonesuch Press, 1930);
'The Witch à la Mode' in Lovat Dickinson's Magazine June 1934;
'The Old Adam' and 'New Eve and Old Adam' in *A Modern Lover* (Secker, 1934);
'Delilah and Mr Bircumshaw' in *Virginia Quarterly* Spring 1940;
'Lessford's Rabbits' and 'A Lesson on a Tortoise' in *Phoenix 2* (Heinemann 1968).

This collection published in Penguin Books 1971
10

Printed in England by Clays Ltd, St Ives plc
Set in Monotype Garamond

*D. H. Lawrence's complete
short stories are also available in Canada
in a Viking/Compass edition*

Contents

Introduction

THIS volume and its companion *The Princess and Other Stories* complete the publication of Lawrence's shorter fiction in Penguin.

The first two sketches are reminiscences of childhood written in middle life. 'Adolf' was written for Lawrence's friend John Middleton Murry when he became editor of *The Athenaeum* in 1919. But, despite Lawrence's willingness to be 'pleasant and a bit old-fashioned' and even to publish under a pseudonym, Murry rejected this harmless sketch as 'unsuitable' for the Great British Public, presumably because it contains the word 'merde', thus shattering Lawrence's hopes of a fruitful collaboration with him and of a steady income from *The Athenaeum*. The following year 'Adolf' was accepted by *The Dial*, for which Lawrence then wrote 'Rex' as a companion piece.

The remaining fourteen stories and sketches were all written in Lawrence's twenties. In them we can trace his development from his first published story, 'A Prelude', and the somewhat callow pieces of the Croydon period, to the mature and tragic art of 'The Mortal Coil'.

In 1907, when Lawrence was twenty-two, the *Nottinghamshire Guardian* offered a prize of three pounds for the best Christmas story. There were three categories, an Amusing Adventure, a Legend, and an Enjoyable Christmas, and Lawrence wrote a story in each: 'The White Stocking', 'Legend', and 'A Prelude to a Happy Christmas'. One person was allowed to enter only one story, but Lawrence cheated by persuading Louie Burrows to submit 'The White Stocking' in her name and Jessie Chambers 'A Prelude' in hers, while Lawrence himself submitted 'Legend'. 'A Prelude' won and was published in the *Nottinghamshire Guardian* on 7 December 1907. The other stories were subsequently rewritten and included in *The Prussian Officer*, 'Legend' under a new title 'A Fragment of Stained Glass'. Lawrence had no regard for 'A Prelude' and towards the end of his life expressed the hope that it had 'gone to glory in the absolute sense'.

From 1908 to 1911 Lawrence taught at Davidson Road School, Croydon, and lodged with Mr and Mrs Jones and their baby daughter Hilda Mary in Colworth Road. The next five pieces date from this period.

7

Shortly before the death of his mother, in December 1910, Lawrence had ended his long engagement to Jessie Chambers and become engaged to Louie Burrows. He continued to see Jessie, and also formed an intimate relationship with Helen Corke in London. But Lawrence was not able to bring any of these relationships on to a satisfactory sexual footing. The frustration contributed to the breakdown in his health at the end of 1911 which forced him to leave the teaching profession. Lawrence's overwrought state at this time is evident in both 'The Old Adam' and 'The Witch à la Mode.'

'The Miner at Home' and 'Her Turn' were occasioned by the strike situation of February 1912, and 'Delilah and Mr Bircumshaw' was written about the same time.

In the spring of 1912 Lawrence and Frieda Weekley, the wife of Professor Ernest Weekley who had taught him modern languages at Nottingham University College, ran away to Germany together to begin a relationship which was to last the rest of Lawrence's life. After spending June and July at Icking, near Munich, Lawrence and Frieda set off on 5 August to walk over the Tyrolese Alps to Mayrhofen, near Innsbruck. 'A Chapel and a Hay Hut among the Mountains' describes the first day and night of that walk. 'Once' appears to follow straight on, with the same characters still in the Tyrol, but Anita's past is not Frieda's; it is closer to her younger sister's. In 'New Eve and Old Adam' the characters are again clearly Lawrence and Frieda, though the incident is probably fictional.

In July 1913 Lawrence wrote: 'Edward Marsh came on Sunday and he took us in to tea with the Herbert Asquiths – jolly nice folk – son of the Prime Minister.' At the outbreak of war Herbert Asquith became a subaltern in the Royal Artillery. He was hit by a flying splinter from a shell burst and sent home. 'The Thimble' is about this incident. In October 1915 Lawrence sent the Ms. to Lady Cynthia Asquith:

This is the story: I don't know what you'll think of it. The fact of resurrection, in this life, is all in all to me now. I don't know what the story is like, as a story. I don't want to read it over – not yet. Send it back to me soon, will you, and tell me what you think of it. Then I can see if it is fit to be typed and offered to an editor, though who will print it, God knows. If you like – if you want the Ms. when I have got typed copies, I will give it you. The fact of resurrection is everything now: whether we dead can rise from the dead and love, and live, in a new life, here.

I tremble very much in front of this. If it could come to pass, one would give anything. If it cannot come to pass, one must go away: you and your

8

husband also. Having known this death, one cannot remain in death. That were profanity. One must go away.

If the war could but end this winter, we might rise to life again, here in this our world. If it sets in for another year, all is lost. One should give anything now, give the Germans England and the whole empire, if they want it, so we may save the hope of a resurrection from the dead, we English, all Europe. What is the whole empire, and kingdom, save the thimble in my story? If we could but bring our souls through, to life.

The following day Lady Cynthia made this entry in her diary:

Lawrence's story arrived by the morning post. It is called The Thimble and is extremely well written, I think, though the symbolism of the thimble is somewhat obscure. I *was* amused to see the 'word-picture' of me. He has quite gratuitously put in the large feet. I think some of his character hints are damnably good. He has kept fairly close to the model in the circumstances.

Lawrence later expressed the hope that it might 'disappear into oblivion'; but it seems to me in some ways preferable to 'The Ladybird' which apparently grew out of it.

'The Mortal Coil', written in Italy before the war and based on an experience of Frieda's father, was rewritten in October 1916. The protagonist, Friedeburg, like Skrebensky in *The Rainbow* and Gerald Crich in *Women in Love*, suffers and causes suffering because he lacks the Lawrentian strengths – independence and integrity. Nevertheless Lawrence writes of him with an unusual depth of inwardness, understanding and compassion. Although in this story Lawrence specifically exculpates God, we seem to be in a Hardy-like world where tragedy, oblivious of human values, hunts down the truly living and leaves the dead to inherit the earth. Lawrence called 'The Mortal Coil' 'a first-class story, one of my purest creations' yet it was never included in any of the collections of short stories published in his lifetime, or, indeed, since.

KEITH SAGAR

Adolf

WHEN we were children our father often worked on the night-shift. Once it was spring-time, and he used to arrive home, black and tired, just as we were downstairs in our nightdresses. Then night met morning face to face, and the contact was not always happy. Perhaps it was painful to my father to see us gaily entering upon the day into which he dragged himself soiled and weary. He didn't like going to bed in the spring morning sunshine.

But sometimes he was happy, because of his long walk through the dewy fields in the first daybreak. He loved the open morning, the crystal and the space, after a night down pit. He watched every bird, every stir in the trembling grass, answered the whinnying of the peewits and tweeted to the wrens. If he could, he also would have whinnied and tweeted and whistled in a native language that was not human. He liked non-human things best.

One sunny morning we were all sitting at table when we heard his heavy slurring walk up the entry. We became uneasy. His was always a disturbing presence, trammelling. He passed the window darkly, and we heard him go into the scullery and put down his tin bottle. But directly he came into the kitchen. We felt at once that he had something to communicate. No one spoke. We watched his black face for a second.

'Give me a drink,' he said.

My mother hastily poured out his tea. He went to pour it out into his saucer. But instead of drinking he suddenly put something on the table among the teacups. A tiny brown rabbit! A small rabbit, a mere morsel, sitting against the bread as still as if it were a made thing.

'A rabbit! A young one! Who gave it you, Father?'

But he laughed enigmatically, with a sliding motion of his yellow-grey eyes, and went to take off his coat. We pounced on the rabbit.

'Is it alive? Can you feel its heart beat?'

My father came back and sat down heavily in his arm-chair. He dragged his saucer to him, and blew his tea, pushing out his red lips under his black moustache.

'Where did you get it, Father?'

'I picked it up,' he said, wiping his naked forearm over his mouth and beard.

'Where?'

'It is a wild one!' came my mother's quick voice.

'Yes, it is.'

'Then why did you bring it?' cried my mother.

'Oh, we wanted it,' came our cry.

'Yes, I've no doubt you did –' retorted my mother. But she was drowned in our clamour of questions.

On the field path my father had found a dead mother rabbit and three dead little ones – this one alive, but unmoving.

'But what had killed them, Daddy?'

'I couldn't say, my child. I s'd think she'd aten something.'

'Why did you bring it!' again my mother's voice of condemnation. 'You know what it will be.'

My father made no answer, but we were loud in protest.

'He must bring it. It's not big enough to live by itself. It would die,' we shouted.

'Yes, and it will die now. And then there'll be *another* outcry.'

My mother set her face against the tragedy of dead pets. Our hearts sank.

'It won't die, Father, will it? Why will it? It won't.'

'I s'd think not,' said my father.

'You know well enough it will. Haven't we had it all before!' said my mother.

'They dunna always pine,' replied my father testily.

But my mother reminded him of other little wild animals he had brought, which had sulked and refused to live, and brought storms of tears and trouble in our house of lunatics.

Trouble fell on us. The little rabbit sat on our lap, unmoving, its eye wide and dark. We brought it milk, warm milk, and held it to its nose. It sat as still as if it was far away, retreated down some deep burrow, hidden, oblivious. We wetted its mouth and whiskers with drops of milk. It gave no sign, did not even shake off the wet white drops. Somebody began to shed a few secret tears.

'What did I say?' cried my mother. 'Take it and put it down in the field.'

Her command was in vain. We were driven to get dressed for school. There sat the rabbit. It was like a tiny obscure cloud. Watching it, the emotions died out of our breast. Useless to love it, to yearn over it. Its little feelings were all ambushed. They must be circumvented. Love and affection were a trespass upon it. A little wild thing, it became more mute and asphyxiated still in its own arrest, when we approached with love. We must not love it. We must circumvent it, for its own existence.

So I passed the order to my sister and my mother. The rabbit was not to be spoken to, nor even looked at. Wrapping it in a piece of flannel I put it in an obscure corner of the cold parlour, and put a saucer of milk before its nose. My mother was forbidden to enter the parlour while we were at school.

'As if I should take any notice of your nonsense,' she cried affronted. Yet I doubt if she ventured into the parlour.

At midday, after school, creeping into the front room, there we saw the rabbit still and unmoving in the piece of flannel. Strange grey-brown neutralization of life, still living! It was a sore problem to us.

'Why won't it drink its milk, Mother?' we whispered. Our father was asleep.

'It prefers to sulk its life away, silly little thing.' A profound problem. Prefers to sulk its life away! We put young dandelion leaves to its nose. The sphinx was not more oblivious. Yet its eye was bright.

At tea-time, however, it had hopped a few inches, out of its flannel, and there it sat again, uncovered, a little solid cloud of muteness, brown, with unmoving whiskers. Only its side palpitated slightly with life.

Darkness came; my father set off to work. The rabbit was still unmoving. Dumb despair was coming over the sisters, a threat of tears before bed-time. Clouds of my mother's anger gathered as she muttered against my father's wantonness.

Once more the rabbit was wrapped in the old pit-singlet. But now it was carried into the scullery and put under the copper fire-place, that it might imagine itself inside a burrow. The saucers were placed about, four or five, here and there on the floor, so that if the little creature *should* chance to hop abroad, it could not fail to come upon some food. After this my mother was allowed to take from the scullery what she wanted and then she was forbidden to open the door.

When morning came and it was light, I went downstairs. Opening the scullery door, I heard a slight scuffle. Then I saw dabbles of milk all over the floor and tiny rabbit-droppings in the saucers. And there the miscreant, the tips of his ears showing behind a pair of boots. I peeped at him. He sat bright-eyed and askance, twitching his nose and looking at me while not looking at me.

He was alive – very much alive. But still we were afraid to trespass much on his confidence.

'Father!' My father was arrested at the door. 'Father, the rabbit's alive.'

'Back your life it is,' said my father.

'Mind how you go in.'

By evening, however, the little creature was tame, quite tame. He was christened Adolf. We were enchanted by him. We couldn't really love him, because he was wild and loveless to the end. But he was an unmixed delight.

We decided he was too small to live in a hutch – he must live at large in the house. My mother protested, but in vain. He was so tiny. So we had him upstairs, and he dropped his tiny pills on the bed and we were enchanted.

Adolf made himself instantly at home. He had the run of the house, and was perfectly happy, with his tunnels and his holes behind the furniture.

We loved him to take meals with us. He would sit on the table humping his back, sipping his milk, shaking his whiskers and his tender ears, hopping off and hobbling back to his saucer, with an air of supreme unconcern. Suddenly he was alert. He hobbled a few tiny paces, and reared himself up inquisitively at the sugar basin. He fluttered his tiny fore-paws, and then reached and laid them on the edge of the basin, while he craned his thin neck and peeped in. He trembled his whiskers at the sugar, then did his best to lift down a lump.

'*Do* you think I will have it! Animals in the sugar pot!' cried my mother, with a rap of her hand on the table.

Which so delighted the electric Adolf that he flung his hind-quarters and knocked over a cup.

'It's your own fault, Mother. If you left him alone –'

He continued to take tea with us. He rather liked warm tea. And he loved sugar. Having nibbled a lump, he would turn to the butter. There he was shooed off by our parent.

He soon learned to treat her shooing with indifference. Still, she hated him to put his nose in the food. And he loved to do it. And one day between them they over-turned the cream-jug. Adolf deluged his little chest, bounced back in terror, was seized by his little ears by my mother and bounced down on the hearth-rug. There he shivered in momentary discomfort, and suddenly set off in a wild flight to the parlour.

This last was his happy hunting ground. He had culti-vated the bad habit of pensively nibbling certain bits of cloth in the hearth-rug. When chased from this pasture he would retreat under the sofa. There he would twinkle in Buddhist meditation until suddenly, no one knew why, he would go off like an alarm clock. With a sudden bumping scuffle he would whirl out of the room, going through the doorway with his little ears flying. Then we would hear his thunderbolt hurtling in the parlour, but before we could follow, the wild streak of Adolf would flash past us, on an electric wind that swept him round the scullery and carried him back, a little mad thing, flying possessed like a ball round the parlour. After which ebullition he would sit in a corner composed and distant, twitching his whiskers in abstract meditation. And it was in vain we questioned him about his outbursts. He just went off like a gun, and was as calm after it as a gun that smokes placidly.

Alas, he grew up rapidly. It was almost impossible to keep him from the outer door.

One day, as we were playing by the stile, I saw his brown shadow loiter across the road and pass into the field that faced the houses. Instantly a cry of 'Adolf!' – a cry he knew full well. And instantly a wind swept him away down the sloping meadow, his tail twinkling and zig-zagging through the grass. After him we pelted. It was a strange sight to see him, ears back, his little loins so powerful, flinging the world behind him. We ran ourselves out of breath, but could not catch him. Then somebody headed him off, and he sat with sudden unconcern, twitching his nose under a bunch of nettles.

His wanderings cost him a shock. One Sunday morning my father had just been quarrelling with a pedlar, and we were hearing the aftermath indoors, when there came a sudden unearthly scream from the yard. We flew out. There sat Adolf cowering under a bench, while a great black and white cat glowered intently at him, a few yards away. Sight not to be forgotten. Adolf rolling back his eyes and parting his strange muzzle in another scream, the cat stretching forward in a slow elongation.

Ha, how we hated that cat! How we pursued him over the chapel wall and across the neighbours' gardens.

Adolf was still only half grown.

'Cats!' said my mother. 'Hideous detestable animals, why do people harbour them?'

But Adolf was becoming too much for her. He dropped too many pills. And suddenly to hear him clumping downstairs when she was alone in the house was startling. And to keep him from the door was impossible. Cats prowled outside. It was worse than having a child to look after.

Yet we would not have him shut up. He became more lusty, more callous than ever. He was a strong kicker, and many a scratch on face and arms did we owe to him. But he brought his own doom on himself. The lace curtains in the parlour – my mother was rather proud of them – fell on the floor very full. One of Adolf's joys was to scuffle wildly through them as though through some foamy undergrowth. He had already torn rents in them.

One day he entangled himself altogether. He kicked, he whirled round in a mad nebulous inferno. He screamed – and brought down the curtain-rod with a smash, right on the best beloved pelargonium, just as my mother rushed in. She extricated him, but she never forgave him. And he never forgave either. A heartless wildness had come over him.

Even we understood that he must go. It was decided, after a long deliberation, that my father should carry him back to the wild-woods. Once again he was stowed into the great pocket of the pit-jacket.

'Best pop him i' th' pot,' said my father, who enjoyed raising the wind of indignation.

And so, next day, our father said that Adolf, set down on the edge of the coppice, had hopped away with utmost indifference, neither elated nor moved. We heard it and believed. But many, many were the heartsearchings. How would the other rabbits receive him? Would they smell his tameness, his humanized degradation, and rend him? My mother pooh-poohed the extravagant idea.

However, he was gone, and we were rather relieved. My father kept an eye open for him. He declared that several times passing the coppice in the early morning, he had seen Adolf peeping through the nettle-stalks. He had called him, in an odd, high-voiced, cajoling fashion. But Adolf had not responded. Wildness gains so soon upon its creatures. And they become so contemptuous then of our tame presence. So it seemed to me. I myself would go to the edge of the coppice, and call softly. I myself would imagine bright eyes between the nettle-stalks, flash of a white, scornful tail past the bracken. That insolent white tail, as Adolf turned his flank on us! It reminded me always of a certain rude gesture, and a certain unprintable phrase, which may not even be suggested.

But when naturalists discuss the meaning of the rabbit's white tail, that rude gesture and still ruder phrase always come to my mind. Naturalists say that the rabbit shows his white tail in order to guide his young safely after him,

as a nursemaid's flying strings are the signal to her todd-
ling charges to follow on. How nice and naïve! I only
know that my Adolf wasn't naïve. He used to whisk his
flank at me, push his white feather in my eye, and say
'*Merde!*' It's a rude word – but one which Adolf was
always semaphoring at me, flag-wagging it with all the
derision of his narrow haunches.

That's a rabbit all over – insolence, and the white flag of
spiteful derision. Yes, and he keeps his flag flying to the
bitter end, sporting, insolent little devil that he is. See him
running for his life. Oh, how his soul is fanned to an
ecstasy of fright, a fugitive whirl-wind of panic. Gone
mad, he throws the world behind him, with astonishing
hind legs. He puts back his head and lays his ears on his
sides and rolls the white of his eyes in sheer ecstatic agony
of speed. He knows the awful approach behind him;
bullet or stoat. He knows! He knows, his eyes are turned
back almost into his head. It is agony. But it is also ecstasy.
Ecstasy! See the insolent white flag bobbing. He whirls
on the magic wind of terror. All his pent-up soul rushes
into agonized electric emotion of fear. He flings himself
on, like a falling star swooping into extinction. White
heat of the agony of fear. And at the same time, bob! bob!
bob! goes the white tail, *merde! merde! merde!* it says to the
pursuer. The rabbit can't help it. In his utmost extremity
he still flings the insult at the pursuer. He is the incon-
querable fugitive, the indomitable meek. No wonder the
stoat becomes vindictive.

And if he escapes, this precious rabbit! Don't you see
him sitting there, in his earthly nook, a little ball of silence
and rabbit triumph? Don't you see the glint on his black
eye? Don't you see, in his very immobility, how the whole
world is *merde* to him? No conceit like the conceit of the
meek. And if the avenging angel in the shape of the
ghostly ferret steals down on him, there comes a shriek of

terror out of that little hump of self-satisfaction sitting motionless in a corner. Falls the fugitive. But even fallen, his white feather floats. Even in death it seems to say: 'I am the meek, I am the righteous, I am the rabbit. All you rest, you are evil doers, and you shall be *bien emmerdés!*'

Rex

SINCE every family has its black sheep, it almost follows that every man must have a sooty uncle. Lucky if he hasn't two. However, it is only with my mother's brother that we are concerned. She had loved him dearly when he was a little blond boy. When he grew up black, she was always vowing she would never speak to him again. Yet when he put in an appearance, after years of absence, she invariably received him in a festive mood, and was even flirty with him.

He rolled up one day in a dog-cart, when I was a small boy. He was large and bullet-headed and blustering, and this time, sporty. Sometimes he was rather literary, sometimes coloured with business. But this time he was in checks, and was sporty. We viewed him from a distance.

The upshot was, would we rear a pup for him. Now my mother detested animals about the house. She could not bear the mix-up of human with animal life. Yet she consented to bring up the pup.

My uncle had taken a large, vulgar public-house in a large and vulgar town. It came to pass that I must fetch the pup. Strange for me, a member of the Band of Hope, to enter the big, noisy, smelly plate-glass and mahogany public-house. It was called The Good Omen. Strange to have my uncle towering over me in the passage, shouting 'Hello, Johnny, what d'yer want?' He didn't know me. Strange to think he was my mother's brother, and that he had his bouts when he read Browning aloud with emotion and éclat.

I was given tea in a narrow, uncomfortable sort of living-room, half kitchen. Curious that such a palatial pub should show such miserable private accommodations, but

21

so it was. There was I, unhappy, and glad to escape with the soft fat pup. It was winter-time, and I wore a big-flapped black overcoat, half cloak. Under the cloak-sleeves I hid the puppy, who trembled. It was Saturday, and the train was crowded, and he whimpered under my coat. I sat in mortal fear of being hauled out for travelling without a dog-ticket. However, we arrived, and my torments were for nothing.

The others were wildy excited over the puppy. He was small and fat and white, with a brown-and-black head: a fox terrier. My father said he had a lemon head – some such mysterious technical phraseology. It wasn't lemon at all, but coloured like a field bee. And he had a black spot at the root of his spine.

It was Saturday night – bath-night. He crawled on the hearth-rug like a fat white teacup, and licked the bare toes that had just been bathed.

'He ought to be called Spot,' said one. But that was too ordinary. It was a great question, what to call him.

'Call him Rex – the King,' said my mother, looking down on the fat, animated little teacup, who was chewing my sister's little toe and making her squeal with joy and tickles. We took the name in all seriousness.

'Rex – the King!' We thought it was just right. Not for years did I realize that it was a sarcasm on my mother's part. She must have wasted some twenty years or more of irony on our incurable naïveté.

It wasn't a successful name, really. Because my father and all the people in the street failed completely to pronounce the monosyllable Rex. They all said Rax. And it always distressed me. It always suggested to me seaweed, and rack-and-ruin. Poor Rex!

We loved him dearly. The first night we woke to hear him weeping and whinnying in loneliness at the foot of the stairs. When it could be borne no more, I slipped down for him, and he slept under the sheets.

'I won't have that little beast in the beds. Beds are not for dogs,' declared my mother callously.

'He's as good as we are!' we cried, injured.

'Whether he is or not, he's not going in the beds.'

I think now, my mother scorned us for our lack of pride. We were a little *infra dig*, we children.

The second night, however, Rex wept the same and in the same way was comforted. The third night we heard our father plod downstairs, heard several slaps administered to the yelling, dismayed puppy, and heard the amiable, but to us heartless voice saying 'Shut it then! Shut thy noise, 'st hear? Stop in thy basket, stop there!'

'It's a shame!' we shouted, in muffled rebellion, from the sheets.

'I'll give you shame, if you don't hold your noise and go to sleep,' called our mother from her room. Whereupon we shed angry tears and went to sleep. But there was a tension.

'Such a houseful of idiots would make me detest the little beast, even if he was better than he is,' said my mother.

But as a matter of fact, she did not detest Rexie at all. She only had to pretend to do so, to balance our adoration. And in truth, she did not care for close contact with animals. She was too fastidious. My father, however, would take on a real dog's voice, talking to the puppy: a funny, high, sing-song falsetto which he seemed to produce at the top of his head. ''S a pretty little dog! 's a pretty little doggy! – ay! – yes! – he is, yes! – Wag thy strunt, then! Wag thy strunt, Rexie! – Ha-ha! Nay, tha munna –' This last as the puppy, wild with excitement at the strange falsetto voice, licked my father's nostrils and bit my father's nose with his sharp little teeth.

''E makes blood come,' said my father.

'Serves you right for being so silly with him,' said my mother. It was odd to see her as she watched the man, my father, crouching and talking to the little dog and laughing strangely when the little creature bit his nose and toused his beard. What does a woman think of her husband at such a moment?

My mother amused herself over the names we called him.

'He's an angel – he's a little butterfly – Rexie, my sweet!'

'Sweet! A dirty little object!' interpolated my mother. She and he had a feud from the first. Of course he chewed boots and worried our stockings and swallowed our garters. The moment we took off our stockings he would dart away with one, we after him. Then as he hung, growling vociferously, at one end of the stocking, we at the other, we would cry:

'Look at him, Mother! He'll make holes in it again.' Whereupon my mother darted at him and spanked him sharply.

'Let go, sir, you destructive little fiend.'

But he didn't let go. He began to growl with real rage, and hung on viciously. Mite as he was, he defied her with a manly fury. He did not hate her, nor she him. But they had one long battle with one another.

'I'll teach you, my Jockey! Do you think I'm going to spend my life darning after your destructive little teeth! I'll show you if I will!'

But Rexie only growled more viciously. They both became really angry, while we children expostulated earnestly with both. He would not let her take the stocking from him.

'You should tell him properly, Mother. He won't be driven,' we said.

'I'll drive him farther than he bargains for. I'll drive him out of my sight for ever, that I will,' declared my mother, truly angry. He would put her into a real temper, with his tiny, growling defiance.

'He's sweet! A Rexie, a little Rexie!'

'A filthy little nuisance! Don't think I'll put up with him.'

And to tell the truth, he was dirty at first. How could he be otherwise, so young! But my mother hated him for it. And perhaps this was the real start of their hostility. For he lived in the house with us. He would wrinkle his nose and show his tiny dagger-teeth in fury when he was thwarted, and his growls of real battle-rage against my mother rejoiced us as much as they angered her. But at last she caught him *in flagrante*. She pounced on him, rubbed his nose in the mess, and flung him out into the yard. He yelped with shame and disgust and indignation. I shall never forget the sight of him as he rolled over, then tried to turn his head away from the disgust of his own muzzle, shaking his little snout with a sort of horror, and trying to sneeze it off. My sister gave a yell of despair, and dashed out with a rag and a pan of water, weeping wildly. She sat in the middle of the yard with the befouled puppy, and shedding bitter tears she wiped him and washed him clean. Loudly she reproached my mother. 'Look how much bigger you are than he is. It's a shame, it's a shame!'

'You ridiculous little lunatic, you've undone all the good it would do him, with your soft ways. Why is my life made a curse with animals! Haven't I enough as it is –'

There was a subdued tension afterwards. Rex was a little white chasm between us and our parent.

He became clean. But then another tragedy loomed. He must be docked. His floating puppy-tail must be docked short. This time my father was the enemy. My mother agreed with us that it was an unnecessary cruelty. But my father was adamant. 'The dog'll look a fool all his life, if he's not docked.' And there was no getting away from it. To add to the horror, poor Rex's tail must be *bitten* off. Why bitten? we asked aghast. We were assured that biting was the only way. A man would take the little tail and just nip it through with his teeth, at a certain joint. My father lifted his lips and bared his incisors, to suit the description. We shuddered. But we were in the hands of fate.

Rex was carried away, and a man called Rowbotham bit off the superfluity of his tail in the Nag's Head, for a quart of best and bitter. We lamented our poor diminished puppy, but agreed to find him more manly and *comme il faut*. We should always have been ashamed of his little whip of a tail, if it had not been shortened. My father said it had made a man of him.

Perhaps it had. For now his true nature came out. And his true nature, like so much else, was dual. First he was a fierce, canine little beast, a beast of rapine and blood. He longed to hunt, savagely. He lusted to set his teeth in his prey. It was no joke with him. The old canine Adam stood first in him, the dog with fangs and glaring eyes. He flew at us when we annoyed him. He flew at all intruders, particularly the postman. He was almost a peril to the neighbourhood. But not quite. Because close second in his nature stood that fatal need to love, the *besoin d'aimer* which at last makes an end of liberty. He had a terrible, terrible necessity to love, and this trammelled the native, savage hunting beast which he was. He was torn between two great impulses: the native impulse to hunt and kill, and the strange, secondary, supervening impulse to love and obey. If he had been left to my father and mother, he would have run wild and got himself shot. As it was, he loved us children with a fierce, joyous love. And we loved him.

When we came home from school we would see him

standing at the end of the entry, cocking his head wistfully at the open country in front of him, and meditating whether to be off or not: a white, inquiring little figure, with green savage freedom in front of him. A cry from a far distance from one of us, and like a bullet he hurled himself down the road, in a mad game. Seeing him coming, my sister invariably turned and fled, shrieking with delighted terror. And he would leap straight up her back, and bite her and tear her clothes. But it was only an ecstasy of savage love, and she knew it. She didn't care if he tore her pinafores. But my mother did.

My mother was maddened by him. He was a little demon. At the least provocation, he flew. You had only to sweep the floor, and he bristled and sprang at the broom. Nor would he let go. With his scruff erect and his nostrils snorting rage, he would turn up the whites of his eyes at my mother, as she wrestled at the other end of the broom. 'Leave go, sir, leave go!' She wrestled and stamped her foot, and he answered with horrid growls. In the end it was she who had to let go. Then she flew at him, and he flew at her. All the time we had him, he was within a hair's-breadth of savagely biting her. And she knew it. Yet he always kept sufficient self-control.

We children loved his temper. We would drag the bones from his mouth, and put him into such paroxysms of rage that he would twist his head right over and lay it on the ground upside-down, because he didn't know what to do with himself, the savage was so strong in him and he must fly at us. 'He'll fly at your throat one of these days,' said my father. Neither he nor my mother dared have touched Rex's bone. It was enough to see him bristle and roll the whites of his eyes when they came near. How near he must have been to driving his teeth right into us, cannot be told. He was a horrid sight snarling and crouching at us. But we only laughed and rebuked him.

And he would whimper in the sheer torment of his need to attack us.

He never did hurt us. He never hurt anybody, though the neighbourhood was terrified of him. But he took to hunting. To my mother's disgust, he would bring large dead bleeding rats and lay them on the hearth-rug, and she had to take them up on a shovel. For he would not remove them. Occasionally he brought a mangled rabbit, and sometimes, alas, fragmentary poultry. We were in terror of prosecution. Once he came home bloody and feathery and rather sheepish-looking. We cleaned him and questioned him and abused him. Next day we heard of six dead ducks. Thank heaven no one had seen him.

But he was disobedient. If he saw a hen he was off, and calling would not bring him back. He was worst of all with my father, who would take him walks on Sunday morning. My mother would not walk a yard with him. Once, walking with my father, he rushed off at some sheep in a field. My father yelled in vain. The dog was at the sheep, and meant business. My father crawled through the hedge, and was upon him in time. And now the man was in a paroxysm of rage. He dragged the little beast into the road and thrashed him with a walking stick.

'Do you know you're thrashing that dog unmercifully?' said a passerby.

'Ay, an' mean to,' shouted my father.

The curious thing was that Rex did not respect my father any the more, for the beatings he had from him. He took much more heed of us children, always.

But he let us down also. One fatal Saturday he disappeared. We hunted and called, but no Rex. We were bathed, and it was bed-time, but we would not go to bed. Instead we sat in a row in our nightdresses on the sofa. and wept without stopping. This drove our mother mad.

'Am I going to put up with it? Am I? And all for that

hateful little beast of a dog! He shall go! If he's not gone now, he shall go.'

Our father came in late, looking rather queer, with his hat over his eye. But in his staccato tippled fashion he tried to be consoling.

'Never mind, my duckie, I s'll look for him in the morning.'

Sunday came – oh, such a Sunday. We cried, and didn't eat. We scoured the land, and for the first time realized how empty and wide the earth is, when you're looking for something. My father walked for many miles – all in vain. Sunday dinner, with rhubarb pudding, I remember, and an atmosphere of abject misery that was unbearable.

'Never,' said my mother, 'never shall an animal set foot in this house again, while I live. I knew what it would be! I knew.'

The day wore on, and it was the black gloom of bed-time, when we heard a scratch and an impudent little whine at the door. In trotted Rex, mud-black, disreputable, and impudent. His air of offhand 'How d'ye do!' was indescribable. He trotted around with *suffisance*, wagging his tail as if to say, 'Yes, I've come back. But I didn't need to. I can carry on remarkably well by myself.' Then he walked to his water, and drank noisily and ostentatiously. It was rather a slap in the eye for us.

He disappeared once or twice in this fashion. We never knew where he went. And we began to feel that his heart was not so golden as we had imagined it.

But one fatal day reappeared my uncle and the dog-cart. He whistled to Rex, and Rex trotted up. But when he wanted to examine the lusty, sturdy dog, Rex became suddenly still, then sprang free. Quite jauntily he trotted round – but out of reach of my uncle. He leaped up, licking our faces, and trying to make us play.

'Why, what ha' you done wi' the dog – you've made a

fool of him. He's softer than grease. You've ruined him. You've made a damned fool of him,' shouted my uncle.

Rex was captured and hauled off to the dog-cart and tied to the seat. He was in a frenzy. He yelped and shrieked and struggled, and was hit on the head, hard, with the butt-end of my uncle's whip, which only made him struggle more frantically. So we saw him driven away, our beloved Rex, frantically, madly fighting to get to us from the high dog-cart, and being knocked down, while we stood in the street in mute despair.

After which, black tears, and a little wound which is still alive in our hearts.

I saw Rex only once again, when I had to call just once at The Good Omen. He must have heard my voice, for he was upon me in the passage before I knew where I was. And in the instant I knew how he loved us. He really loved us. And in the same instant there was my uncle with a whip, beating and kicking him back, and Rex cowering, bristling, snarling.

My uncle swore many oaths, how we had ruined the dog for ever, made him vicious, spoiled him for showing purposes, and been altogether a pack of mard-soft fools not fit to be trusted with any dog but a gutter-mongrel.

Poor Rex! We heard his temper was incurably vicious, and he had to be shot.

And it was our fault. We had loved him too much, and he had loved us too much. We never had another pet.

It is a strange thing, love. Nothing but love has made the dog lose his wild freedom, to become the servant of man. And this very servility or completeness of love makes him a term of deepest contempt – 'You dog!'

We should not have loved Rex so much, and he should not have loved us. There should have been a measure. We tended, all of us, to overstep the limits of our own natures. He should have stayed outside human limits, we should have stayed outside canine limits. Nothing is more fatal than the disaster of too much love. My uncle was right, we had ruined the dog.

My uncle was a fool, for all that.

A Prelude

'Sweet is pleasure after pain . . .'

In the kitchen of a small farm a little woman sat cutting bread and butter. The glow of the clear, ruddy fire was on her shining cheek and white apron; but grey hair will not take the warm caress of firelight.

She skilfully spread the softened butter, and cut off great slices from the floury loaf in her lap. Already two plates were piled, but she continued to cut.

Outside the naked ropes of the creeper tapped and lashed at the window.

The grey-haired mother looked up, and, setting the butter on the hearth, rose and went to look out. The sky was heavy and grey as she saw it in the narrow band over the near black wood. So she turned and went to look through the tiny window which opened from the deep recess on the opposite side of the room. The northern sky was blacker than ever.

She turned away with a little sigh, and took a duster from the red, shining warming-pan to take the bread from the oven. Afterwards she laid the table for five.

There was a rumbling and a whirring in the corner, and the clock struck five. Like many clocks in farmers' kitchens it was more than half an hour fast. The little woman hurried about, bringing milk and other things from the dairy; lifting the potatoes from the fire, peeping through the window anxiously. Very often her neck ached with watching the gate for a sign of approach. There was a click of the yard gate. She ran to the window, but turned away again, and catching up the blue enamelled teapot, dropped into it a handful of tea from the caddy, and poured on the water. A clinking scrape of iron-shod boots sounded outside, then the door opened with a burst as a burly, bearded man entered. He drooped at the shoulders, and leaned forward as a man who has worked all his life.

'Hello, Mother,' he said loudly and cheerfully. 'Am I first? Aren't any of the lads down yet? Fred will be here in a minute.'

'I wish they would come,' said his wife, 'or else it'll rain before they're here.'

'Ay,' he assented, 'it's beginning, and it's cold rain an' all. Bit of sleet, I think,' and he sat down heavily in his armchair, looking at his wife as she knelt and turned the bread, and took a large jar of stewed apples from the oven.

'Well, Mother,' he said with a pleasant, comfortable little smile, 'here's another Christmas for you and me. They keep passing us by.'

'Ay,' she answered, the effects of her afternoon's brooding now appearing. 'They come and go, but they never find us any better off.'

'It seems so,' he said, a shade of regret appearing momentarily over his cheerfulness. 'This year we've certainly had some very bad luck. But we keep straight . . . and we never regret that Christmas – see, it's twenty-seven years since . . . twenty-seven years.'

'No, perhaps not, but there's Fred as hasn't had above three pounds for the whole year's work, and the other two at the pit.'

'Well, what can I do? If I hadn't lost the biggest part of the hay, and them two beasts . . .'

'If . . . Besides, what prospects has he? Here he is working year in, year out for you and getting nothing at the end of it. When you were his age, when you were twenty-five, you were married and had two children. How can he ask anybody to marry him?'

'I don't know that he wants to. He's fairly contented. Don't be worrying about him and upsetting him. Besides, we may have a good year next year, and we can make this up.'

'Ay, so you say.'

'Don't fret yourself tonight, lass. It's true things haven't gone as we hoped they would. I never thought to see you doing all the work you have to do, but we've been very comfortable, all things considered, haven't we?'

'I never thought to see my first lad a farm labourer at twenty-five, and the other two in the pit. Two of my sons in the pit.'

'I'm sure I've done what I could, and . . .' but he heard a scraping outside, and he said no more.

The eldest son tramped in, his great boots and his leggings all covered with mud. He took off his wet overcoat, and stood on the hearth-rug, his hands spread out behind him in the warmth of the fire. Looking smilingly at his mother, as she moved about the kitchen, he said: 'You do look warm and cosy, Mother. When I was coming up with the last load I thought of you trotting about in that big, white apron, getting tea ready, watching the weather. There are the lads. Aren't you quite contented now . . . perfectly happy?'

She laughed an odd little laugh, and poured out the tea. The boys came in from the pit, wet and dirty, with clean streaks down their faces where the rain had trickled. They changed their clothes and sat at the table. The elder was a big, heavy loosely-made fellow, with a long nose and chin, and comical wrinkling round his eyes. The younger, Arthur, was a handsome lad, dark-haired, with ruddy colour glowing through his dirt, and dark eyes. When he talked and laughed the red of his lips and the whiteness of his teeth and eyeballs stood out in startling contrast to the surrounding black.

'Mother, I'm glad to see thee,' he said, looking at her with frank, boyish affection.

'There, Mother, what more can you want?' asked her husband.

She took a bite of bread and butter, and looked up with a quaint, comical glance, as if she were given only her just dues, but for all that it pleased and amused her, only she was half shy and a grain doubtful.

'Lad,' said Henry, 'it's Christmas Eve. The fire ought to burn its brightest.'

'Yes, I will have just another potato, seeing as Christmas is the time for feeding. What are we going to do? Are we going to have a party, Mother?'

'Yes, if you want one.'

'Party,' laughed the father, 'who'd come?'

'We might ask somebody. We could have Nellie Wycherley who used to come, an' David Garton.'

'We shall not do for Nellie nowadays,' said the father. 'I saw her on Sunday morning on the top road. She was drivin' home with another young woman, an' she stopped an' asked me if we'd got any holly with berries on, an' I said we hadn't.'

Fred looked up from the book he was reading over tea. He had dark brown eyes, something like his mother's, and they always drew attention when he turned them on anyone.

'There is a tree covered in the wood,' he said.

'Well,' answered the irrepressible Henry, 'that's not ours, is it? An' if she's got that proud she won't come near to see us, am I goin' choppin' trees down for her? If she'd come here an' say she wanted a bit, I'd fetch her half the wood in. But when she sits in the trap and looks down on you an' asks, "Do you happen to hev a bush of berried holly in your hedges? Preston can't find a sprig to decorate the house, and I hev some people coming down from town," then I tell her we're all crying because we've none to decorate ourselves, and we want it the more because nobody's coming, neither from the town nor th' country, an' we're likely to forget it's Christmas if we've neither folks nor things to remind us.'

'What did she say?' asked the mother.

'She said she was sorry, an' I told her not to bother, it's better lookin' at folks than at bits o' holly. The other lass was laughing, an' she wanted to know what folks. I told her any as hadn't got more pricks than a holly bush to keep you off.'

'Ha! ha!' laughed the father, 'did she take it?'

'The other girl nudged her, and they both began a-laughing. Then Nellie told me to send down the guysers tonight. I said I would, but they're not going now.'

'Why not?' asked Fred.

'Billy Simpson's got a gathered face, and Ward's gone to Nottingham.'

'The company down at Ramsley Mill will have nobody to laugh at tonight,' said Arthur.

'Tell you what,' exclaimed Henry, 'we'll go.'

'How can we, three of us?' asked Arthur.

'Well,' persisted Henry, 'we could dress up so as they'd niver know us, an' hae a bit o' fun.'

'Hey!' he suddenly shouted to Fred, who was reading, and taking no notice. 'Hey, we're going to the Mill guysering.'

'Who is?' asked the elder brother, somewhat surprised.

'You an' me, an' our Arthur. I'll be Beelzebub.'

Here he distorted his face to look diabolic, so that everybody roared.

'Go,' said his father, 'you'll make our fortunes.'

'What!' he exclaimed, 'by making a fool of myself? They say fools for luck. What fools wise folk must be.

Well, I'll be the devil – are you shocked, Mother? What will you be, Arthur?'

'I don' care,' was the answer. 'We can put some of that red paint on our faces, and some soot, they'd never know us. Shall we go, Fred?'

'I don't know.'

'Why, I should like to see her with her company, to see if she has very fine airs. We could leave some holly for her in the scullery.'

'All right, then.'

After tea all helped with the milking and feeding. Then Fred took a hedge knife and a hurricane lamp and went into the wood to cut some of the richly-berried holly. When he got back he found his brothers roaring with laughter before the mirror. They were smeared with red and black, and had fastened on grotesque horsehair moustaches, so that they were entirely unrecognizable.

'Oh, you are hideous,' cried their mother. 'Oh, it's shameful to disfigure the work of the Almighty like that.'

Fred washed and proceeded to dress. They could not persuade him to use paint or soot. He rolled his sleeves up to the shoulder, and wrapped himself in a great striped horse rug. Then he tied a white cloth round his head, as the Bedouins do, and pulled out his moustaches to fierce points. He looked at himself with approval, took an old sword from the wall, and held it in one naked muscular arm.

'Decidedly,' he thought, 'it is very picturesque, and I look very fine.'

'Oh, that is grand,' said his mother, as he entered the kitchen. His dark eyes glowed with pleasure to hear her say it. He seemed somewhat excited, this bucolic young man. His tanned skin shone rich and warm under the white cloth, its coarseness hidden by the yellow lamplight. His eyes glittered like a true Arab's and it was to be noticed that the muscles of his sun-browned arm were tense with the grip of the broad hand.

It was remarkable how the dark folds of the rug and the flowing burnous glorified this young farmer, who in his best clothes looked awkward and ungainly, and whose face in a linen collar showed coarse, owing to exposure from the weather, and long application to heavy labour.

They set out to cross the two of their own fields, and two of their neighbour's, which separated their home from the Mill. A few uncertain flakes of snow were eddying down, melting as they settled. The ground was wet, and the night very dark. But they knew the way well, and were soon at the gate leading to the mill yard. The dog began to bark furiously, but they called to him, 'Trip, Trip,' and, knowing their voices, he was quieted.

Henry gave a thundering knock, and bawled in stentorian tones, 'Dun yer want guysers?'

A man came to the door, very tall, very ungainly, very swarthy.

'We non want yer,' he said, talking down his nose.

'Here comes Beelzebub,' banged away Henry, thumping a pan which he carried. 'Here comes Beelzebub, an' he's come to th' right place.'

A big, bonny farm girl came to the door.

'Who is it?' she asked.

'Beelzebub, you know him well,' was the answer.

'I'll ask Miss Ellen if she wants you.'

Henry winked a red and black wink at the maid, saying, 'Never keep Satan on the doorstep,' and he stepped into the scullery.

The girl ran away and soon was heard a laughing and bright talking of women's voices drawing nearer to the kitchen.

'Tell them to come in,' said a voice.

The three trooped in, and glanced round the big

kitchen. They could only see Betty, seated to them as near as possible on the squab, her father, black and surly, in his armchair, and two women's figures in the deep shadows of one of the great ingle-nook seats.

'Ah,' said Beelzebub, 'this is a bit more like it, a bit hotter. The Devils feel at home here.'

They began the ludicrous old Christmas play that everyone knows so well. Beelzebub acted with much force, much noise, and some humour. St George, that is Fred, played his part with zeal and earnestness most amusing, but at one of the most crucial moments he entirely forgot his speech, which, however, was speedily rectified by Beelzebub. Arthur was nervous and awkward, so that Beelzebub supplied him with most of the speeches.

After much horseplay, stabbing, falling on the floor, bangings of dripping-pans, and ludicrous striving to fill in the blanks, they came to an end.

They waited in silence.

'Well, what next?' asked a voice from the shadows.

'It's your turn,' said Beelzebub.

'What do you want?'

'As little as you have the heart to give.'

'But,' said another voice, one they knew well, 'we have no heart to give at all.'

'You did not know your parts well,' said Blanche, the stranger. 'The big fellow in the blanket deserves nothing.'

'What about me?' asked Arthur.

'You,' answered the same voice, 'oh, you're a nice boy, and a lady's thanks are enough reward for you.'

He blushed and muttered something unintelligible.

'There'll be the Devil to pay,' suggested Beelzebub.

'Give the Devil his dues, Nell,' said Blanche, choking again with laughter. Nellie threw a large silver coin on the flagstone floor, but she was nervous, and it rolled to the feet of Preston in his armchair.

''Alf-a-crern!' he exclaimed, 'gie 'em thrippence, an' they're non worth that much.'

This was too much for the chivalrous St George. He could bear no longer to stand in the ridiculous garb before his scornful lady-love and her laughing friend.

He snatched off his burnous and his robe, flung them over one arm, and with the other caught back Beelzebub, who would have gone to pick up the money. There he stood, St George metamorphosed into a simple young farmer, with ruffled curly black hair, a heavy frown, and bare arms.

'Won't you let him have it?' asked Blanche. 'Well, what do you want?' she continued.

'Nothing, thanks. I'm sorry we troubled you.'

'Come on,' he said, drawing the reluctant Beelzebub, and the three made their exit. Blanche laughed and laughed again to see the discomfited knight tramp out, rolling down his shirt sleeves.

Nellie did not laugh. Seeing him turn, she saw him again as a child, before her father had made money by the cattle-dealing, when she was a poor, wild little creature. But her father had grown rich, and the mill was a big farm, and when the old cattle dealer had died, she became sole mistress. Then Preston, their chief man, came with Betty and Sarah, to live in, and take charge of the farm.

Nellie had seen little of her old friends since then. She had stayed a long time in town, and when she called on them after her return found them cool and estranged. So she had not been again, and now it was almost a year since she had spoken many words to Fred.

Her brief meditations were disturbed by a scream from Betty in the scullery, followed by the wild rush of that damsel into the kitchen.

'What's up?' asked her father.

'There's somebody there got hold of my legs.'

Nellie felt suddenly her own loneliness. Preston struck a match and investigated. He returned with a bunch of glittering holly, thick with scarlet berries.

'Here's yer somebody,' said he, flinging the bunch down on the table.

'Oh, that is pretty,' exclaimed Blanche. Nellie rose, looked, then hurried down the passage to the sitting-room, followed by her friend. There, to the consternation of Blanche, she sat down and began to cry.

'Whatever is the matter?' asked Blanche.

It was some time before she had a reply, then, 'It's so miserable and so lonely. I do think Will and Harry and Louie and all the others were mean not to come, then this wouldn't have happened. It was such a shame – such a shame.'

'What was a shame?' asked Blanche.

'Why, when he had got me that holly, and come down to see . . .' she ended, blushing.

'Whom do you mean – the Bedouin?'

'And I had not seen him for months, and he will think I am just a mean, proud thing.'

'You don't mean to say you care for him?'

Nellie's tears began to flow again. 'I do, and I wish this miserable farm and bit of money had never come between us. He'll never come again, never, I know.'

'Then,' said Blanche, 'you must go to him.'

'Yes, and I will.'

'Come along, then.'

In the meantime the disappointed brothers had reached home. Fred had thrown down his Bedouin wardrobe, and put on his coat, muttering something about having a walk up the village. Then he had gone out, his mother's eyes watching his exit with helpless grief, his father looking over his spectacles in a half-surprised paternal sympathy.

However, they heard him tramp down the yard and enter the barn, and they knew he would soon recover. Then the lads went out, and nothing was heard in the kitchen save the beat of the clock and the rustle of the newspaper, or the rattle of the board, as the mother rolled out paste for the mince-pies.

In the pitch-dark barn, the rueful Bedouin told himself that he expected no other than this, and that it was high time he ceased fooling himself with fancies, that he was well-cured, that even if she had invited himself to stay, how could he; she must think he wanted badly to become master of Ramsley Mill. What a fool he had been to go – what a fool!

'But,' he argued, 'let her think what she likes, I don't care. She may remember if she can that I used to sole her boots with my father's leather, and she went home in mine. She can remember that my mother taught her how to write and sew decently. I should say she must sometimes.' Then he admitted to himself that he was sure she did not forget. He could feel quite well that she was wishing that this long estrangement might cease.

'But,' came the question, 'why doesn't she end it? Pah, it's only my conceit; she thinks more of those glib, grinning fellows from the clerks' stools. Let her, what do I care!'

Suddenly he heard voices from the field at the back, and sat up listening.

'Oh, it's a regular slough,' said someone. 'We can never get through the gate. See, let us climb the stackyard fence. They've put some new rails in. Can you manage, Blanche? Here, just between the lilac bush and the stack. What a blessing they keep Chris at the front! Mind, bend under this plum tree. Dare we go, Blanche?'

'Go on, go on,' whispered Blanche, and they crept up to the tiny window, through which the lamplight streamed uninterrupted. Fred stole out of the barn, and hid behind the great water-butt. He saw them stoop and creep to the window and peep through.

In the kitchen sat the father, smoking and appearing to read, but really staring into the fire. The mother was putting the top crusts on the little pies, but she was interrupted by the need to wipe her eyes.

'Oh, Blanche,' whispered Nellie, 'he's gone out.'

'It looks like it,' assented the other.

'Perhaps he's not,' resumed the former bravely. 'He's very likely only in the parlour.'

'That's all right, then,' said Blanche, 'I thought we should have seen him looking so miserable. But, of course, he wouldn't let his mother see it.'

'Certainly not,' said Nellie.

Fred chuckled.

'But,' she continued doubtfully, 'if he has gone out, whatever shall we do? What can we tell his mother?'

'Tell her, we came up for fun.'

'But if he's out?'

'Stay till he comes home.'

'If it's late?'

'It's Christmas Eve.'

'Perhaps he doesn't care after all.'

'You think he does, so do I; and you're quite sure you want him?'

'You know I do, Blanche, and I always have done.'

'Let us begin, then.'

'What? Good King Wenceslas?'

The mother and father started as the two voices suddenly began to carol outside. She would have run to the door, but her husband waved her excitedly back. 'Let them finish,' his eyes shining, 'let them finish.'

The girls had retired from the window lest they should be seen, and stood near the water-butt. When the old carol was finished, Nellie began the beautiful song of Giordani's:

> Turn once again, heal thou my pain,
> Parted from thee my heart is sore.

As she sang she stood holding a bough of the old plum tree, so close to Fred that by leaning forward he could have touched her coat. Carried away by the sweet pathos of her song, he could hardly refrain from rising and flinging his arms round her.

She finished; the door opened, showing a little woman holding out her hands.

Both girls made a motion towards her, but –

'Nell, Nell,' he whispered, and caught her in his arms. She gave a little cry of alarm and delight. Blanche stepped into the kitchen and shut the door, laughing.

She sat in the low rocking-chair, swinging to and fro in a delighted excitement, chattering brightly about a hundred things. And with a keen woman's eye she noticed the mother put her hands on her husband's as she sat on the sofa by his chair, and saw him hold the shining stiffened hand in one of his, and stroke it with old undiminished affection.

Soon the two came in, Nellie all blushing. Without a word she ran and kissed the little mother, lingering a moment over her before she turned to the quiet embrace of the father. Then she took off her hat, and brushed back the brown tendrils all curled so prettily by the damp.

Already she was at home.

Lessford's Rabbits

On Tuesday mornings I have to be at school at half past eight to administer the free breakfasts. Dinners are given in the canteen in one of the mean streets, where the children feed in a Church Mission room appropriately adorned by Sunday School cartoons showing the blessing of the little ones, and the feeding of the five thousand. We serve breakfasts, however, in school, in the wood-work room high up under the roof.

Tuesday morning sees me rushing up the six short flights of stone stairs, at twenty-five minutes to nine. It is my disposition to be late. I generally find a little crowd of children waiting in the 'art' room – so called because it is surrounded with a strip of blackboard too high for the tallest boy to reach – which is a sort of ante-room to the workshop where breakfast is being prepared. I hasten through the little throng to see if things are ready. There are two big girls putting out the basins, and another one looking in the pan to see if the milk is boiling. The room is warm, and seems more comfortable because the windows are high up under the beams of the slanting roof and the walls are all panelled with ruddy gold, varnished wood. The work bench is in the form of three sides of a square – or of an oblong – as the dining tables of the ancients used to be, I believe. At one of the extremities are the three vises, and at the other the great tin pan, like a fish kettle, standing on a gas ring. When the boys' basins are placed along the outer edge of the bench, the girls' on the inner, and the infants' on the lockers against the wall, we are ready. I look at the two rows of assorted basins, and think of the three bears. Then I admit the thirty, who bundle to their places and stand in position, girls on the inside facing boys on the outside, and quaint little infants with their toes kicking the lockers along the walls.

Last week the infant mistress did not come up, so I was alone. She is an impressive woman, who always commands the field. I stand in considerable awe of her. I feel like a reckless pleasure boat with one extravagant sail misbehaving myself in the track of a heavy earnest coaster when she bears down on me. I was considerably excited to find myself in sole charge. As I ushered in the children, the caretaker, a little fierce-eyed man with hollow cheeks and walrus moustache, entered with the large basket full of chunks of bread. He glared around without bidding me good morning.

'Miss Culloch not come?' he asked.

'As you see,' I replied.

He grunted, and put down the basket. Then he drew himself up like a fiery prophet, and stretching forth his hairy arm towards the opposite door, shouted loudly to the children:

'None of you's got to touch that other door there! You hear – you're to leave it alone!'

The children stared at him without answering.

'A brake as I'm making for these doors,' he said confidentially to me, thrusting forward his extraordinarily hairy lean arms, and putting two fingers of one hand into the palm of the other, as if to explain his invention. I bowed.

'Nasty things them swing doors' – he looked up at me with his fierce eyes, and suddenly swished aside his right arm:

'They come to like *that*!' he exclaimed, 'and a child's fingers is cut off – clean!' – he looked at me for ratification. I bowed.

'It'll be a good thing, I think,' he concluded, considerably damped. I bowed again. Then he left me. The chief, almost the only duty of a caretaker, is to review the works of the head and of the staff, as a reviewer does books: at length and according to his superior light.

I told one of the girls to give three chunks of bread to each child, and, having fished a mysterious earwig out of the scalding milk, I filled the large enamelled jug – such as figures and has figured in the drawing lessons of every school in England, I suppose – and doled out the portions – about three-quarters of a pint per senior, and half a pint per infant. Everything was ready. I had to say grace. I dared not launch into the Infant mistress' formula, thanking the Lord for his goodness – 'and may we eat and drink to thine everlasting glory – Amen.' I looked at the boys, dressed in mouldering garments of remote men, at the girls with their rat-tailed hair, and at the infants, quaint little mites on whom I wished, but could not bring myself, to expend my handkerchief, and I wondered what I should say. The only other grace I knew was 'For these and for all good things may the Lord make us truly thankful.' But I wondered whom we should thank for the bad things. I was becoming desperate. I plunged:

'Ready now – hands together, close eyes. "Let us eat, drink and be merry, for tomorrow we die." ' I felt myself flushing with confusion – what did I mean? But there was a universal clink of iron spoons on the basins, and a snuffling, slobbering sound of children feeding. They had not noticed, so it was all right. The infants were kneeling and squalling by the lockers, the boys were stretching wide their eyes and their mouths at the same time, to admit the spoon. They spilled the milk on their jackets and wiped it off with their sleeves, continuing to eat all the time.

'Don't slobber, lads, be decent,' I said, rebuking them from my superior sphere. They ate more carefully, glancing up at me when the spoon was at their mouths.

I began to count the number – nine boys, seven girls, and eleven infants. Not many. We could never get many boys to give in their names for free meals. I used to ask the Kelletts, who were pinched and pared thin with poverty:

'Are you sure you don't want either dinners or breakfasts, Kellet?'

He would look at me curiously, and say, with a peculiar small movement of his thin lips.

'No Sir.'

'But have you plenty – quite plenty?'

'Yes Sir' – he was very quiet, flushing at my questions. None – or very few – of the boys could endure to accept the meals. Not many parents would submit to the indignity of the officer's inquirer and the boys, the most foolishly sensitive animals in the world, would, many of them, prefer to go short rather than to partake of charity meals of which all their school-mates were aware.

'Halket – where is Halket?' I asked.

'Please Sir, his mother's got work,' replied Lessford, one of my own boys, a ruddy, bonny lad – many of those at breakfast were pictures of health. Lessford was brown-skinned and had fine dark eyes. He was a reticent, irresponsible creature, with a radical incapacity to spell and to read and to draw, but who sometimes scored at arithmetic. I should think he came of a long line of unrelievedly poor people. He was skilled in street lore, and cute at arithmetic, but blunt and blind to everything that needed a little delicacy of perception. He had an irritating habit of looking at me furtively, with his handsome dark eyes, glancing covertly again and again. Yet he was not a sneak; he gave himself the appearance of one. He was a well-built lad, and he looked well in the blue jersey he wore – there were great holes at the elbows, showing the whitish shirt and a brown bit of Lessford. At breakfasts he was a great eater. He would have five solid pieces of bread, and then ask for more.

We gave them bread and milk one morning, cocoa and currant bread the next. I happened to go one cocoa morning to take charge. Lessford, I noticed, did not eat by any means so much as on bread mornings. I was surprised. I asked him if he did not care for currant loaf, but he said he did. Feeling curious, I asked the other teachers what they thought of him. Mr Hayward, who took a currant bread morning, said he was sure the boy had a breakfast before he came to school; – Mr Jephson, who took a milk morning, said the lad was voracious, that it amused him to try to feed him up. I watched – turning suddenly to ask if anyone wanted a little more milk, and glancing over the top of the milk pan as I was emptying it.

I caught him: I saw him push a piece of bread under his jersey, glancing furtively with a little quiver of apprehension up at me. I did not appear to notice, but when he was going downstairs I followed him and asked him to go into the class-room with me. I closed the door and sat down at my table: he stood hanging his head and marking with his foot on the floor. He came to me, very slowly, when I bade him. I put my hand on his jersey, and felt something underneath. He did not resist me, and I drew it out. It was his cap. He smiled, he could not help it, at my discomfiture. Then he pulled his lips straight and looked sulky. I tried again – and this time I found three pieces of bread in a kind of rough pocket inside the waist of his trousers. He looked at them blackly as I arranged them on the table before him, flushing under his brown skin.

'What does this mean?' I asked. He hung his head, and would not answer.

'You may as well tell me – what do you want this for?'

'Eat,' he muttered, keeping his face bent. I put my hand under his chin and lifted up his face. He shut his eyes, and tried to move his face aside, as if from a very strong light which hurt him.

'That is not true,' I said. 'I know perfectly well it is not true. You have a breakfast before you come. You do not come to eat. You come to take the food away.'

'I never!' he exclaimed sulkily.

'No,' I said. 'You did not take any yesterday. But the day before you did.'

'I never, I never!!' he declared, more emphatically, in the tone of one who scores again. I considered.

'Oh no – the day before was Sunday. Let me see. You took some on Thursday – yes, that was the last time – You took four or five pieces of bread –' I hung fire; he did not contradict; 'five, I believe,' I added. He scraped his toe on the ground. I had guessed aright. He could not deny the definite knowledge of a number.

But I could not get another word from him. He stood and heard all I had to say, but he would not look up, or answer anything. I felt angry.

'Well,' I said, 'if you come to breakfasts any more, you will be reported.'

Next day, when asked why he was absent from breakfast, he said his father had got a job.

He was a great nuisance for coming with dirty boots. Evidently he went roaming over fields and everywhere. I concluded he must have a strain of gipsy in him, a mongrel form common in the south of London. Halket was his great friend. They never played together at school, and they had no apparent common interests. Halket was a debonair, clever lad who gave great promise of turning out a neer-do-well. He was very lively, soon moved from tears to laughter; Lessford was an inveterate sulker. Yet they always hung together.

One day my bread-stealer arrived at half past two, when the register was closed. He was sweating, dishevelled, and his breast was heaving. He gave no word of explanation, but stood near the great blackboard, his head dropped, one leg loosely apart, panting.

'Well!' I exclaimed, 'this is a nice thing! What have you to say?' I rose from my chair.

Evidently he had nothing to say.

'Come on,' I said finally. 'No foolery! Let me hear it.' He knew he would have to speak. He looked up at me, his dark eyes blazing:

'My rabbits has all gone!' he cried, as a man would announce his wife and children slain. I heard Halket exclaim. I looked at him. He was half-out of the desk, his mercurial face blank with dismay.

'Who's 'ad 'em?' he said, breathing the words almost in a whisper.

'Did you leave th' door open?' Lessford bent forward like a serpent about to strike as he asked this. Halket shook his head solemnly:

'No! I've not been near 'em today.'

There was a pause. It was time for me to reassume my position of authority. I told them both to sit down, and we continued the lesson. Halket crept near his comrade and began to whisper to him, but he received no response. Lessford sulked fixedly, not moving his head for more than an hour.

At playtime I began to question Halket: 'Please Sir – we had some rabbits in a place on the allotments. We used to gather manure for a man, and he let us have half of his tool-house in the garden –.'

'How many had you – rabbits?'

'Please Sir – they varied. When we had young ones we used to have sixteen sometimes. We had two brown does and a black buck.'

I was somewhat taken back by this.

'How long have you had them?'

51

'A long time now Sir. We've had six lots of young ones.'

'And what did you do with them?'

'Fatten them, Sir' – he spoke with a little triumph, but he was reluctant to say much more.

'And what did you fatten them on?'

The boy glanced swiftly at me. He reddened, and for the first time became confused.

'Green stuff, what we had given us out of the gardens, and what we got out of the fields.'

'And bread,' I answered quietly.

He looked at me. He saw I was not angry, only ironical. For a few moments he hesitated, whether to lie or not. Then he admitted, very subdued:

'Yes Sir.'

'And what did you do with the rabbits?' – he did not answer – 'Come, tell me. I can find out whether or not.'

'Sold them,' – he hung his head guiltily.

'Who did the selling?'

'I, Sir – to a greengrocer.'

'For how much?'

'Eightpence each.'

'And did your mothers know?'

'No Sir.' He was very subdued and guilty.

'And what did you do with the money?'

'Go to the Empire – generally.'

I asked him a day or two later if they had found the rabbits. They had not. I asked Halket what he supposed had become of them.

'Please Sir – I suppose somebody must 'a stole them. The door was not broken. You could open our padlock with a hair-pin. I suppose somebody must have come after us last night when we'd fed them. I think I know who it is, too, Sir.' He shook his head widely – 'There's a place where you can get into the allotments off the field –'

A Lesson on a Tortoise

It was the last lesson on Friday afternoon, and this, with Standard VI, was Nature Study from half-past three till half-past four. The last lesson of the week is a weariness to teachers and scholars. It is the end; there is no need to keep up the tension of discipline and effort any longer, and, yielding to weariness, a teacher is spent.

But Nature Study is a pleasant lesson. I had got a big old tortoise, who had not yet gone to sleep, though November was darkening the early afternoon, and I knew the boys would enjoy sketching him. I put him under the radiator to warm while I went for a large empty shell that I had sawn in two to show the ribs of some ancient tortoise absorbed in his bony coat. When I came back I found Joe, the old reptile, stretching slowly his skinny neck, and looking with indifferent eyes at the two intruding boys who were kneeling beside him. I was too good-tempered to send them out again into the playground, too slack with the great relief of Friday afternoon. So I bade them put out the Nature books ready. I crouched to look at Joey, and stroked his horny, blunt head with my finger. He was quite lively. He spread out his legs and gripped the floor with his flat hand-like paws, then he slackened again as if from a yawn, dropping his head meditatively.

I felt pleased with myself, knowing that the boys would be delighted with the lesson. 'He will not want to walk,' I said to myself, 'and if he takes a sleepy stride, they'll be just in ecstasy, and I can easily calm him down to his old position.' So I anticipated their entry. At the end of playtime I went to bring them in. They were a small class of about thirty – my own boys. A difficult, mixed class, they were, consisting of six London Home boys, five boys

53

from a fairly well-to-do Home for the children of actors, and a set of commoners varying from poor lads who hobbled to school, crippled by broken enormous boots, to boys who brought soft, light shoes to wear in school on snowy days. The Gordons were a difficult set; you could pick them out: crop haired, coarsely dressed lads, distrustful, always ready to assume the defensive. They would lie till it made my heart sick, if they were charged with offence, but they were willing, and would respond beautifully to an appeal. The actors were of different fibre: some gentle, a pleasure even to look at; others polite and obedient, but indifferent, covertly insolent and vulgar; all of them more or less gentlemanly.

The boys crowded round the table noisily as soon as they discovered Joe. 'Is he alive? – Look, his head's coming out! He'll bite you? – He *won't*!' – with much scorn – 'Please Sir, do tortoises bite?' I hurried them off to their seats in a little group in front, and pulled the table up to the desks. Joe kept fairly still. The boys nudged each other excitedly, making half audible remarks concerning the poor reptile, looking quickly from me to Joe and then to their neighbours. I set them sketching, but in their pleasure at the novelty they could not be still:

'Please Sir – shall we draw the marks on the shell? Please Sir, has he only got four toes?' – 'Toes!' echoes somebody, covertly delighted at the absurdity of calling the grains of claws 'toes'. 'Please Sir, he's moving – Please Sir!'

I stroked his neck and calmed him down:

'Now don't make me wish I hadn't brought him. That's enough. Miles – you shall go to the back and draw twigs if I hear you again! Enough now – be still, get on with the drawing, it's hard!'

I wanted peace for myself. They began to sketch

diligently. I stood and looked across at the sunset, which I could see facing me through my window, a great gold sunset, very large and magnificent, rising up in immense gold beauty beyond the town, that was become a low dark strip of nothingness under the wonderful up-building of the western sky. The light, the thick, heavy golden sunlight which is only seen in its full dripping splendour in town, spread on the desks and the floor like gold lacquer. I lifted my hands, to take the sunlight on them, smiling faintly to myself, trying to shut my fingers over its tangible richness.

'Please Sir!' – I was interrupted – 'Please Sir, can we have rubbers?'

The question was rather plaintive. I had said they should have rubbers no more. I could not keep my stock, I could not detect the thief among them, and I was weary of the continual degradation of bullying them to try to recover what was lost among them. But it was Friday afternoon, very peaceful and happy. Like a bad teacher, I went back on my word:

'Well –!' I said, indulgently.

My monitor, a pale, bright, erratic boy, went to the cupboard and took out a red box.

'Please Sir!' he cried, then he stopped and counted again in the box. 'Eleven! There's only eleven, Sir, and there were fifteen when I put them away on Wednesday –!'

The class stopped, every face upturned. Joe sunk, and lay flat on his shell, his legs limp. Another of the hateful moments had come. The sunset was smeared out, the charm of the afternoon was smashed like a fair glass that falls to the floor. My nerves seemed to tighten, and to vibrate with sudden tension.

'Again!' I cried, turning to the class in passion, to the upturned faces, and the sixty watchful eyes.

'Again! I am sick of it, sick of it I am! A thieving,

wretched set! – a skulking, mean lot!' I was quivering with anger and distress.

'Who is it? You must know! You are all as bad as one another, you hide it – a miserable –!' I looked round the class in great agitation. The 'Gordons' with their distrustful faces, were noticeable:

'Marples!' I cried to one of them, 'where are those rubbers?'

'I don't know where they are – I've never 'ad no rubbers' – he almost shouted back, with the usual insolence of his set. I was more angry:

'You must know! They're gone – they don't melt into air, they don't fly – who took them then? Rawson, do you know anything of them?'

'No Sir!' he cried, with impudent indignation.

'No, you intend to know nothing! Wood, have you any knowledge of these four rubbers?'

'No!' he shouted, with absolute insolence.

'Come here!' I cried, 'come here! Fetch the cane, Burton. We'll make an end, insolence and thieving and all.'

The boy dragged himself to the front of the class, and stood slackly, almost crouching, glaring at me. The rest of the 'Gordons' sat upright in their desks, like animals of a pack ready to spring. There was tense silence for a moment. Burton handed me the cane, and I turned from the class to Wood. I liked him best among the Gordons.

'Now my lad!' I said. 'I'll cane you for impudence first.'

He turned swiftly to me; tears sprang to his eyes.

'Well,' he shouted at me, 'you always pick on the Gordons – you're always on to us –!' This was so manifestly untrue that my anger fell like a bird shot in a midflight.

'Why!' I exclaimed, 'what a disgraceful untruth! I am always excusing you, letting you off –!'

'But you pick on us – you start on us – you pick on Marples, an' Rawson, an' on me. You always begin with the Gordons.'

'Well,' I answered, justifying myself, 'isn't it natural? Haven't you boys stolen – haven't these boys stolen – several times – and been caught?'

'That doesn't say as we do now,' he replied.

'How am I to know? You don't help me. How do I know? Isn't it natural to suspect you –?'

'Well, it's not us. We know who it is. Everybody knows who it is – only they won't tell.'

'Who know?' I asked.

'Why Rawson, and Maddock, and Newling, and all of 'em.'

I asked these boys if they could tell me. Each one shook his head, and said 'No Sir.' I went round the class. It was the same. They lied to me every one.

'You see,' I said to Wood.

'Well – they won't own up,' he said. 'I shouldn't 'a done if you hadn't 'a been goin' to cane me.'

This frankness was painful, but I preferred it. I made them all sit down. I asked Wood to write his knowledge on a piece of paper, and I promised not to divulge. He would not. I asked the boys he had named, all of them. They refused. I asked them again – I appealed to them.

'Let them all do it then!' said Wood. I tore up scraps of paper, and gave each boy one.

'Write on it the name of the boy you suspect. He is a thief and a sneak. He gives endless pain and trouble to us all. It is your duty.'

They wrote furtively, and quickly doubled up the papers. I collected them in the lid of the rubber box, and sat at the table to examine them. There was dead silence, they all watched me. Joe had withdrawn into his shell, forgotten.

A few papers were blank; several had 'I suspect nobody' – these I threw in the paper basket; two had the name of an old thief, and these I tore up; eleven bore the name of my assistant monitor a splendid, handsome boy, one of the oldest of the actors. I remembered how deferential and polite he had been when I had asked him, how ready to make barren suggestions; I remembered his shifty, anxious look during the questioning; I remembered how eager he had been to do things for me before the monitor came in the room. I knew it was he – without remembering.

'Well!' I said, feeling very wretched when I was convinced that the papers were right. 'Go on with the drawing.'

They were very uneasy and restless, but quiet. From time to time they watched me. Very shortly, the bell rang. I told the two monitors to collect up the things, and I sent the class home. We did not go into prayers. I, and they, were in no mood for hymns and the evening prayer of gratitude.

When the monitors had finished, and I had turned out all the lights but one, I sent home Curwen, and kept my assistant-monitor a moment.

'Ségar, do you know anything of my rubbers?'

'No Sir' – he had a deep, manly voice, and he spoke with earnest protestation – flushing.

'No? Nor my pencils – nor my two books?'

'No Sir! I know nothing about the books.'

'No? The pencils then –?'

'No Sir! Nothing! I don't know anything about them.'

'Nothing, Ségar?'

'No Sir.'

He hung his head, and looked so humiliated, a fine, handsome lad, that I gave it up. Yet I knew he would be dishonest again, when the opportunity arrived.

'Very well! You will not help as monitor any more. You will not come into the classroom until the class comes in – any more. You understand?'

'Yes Sir' – he was very quiet.

'Go along then.'

He went out, and silently closed the door. I turned out the last light, tried the cupboards, and went home.

I felt very tired, and very sick. The night had come up, the clouds were moving darkly, and the sordid streets near the school felt like disease in the lamplight.

The Fly in the Ointment

MURIEL had sent me some mauve primroses, slightly weather-beaten, and some honeysuckle – twine threaded with grey-green rosettes, and some timid hazel catkins. They had arrived in a forlorn little cardboard box just as I was rushing off to school.

'Stick 'em in water!' I said to Mrs Williams; and I left the house. But those mauve primroses had set my tone for the day: I was dreamy and reluctant; school and the sounds of the boys were unreal, unsubstantial; beyond these were the realities of my poor winter – trodden primroses and the pale hazel catkins that Muriel had sent me. Altogether the boys must have thought me a vacant fool; I regarded them as a punishment upon me.

I rejoiced exceedingly when night came, with the evening star, and the sky flushed dark blue, purple over the golden pomegranates of the lamps. I was as glad as if I had been hurrying home to Muriel, as if she would open the door to me, would keep me a little while in the fire-glow, with the splendid purple of the evening against the window, before she laughed and drew up her head proudly and flashed on the light over the tea-cups. But Eleanor, the girl, opened the door to me, and I poured out my tea in solitary state.

Mrs Williams had set out my winter posy for me on the table, and I thought of all the beautiful things we had done, Muriel and I, at home in the Midlands, of all the beautiful ways she had looked at me, of all the beautiful things I had said to her – or had meant to say. I went on imagining beautiful things to say to her, while she looked at me with her wonderful eyes from among the fir boughs in the wood. Meanwhile, I talked to my landlady about the neighbours.

Although I had much work to do, and although I laboured away at it, in the end there was nothing done. Then I felt very miserable, and sat still and sulked. At a quarter to eleven I said to myself:

'This will never do,' and I took up my pen and wrote a letter to Muriel.

'It was not fair to send me those robins' – we called the purple primroses 'robins', for no reason, unless that they bloomed in winter – 'they have bewitched me. Their wicked, bleared little pinkish eyes follow me about, and I have to think of you and home, instead of doing what I've got to do. All the time while I was teaching I had a grasshopper chirruping away in my head and the arithmetic rattled like the carts on the street. Poor lads! I read their miserable pieces of composition on "Pancakes" over and over, and never saw them, thinking "the primroses flower now because it is so sheltered under the plum-trees – those old trees with gummy bark". You like biting through a piece of hard, bright gum. If your lips did not get so sticky . . .'

I will not say at what time I finished my letter. I can recall a sensation of being dim, oblivious of everything, smiling to myself as I sealed the envelope; of putting my books and papers in their places without the least knowledge of so doing, keeping the atmosphere of Strelley Mill close round me in my London lodging. I cannot remember turning off the electric light. The next thing of which I am conscious is pushing at the kitchen door.

The kitchen is at the back of the house. Outside in the dark was a little yard and a hand's breadth of garden backed by the railway embankment. I had come down the passage from my room in the front of the house, and stood pushing at the kitchen door to get a glass for some water. Evidently the oilcloth had turned up a little, and the edge of the door was under it. I woke up irritably, swore a little, pushed harder, and heard the oilcloth rip. Then I bent and put my hand through the small space of the door to flatten the oilcloth.

The kitchen was in darkness save for the red embers lying low in the stove. I started, but rather from sleepy wonder than anything else. The shock was not quite enough to bring me to. Pressing himself flat into the corner between the stove and the wall was a fellow. I wondered, and was disturbed; the greater part of me was away in the Midlands still. So I stood looking and blinking.

'Why?' I said helplessly. I think this very mildness must have terrified him. Immediately he shrank together and began to dodge about between the table and stove, whining, snarling, with an incredibly mongrel sound:

'Don't yer touch me! Don't yer come grabbin' at me! I'll hit you between the eyes with this poker. I ain't done nothin' to you. Don't yer touch me, yer bloody coward!'

All the time he was writhing about in the space in which I had him trapped, between the table and stove. I was much too dazed to do anything but stare. Then my blood seemed to change its quality. I came awake, sick and sharp with pain. It was such a display as I had seen before in school, and I felt again the old misery of helplessness and disgust. He dared not, I knew, strike, unless by trying to get hold of him I terrified him to the momentary madness of such a slum-rat.

'Stop your row!' I said, standing still and leaving him his room. 'Shut your miserable row! Do you want to waken the children?'

'Ah, but don't you touch me, don't you come no nearer!'

He had stopped writhing about, and was crouching at the

defensive. The little frenzy, too, had gone out of his voice.

'Put the poker down, you fool' – I pointed to the corner of the stove, where the poker used to stand. I supplied him with the definite idea of placing the poker in the corner, and in his crazy witless state he could not reject it. He did as I told him, but indefinitely, as if the action were secondhand. The poker, loosely dropped into the corner, slid to the ground with a clatter.

I looked from it to him, feeling him like a burden upon me, and in some way I was afraid of him, for my heart began to beat heavily. His own indefinite clumsiness, and the jangle of the poker on the hearth, and then my sudden spiritual collapse, unnerved him still more. He crouched there abjectly.

I took a box of matches from the mantelpiece and lit the gas at the pendant that hung in the middle of the bare little room. Then I saw that he was a youth of nineteen or so, narrow at the temples, with thin, pinched-looking brows. He was not ugly, nor did he look ill-fed. But he evidently came of a low breed. His hair had been cut close to his skull, leaving a tussocky fringe over his forehead to provide him with a 'topping', and to show that it was no prison crop which had bared him.

'I wasn't doin' no harm,' he whined resentfully, with still an attempt at a threat in his tones. 'I 'aven't done nuffin' to you; you leave me alone. What harm have I done?'

'Be quiet,' I said. 'You'll wake the children and the people.'

I went to the door and listened. No one was disturbed. Then I closed the door and pulled down the wide-opened window, which was letting in the cold night air. As I did so I shivered, noting how ugly and shapeless the mangle looked in the yard, with the moonlight on its frosty cover.

The fellow was standing abjectly in the same place. He had evidently been rickety as a child. I sat down in the rocking-chair.

'What did you come in here for?' I asked, almost pleading.

'Well,' he retorted insolently. 'An' wouldn't you go somewhere if you 'edn't a place to go to of a night like this?'

'Look here,' I said coldly, a flash of hate in my blood; 'None of your chelp.'

'Well, I only come in for a warm,' he said, afraid not to appear defiant.

'No you didn't,' I replied. 'You came to take something. What did you want from here?' I looked round the kitchen unhappily. He looked back at me uneasily, then at his dirty hands, then at me again. He had brown eyes, in which low cunning floated like oil on the top of much misery.

'I might 'a took some boots' he said, with a little vaunt.

My heart sank. I hoped he would say 'food'. And I was responsible for him. I hated him.

'You want your neck breaking,' I said. 'We can hardly afford boots as it is.'

'I ain't never done it before! This is the first time –'

'You miserable swine!' I said. He looked at me with a flash of rat-fury.

'Where do you live?' I asked.

'Exeter Road.'

'And you don't do any work?'

'I couldn't never get a job – except – I used to deliver laundry –'

'And they turned you off for thieving?'

He shifted and stirred uneasily in his chair. As he was so manifestly uncomfortable, I did not press him.

'Who do you live with?'

'I live at 'ome.'

'What does your father do?'

But he sat stubborn and would not answer. I thought of the gangs of youths who stood at the corner of the mean streets near the school, there all day long, month after month, fooling with the laundry girls and insulting passers-by.

'But,' I said, 'what are you going to do?'

He hung his head again and fidgeted in his chair. Evidently what little thought he gave to the subject made him uncomfortable. He could not answer.

'Get a laundry girl to marry you and live on her?' I asked sarcastically.

He smiled sicklily, evidently even a little bit flattered. What was the good of talking to him?

'And loaf at the street corners till you go rotten?' I said.

He looked up at me sullenly.

'Well, I can't get a job,' he replied with insolence. He was not hopeless, but like a man born without expectations, apathetic, looking to be provided for, sullenly allowing everything.

'No,' I said, 'if a man is worthy of his hire, the hire is worthy of a man – and I'm damned if you *are* a man!'

He grinned at me with sly insolence.

'And would any woman have you?' I asked.

Then he grinned slyly to himself, ducking his head to hide the joke. And I thought of the coloured primroses and of Muriel's beautiful, pensive face. Then of him with his dirty clothes and his nasty skin! Then that, given a woman, he would be a father.

'Well,' I said, 'it's a knock-out.'

He gave me a narrow, sleering look.

'You don't know everyfing,' he said in contempt.

I sat and wondered. And I knew I could not understand

him, that I had no fellow feeling with him. He was something beyond me.

'Well,' I said helplessly, 'you'd better go.'

I rose, feeling he had beaten me. He could affect and alter me: I could not affect nor alter him. He shambled off down the path. I watched him skulk under the lamp-posts, afraid of the police. Then I shut the door.

In the silence of the sleeping house I stood quite still for some minutes, up against the impassable fact of this man, beyond which I could not get. I could not accept him. I simply hated him. Then I climbed the stairs. It was like a nightmare. I thought he was a blot, like a blot fallen on my mind, something black and heavy out of which I could not extricate myself.

As I hung up my coat I felt Muriel's fat letter in my pocket. It made me a trifle sick. 'No!' I said, with a flush of rage against her perfect, serene purity, 'I don't want to think of her.' And I wound my watch up sullenly, feeling alone and wretched.

The Old Adam

THE maid who opened the door was just developing into a handsome womanhood. Therefore she seemed to have the insolent pride of one newly come to an inheritance. She would be a splendid woman to look at, having just enough of Jewish blood to enrich her comeliness into beauty. At nineteen her fine grey eyes looked challenge, and her warm complexion, her black hair looped up slack, enforced the sensuous folding of her mouth.

She wore no cap nor apron, but a well-looking sleeved overall such as even very ladies don.

The man she opened to was tall and thin, but graceful in his energy. He wore white flannels, carried a tennis-racket. With a light bow to the maid he stepped beside her on the threshold. He was one of those who attract by their movement, whose movement is watched unconsciously, as we watch the flight of a sea-bird waving its wing leisurely. Instead of entering the house, the young man stood beside the maid-servant and looked back into the blackish evening. When in repose, he had the diffident, ironic bearing so remarkable in the educated youth of today, the very reverse of that traditional aggressiveness of youth.

'It is going to thunder, Kate,' he said.

'Yes, I think it is,' she replied, on an even footing.

The young man stood a moment looking at the trees across the road, and on the oppressive twilight.

'Look,' he said, 'there's not a trace of colour in the atmosphere, though it's sunset; all a dark, lustrous grey; and those oaks kindle green like a low fire – see!'

'Yes,' said Kate, rather awkwardly.

'A troublesome sort of evening; must be, because it's your last with us.'

67

'Yes,' said the girl, flushing and hardening.

There was another pause; then:

'Sorry you're going?' he asked, with a faint tang of irony.

'In some ways,' she replied, rather haughtily.

He laughed, as if he understood what was not said, then, with an 'Ah well!' he passed along the hall.

The maid stood for a few moments clenching her young fists, clenching her very breast in revolt. Then she closed the door.

Edward Severn went into the dining-room. It was eight o'clock, very dark for a June evening; on the dusk-blue walls only the gilt frames of the pictures glinted pale. The clock occupied the room with its delicate ticking.

The door opened into a tiny conservatory that was lined with a grape-vine. Severn could hear, from the garden beyond, the high prattling of a child. He went to the glass door.

Running down the grass by the flower-border, was a little girl of three, dressed in white. She was very bonny, very quick and intent in her movements; she reminded him of a field-mouse which plays alone in the corn, for sheer joy. Severn lounged in the doorway, watching her. Suddenly she perceived him. She started, flashed into greeting, gave a little gay jump, and stood quite still again, as if pleading.

'Mr Severn,' she cried, in wonderfully coaxing tones: 'Come and see this.'

'What?' he asked.

'Com' and see it,' she pleaded.

He laughed, knowing she only wanted to coax him into the garden; and he went.

'Look,' she said spreading out her plump little arm.

'What?' he asked.

The baby was not going to admit that she had tricked him thither for her amusement.

'All gone up to buds,' she said, pointing to the closed marigolds. Then 'See!' she shrieked, flinging herself at his legs, grasping the flannel of his trousers, and tugging at him wildly. She was a wild little Maenad. She flew shrieking like a revelling bird down the garden, glancing back to see if he were coming. He had not the heart to desist, but went swiftly after her. In the obscure garden, the two white figures darted through the flowering plants, the baby, with her full silk skirts, scudding like a ruffled bird, the man, lithe and fleet, snatching her up and smothering his face in hers. And all the time her piercing voice re-echoed from his low calls of warning and of triumph as he hunted her. Often she was really frightened of him; then she clung fast round his neck, and he laughed and mocked her in a low, stirring voice, while she protested.

The garden was large for a London suburb. It was shut in by a high, dark embankment, that rose above a row of black poplar trees. And over the spires of the trees, high up, slid by the golden-lighted trains, with the soft movement of caterpillars and a hoarse, subtle noise.

Mrs Thomas stood in the dark doorway watching the night, the trains, the flash and run of the two white figures.

'And now we must go in,' she heard Severn say.

'No,' cried the baby, wild and defiant as a bacchanal. She clung to him like a wild-cat.

'Yes,' he said. 'Where's your mother?'

'Give me a swing,' demanded the child.

He caught her up. She strangled him hard with her young arms.

'I said, where's your mother?' he persisted, half-smothered.

'She's op'tairs,' shouted the child. 'Give me a swing.'

'I don't think she is,' said Severn.

'She is. Give me a swing, a swi-i-ing!'

He bent forward, so that she hung from his neck like a great pendant. Then he swung her, laughing low to himself while she shrieked with fear. As she slipped he caught her to his breast.

'Mary!' called Mrs Thomas, in that low, songful tone of a woman when her heart is roused and happy.

'Mary!' she called, long and sweet.

'Oh, no!' cried the child quickly.

But Severn bore her off. Laughing, he bowed his head and offered to the mother the baby who clung round his neck.

'Come along here,' said Mrs Thomas roguishly, clasping the baby's waist with her hands.

'Oh, no,' cried the child, tucking her head into the young man's neck.

'But it's bed-time,' said the mother. She laughed as she drew at the child to pull her loose from Severn. The baby clung tighter, and laughed, feeling no determination in her mother's grip. Severn bent his head to loosen the child's hold, bowed, and swung the heavy baby on his neck. The child clung to him, bubbling with laughter; the mother drew at her baby, laughing low, while the man swung gracefully, giving little jerks of laughter.

'Let Mr Severn undress me,' said the child, hugging close to the young man, who had come to lodge with her parents when she was scarce a month old.

'You're in high favour tonight,' said the mother to Severn. He laughed, and all three stood a moment watching the trains pass and re-pass in the sky beyond the garden-end. Then they went indoors, and Severn undressed the child.

She was a beautiful girl, a bacchanal with her wild, dull-gold hair tossing about like a loose chaplet, her hazel eyes shining daringly, her small, spaced teeth glistening in little passions of laughter within her red, small mouth. The young man loved her. She was such a little bright wave of wilfulness, so abandoned to her impulses, so white and smooth as she lay at rest, so startling as she flashed her naked limbs about. But she was growing too old for a young man to undress.

She sat on his knee in her high-waisted night-gown, eating her piece of bread-and-butter with savage little bites of resentment: she did not want to go to bed. But Severn made her repeat a Pater Noster. She lisped over the Latin, and Mrs Thomas, listening, flushed with pleasure; although she was a Protestant, and although she deplored the unbelief of Severn, who had been a Catholic.

The mother took the baby to carry her to bed. Mrs Thomas was thirty-four years old, full-bosomed and ripe. She had dark hair that twined lightly round her low, white brow. She had a clear complexion, and beautiful brows, and dark-blue eyes. The lower part of her face was heavy.

'Kiss me,' said Severn to the child.

He raised his face as he sat in the rocking-chair. The mother stood beside, looking down at him, and holding the laughing rogue of a baby against her breast. The man's face was uptilted, his heavy brows set back from the laughing tenderness of his eyes, which looked dark, because the pupil was dilated. He pursed up his handsome mouth, his thick close-cut moustache roused.

He was a man who gave tenderness, but who did not ask for it. All his own troubles he kept, laughingly, to himself. But his eyes were very sad when quiet, and he was too quick to understand sorrow, not to know it.

Mrs Thomas watched his fine mouth lifted for kissing. She leaned forward, lowering the baby, and suddenly, by a quick change in his eyes, she knew he was aware of her heavy woman's breasts approaching down to him. The wild rogue of a baby bent her face to his, and then, instead

71

of kissing him, suddenly licked his cheek with her wet, soft tongue. He started back in aversion, and his eyes and his teeth flashed with a dangerous laugh.

'No, no,' he laughed, in low strangled tones. 'No dog-lick, my dear, oh no!'

The baby chuckled with glee, gave one wicked jerk of laughter, that came out like a bubble escaping.

He put up his mouth again, and again his face was horizontal below the face of the young mother. She looked down on him as if by a kind of fascination.

'Kiss me, then,' he said with thick throat.

The mother lowered the baby. She felt scarcely sure of her balance. Again the child, when near to his face, darted out her tongue to lick him. He swiftly averted his face, laughing in his throat.

Mrs Thomas turned her face aside; she would see no more.

'Come then,' she said to the child. 'If you won't kiss Mr Severn nicely –'

The child laughed over the mother's shoulder like a squirrel crouched there. She was carried to bed.

It was still not quite dark; the clouds had opened slightly. The young man flung himself into an arm-chair, with a volume of French verse. He read one lyric, then he lay still.

'What, all in the dark!' exclaimed Mrs Thomas, coming in. 'And reading by *this* light.' She rebuked him with timid affectionateness. Then, glancing at his white-flannelled limbs sprawled out in the gloom, she went to the door. There she turned her back to him, looking out.

'Don't these flags smell strongly in the evening?' she said at length.

He replied with a few lines of the French he had been reading.

She did not understand. There was a peculiar silence.

'A peculiar brutal, carnal scent, iris,' he drawled at length. 'Isn't it?'

She laughed shortly, saying: 'Eh, I don't know about that.'

'It is,' he asserted calmly.

He rose from his chair, went to stand beside her at the door.

There was a great sheaf of yellow iris near the window. Farther off, in the last twilight, a gang of enormous poppies balanced and flapped their gold-scarlet, which even the darkness could not quite put out.

'We ought to be feeling very sad,' she said after a while.

'Why?' he asked.

'Well – isn't it Kate's last night?' she said, slightly mocking.

'She's a tartar, Kate,' he said.

'Oh, she's too rude, she is really! The way she criticizes the things you do, and her insolence –'

'The things *I* do?' he asked.

'Oh no; you can't do anything wrong. It's the things *I* do.' Mrs Thomas sounded very much incensed.

'Poor Kate, she'll have to lower her key,' said Severn.

'Indeed she will, and a good thing too.'

There was silence again.

'It's lightning,' he said at last.

'Where?' she asked, with a suddenness that suprised him. She turned, met his eyes for a second. He sank his head, abashed.

'Over there in the north-east,' he said, keeping his face from her. She watched his hand rather than the sky.

'Oh,' she said uninterestedly.

'The storm will wheel round, you'll see,' he said.

'I hope it wheels the other way, then.'

'Well, it won't. You don't like lightning, do you? You'd even have to take refuge with Kate if I weren't here.'

She laughed quietly at his irony.

'No,' she said, quite bitterly. 'Mr Thomas is never in when he's wanted.'

'Well, as he won't be urgently required, we'll acquit him, eh?'

At that moment a white flash fell across the blackness. They looked at each other, laughing. The thunder came broken and hesitatingly.

'I think we'll shut the door,' said Mrs Thomas, in normal, sufficiently distant tones. A strong woman, she locked and bolted the stiff fastenings easily. Severn pressed on the light. Mrs Thomas noticed the untidiness of the room. She rang, and presently Kate appeared.

'Will you clear baby's things away?' she said, in the contemptuous tone of a hostile woman. Without answering, and in her superb, unhastening way, Kate began to gather up the small garments. Both women were aware of the observant, white figure of the man standing on the hearth. Severn balanced with a fine, easy poise, and smiled to himself, exulting a little to see the two women in this state of hostility. Kate moved about with bowed defiant head. Severn watched her curiously; he could not understand her. And she was leaving tomorrow. When she had gone out of the room, he remained still standing, thinking. Something in his lithe, vigorous balance, so alert, and white, and independent, caused Mrs Thomas to glance at him from her sewing.

'I will let the blinds down,' he said, becoming aware that he was attracting attention.

'Thank you,' she replied conventionally.

He let the lattice blinds down, then flung himself into his chair.

Mrs Thomas sat at the table, near him, sewing. She was a good-looking woman, well made. She sat under the one light that was turned on. The lamp-shade was of red silk lined with yellow. She sat in the warm-gold light. There was established between the two a peculiar silence, like suspense, almost painful to each of them, yet which neither would break. Severn listened to the snap of her needle, looked from the movement of her hand to the window, where the lightning beat and fluttered through the lattice. The thunder was as yet far off.

'Look,' he said, 'at the lightning.'

Mrs Thomas started at the sound of his voice, and some of the colour went from her face. She turned to the window.

There, between the cracks of the venetian blinds, came the white flare of lightning, then the dark. Several storms were in the sky. Scarcely had one sudden glare fluttered and palpitated out, than another covered the window with white. It dropped, and another flew up, beat like a moth for a moment, then vanished. Thunder met and over-lapped; two battles were fought together in the sky.

Mrs Thomas went very pale. She tried not to look at the window, yet, when she felt the lightning blench the lamp-light, she watched, and each time a flash leaped on the window, she shuddered. Severn, all unconsciously, was smiling with roused eyes.

'You don't like it?' he said, at last, gently.

'Not much,' she answered, and he laughed.

'Yet all the storms are a fair way off,' he said. 'Not one near enough to touch us.'

'No, but,' she replied, at last laying her hands in her lap, and turning to him, 'it makes me feel worked up. You don't know how it makes me feel, as if I couldn't contain myself.'

She made a helpless gesture with her hand. He was watching her closely. She seemed to him pathetically help-less and bewildered; she was eight years older than he. He smiled in a strange, alert fashion, like a man who feels in jeopardy. She bent over her work, stitching nervously. There was a silence in which neither of them could breathe freely.

Presently a bigger flash than usual whitened through the yellow lamplight. Both glanced at the window, then at each other. For a moment it was a look of greeting; then his eyes dilated to a smile, wide with recklessness. He felt her waver, lose her composure, become incoherent. Seeing the faint helplessness of coming tears, he felt his heart thud to a crisis. She hid her face at her sewing.

Severn sank in his chair, half suffocated by the beating of his heart. Yet, time after time, as the flashes came, they looked at each other, till in the end they both were panting, and afraid, not of the lightning but of themselves and of each other.

He was so much moved that he became conscious of his perturbation. 'What the deuce is up?' he asked himself, wondering. At twenty-seven, he was quite chaste. Being highly civilized, he prized women for their intuition, and because of the delicacy with which he could transfer to them his thoughts and feelings, without cumbrous argument. From this to a state of passion he could only proceed by fine gradations, and such a procedure he had never begun. Now he was startled, astonished, perturbed, yet still scarcely conscious of his whereabouts. There was a pain in his chest that made him pant, and an involuntary tension in his arms, as if he must press someone to his breast. But the idea that this someone was Mrs Thomas would have shocked him too much had he formed it. His passion had run on subconsciously, till now it had come to such a pitch it must drag his conscious soul into allegiance. This, however, would probably never happen; he would not yield allegiance, and blind emotion, in this direction, could not carry him alone.

Towards eleven o'clock Mr Thomas came in.

'I wonder you come home at all,' Severn heard Mrs Thomas say as her husband stepped indoors.

'I left the office at half-past ten,' the voice of Thomas replied, disagreeably.

'Oh, don't try to tell me that old tale,' the woman answered contemptuously.

'I didn't try anything at all, Gertie,' he replied with sarcasm. 'Your question was answered.'

Severn imagined him bowing with affected, magisterial dignity, and he smiled. Mr Thomas was something in the law.

Mrs Thomas left her husband in the hall, came and sat down again at table, where she and Severn had just finished supper, both of them reading the while.

Thomas came in, flushed very red. He was of middle stature, a thickly-built man of forty, good-looking. But he had grown round-shouldered with thrusting forward his chin in order to look the aggressive, strong-jawed man. He *had* a good jaw; but his mouth was small and nervously pinched. His brown eyes were of the emotional, affectionate sort, lacking pride or any austerity.

He did not speak to Severn nor Severn to him. Although as a rule the two men were very friendly, there came these times when, for no reason whatever, they were sullenly hostile. Thomas sat down heavily, and reached his bottle of beer. His hands were thick, and in their movement rudimentary. Severn watched the thick fingers grasp the drinking-glass as if it were a treacherous enemy.

'Have you *had* supper, Gertie?' he asked, in tones that sounded like an insult. He could not bear that these two should sit reading as if he did not exist.

'Yes,' she replied, looking up at him in impatient surprise. 'It's late enough.' Then she buried herself again in her book.

Severn ducked low and grinned. Thomas swallowed a mouthful of beer.

'I wish you could answer my questions, Gertie, without superfluous *de*-tail,' he said nastily, thrusting out his chin at her as if cross-examining.

'Oh,' she said indifferently, not looking up. 'Wasn't my answer right, then?'

'Quite – I thank you,' he answered, bowing with great sarcasm. It was utterly lost on his wife.

'Hm-hm!' she murmured in abstraction, continuing to read.

Silence resumed. Severn was grinning to himself, chuckling.

'I *had* a compliment paid me tonight, Gertie,' said Thomas, quite amicably, after a while. He still ignored Severn.

'Hm-hm!' murmured his wife. This was a well-known beginning. Thomas valiantly struggled on with his courtship of his wife, swallowing his spleen.

'Councillor Jarndyce, in full committee – Are you listening, Gertie?'

'Yes,' she replied, looking up for a moment.

'You know Councillor Jarndyce's style,' Thomas continued, in the tone of a man determined to be patient and affable: '– the courteous Old English Gentleman –'

'Hm-hm!' replied Mrs Thomas.

'He was speaking in reply to . . .' Thomas gave innumerable wearisome details, which no one heeded.

'Then he bowed to me, then to the Chairman – "I am compelled to say, Mr Chairman, that we have *one* cause for congratulation; we are inestimably fortunate in *one* member of our staff; there is one point of which we can always be sure – the point of *law*; and it is an important point, Mr Chairman."'

'He bowed to the Chairman, he bowed to me. And you

should have heard the applause all round that Council Chamber – that great, horse-shoe table, you don't know how impressive it is. And every face turned to me, and all round the board: "Hear – Hear!" You don't know what respect I command in *business*, Mrs Thomas.'

'Then let it suffice you,' said Mrs Thomas, calmly indifferent.

Mr Thomas bit his bread-and-butter.

'The fat-head's had two drops of Scotch, so he's drawing on his imagination,' thought Severn, chuckling deeply.

'I thought you said there was no meeting tonight,' Mrs Thomas suddenly and innocently remarked after a while.

'There was a meeting *in camera*,' replied her husband, drawing himself up with official dignity. His excessive and wounded dignity convulsed Severn; the lie disgusted Mrs Thomas in spite of herself.

Presently Thomas, always courting his wife and insultingly overlooking Severn, raised a point of politics, passed a lordly opinion very offensive to the young man. Severn had risen, stretched himself, and laid down his book. He was leaning on the mantelpiece in an indifferent manner, as if he scarcely noticed the two talkers. But hearing Thomas pronounce like a boor upon the Woman's Bill, he roused himself, and coolly contradicted his landlord. Mrs Thomas shot a look of joy at the white-clad young man who lounged so scornfully on the hearth. Thomas cracked his knuckles one after another, and lowered his brown eyes, which were full of hate. After a sufficient pause, for his timidity was stronger than his impulse, he replied with a phrase that sounded final. Severn flipped the sense out of it with a few words. In the argument Severn, more cultured and far more nimble-witted than his antagonist, who hauled up his answers with a lawyer's show of invincibility, but who had not any fineness of perception, merely spiked his opponent's pieces and smiled at him. Also the young man enjoyed himself by looking down scornfully, straight into the brown eyes of his senior all the time, so that Thomas writhed.

Mrs Thomas, meantime, took her husband's side against women, without reserve. Severn was angry; he was scornfully angry with her. Mrs Thomas glanced at him from time to time, a little ecstasy lighting her fine blue eyes. The irony of her part was delicious to her. If she had sided with Severn, that young man would have pitied the forlorn man, and been gentle with him.

The battle of words had got quieter and more intense. Mrs Thomas made no move to check it. At last Severn was aware he and Thomas were both getting overheated. Thomas had doubled and dodged painfully, like a half-frenzied rabbit that will not realize it is trapped. Finally his efforts had moved even his opponent to pity. Mrs Thomas was not pitiful. She scorned her husband's dexterity of argument, when his intellectual dishonesty was so evident to her. Severn uttered his last phrases, and would say no more. Then Thomas cracked his knuckles one after the other, turned aside, consumed with morbid humiliation, and there was silence.

'I will go to bed,' said Severn. He would have spoken some conciliatory words to his landlord; he lingered with that purpose; but he could not bring his throat to utter his purpose.

'Oh, before you go, do you mind, Mr Severn, helping Mr Thomas down with Kate's box? You may be gone before he's up in the morning, and the cab comes at ten. Do you mind?'

'Why should I?' replied Severn.

'Are you ready, Joe?' she asked her husband.

Thomas rose with the air of a man who represses himself and is determined to be patient.

'Where is it?' he asked.

'On the top landing. I'll tell Kate, and then we shan't frighten her. She has gone to bed.'

Mrs Thomas was quite mistress of the situation; both men were humble before her. She led the way, with a candle, to the third floor. There on the little landing, outside the closed door, stood a large tin trunk. The three were silent because of the baby.

'Poor Kate,' Severn thought. 'It's a shame to kick her out into the world, and all for nothing.' He felt an impulse of hate towards womankind.

'Shall I go first, Mr Severn?' asked Thomas.

It was surprising how friendly the two men were, as soon as they had something to do together, or when Mrs Thomas was absent. Then they were comrades, Thomas, the elder, the thick-set, playing the protector's part, though always deferential to the younger, whimsical man.

'I had better go first,' said Thomas kindly. 'And if you put this round the handle, it won't cut your fingers.'

He offered the young man a little flexible book from his pocket. Severn had such small, fine hands that Thomas pitied them.

Severn raised one end of the trunk. Leaning back, and flashing a smile to Mrs Thomas, who stood with the candle, he whispered: 'Kate's got a lot more impediments than I have.'

'I know it's heavy,' laughed Mrs Thomas.

Thomas, waiting at the brink of the stairs, saw the young man tilting his bare throat towards the smiling woman, and whispering words which pleased her.

'At your pleasure, sir,' he said in his most grating and official tones.

'Sorry,' Severn flung out scornfully.

The elder man retreated very cautiously, stiffly lowering himself down one stair, looking anxiously behind.

'Are you holding the light for *me*, Gertie?' he snapped sarcastically, when he had managed one stair. She lifted the candle with a swoop. He was in a bustle and a funk. Severn, always indifferent, smiled slightly, and lowered the box with negligent ease of movement. As a matter of fact, three-quarters of the heavy weight pressed on Thomas. Mrs Thomas watched the two figures from above.

'If I slip now,' thought Severn, as he noticed the anxious, red face of his landlord, 'I should squash him like a shrimp,' and he laughed to himself.

'Don't come yet,' he called softly to Mrs Thomas, whom he heard following. 'If you slip, your husband's bottom-most under the smash. "Beware the fearful avalanche!"'

He laughed, and Mrs Thomas gave a little chuckle. Thomas, very red and flustered, glanced irritably back at them, but said nothing.

Near the bottom of the staircase there was a twist in the stairs. Severn was feeling particularly reckless. When he came to the turn, he chuckled to himself, feeling his house-slippers unsafe on the narrowed, triangular stairs. He loved a risk above all things, and a subconscious instinct made the risk doubly sweet when his rival was under the box. Though Severn would not knowingly have hurt a hair of his landlord's head.

When Thomas was beginning to sweat with relief, being only one step from the landing, Severn did slip, quite accidentally. The great box crashed as if in pain, Severn glissaded down the stairs, Thomas was flung backwards across the landing, and his head went thud against the banister post. Severn, seeing no great harm done, was struggling to his feet, laughing and saying: 'I'm awfully sorry –' when Thomas got up. The elder man was infuriated like a bull. He saw the laughing face of Severn and he went mad. His brown eyes flared.

'You –, you did it on purpose!' he shouted, and straightway he fetched the young man two heavy blows, upon the jaw and ear. Thomas, a footballer and boxer in his youth, had been brought up among the roughs of Swansea; Severn in a religious college in France. The young man had never been struck in the face before. He instantly went white and mad with rage. Thomas stood on guard, fists up. But on the small, lumbered landing there was no room for fight. Moreover, Severn had no instinct of fisticuffs. With open, stiff fingers, the young man sprang on his adversary. In spite of the blow he received, but did not feel, he flung himself again forward, and then, catching Thomas's collar, brought him down with a crash. Instantly his exquisite hands were dug in the other's thick throat, the linen collar having been torn open. Thomas fought madly, with blind, brute strength. But the other lay wrapped on him like a white steel, his rare intelligence concentrated, not scattered; concentrated on strangling Thomas swiftly. He pressed forward, forcing his landlord's head over the edge of the next flight of stairs. Thomas, stout and full-blooded, lost every trace of self-possession; he struggled like an animal at slaughter. The blood came out of his nose over his face; he made horrid choking sounds as he struggled.

Suddenly Severn felt his face turned between two hands. With a shock of real agony, he met the eyes of Kate. She bent forward, she captured his eyes.

'What do you think you're doing?' she cried in frenzy of indignation. She leaned over him in her night-dress, her two black plaits hanging perpendicular. He hid his face, and took his hands away. As he kneeled to rise, he glanced up the stairs. Mrs Thomas stood against the banisters, motionless in a trance of horror and remorse. He saw the remorse plainly. Severn turned away his face, and was wild with shame. He saw his landlord kneeling, his hands at his throat, choking, rattling, and gasping. The young man's heart filled with remorse and grief. He put his arms round the heavy man, and raised him, saying tenderly:

'Let me help you up.'

He had got Thomas up against the wall, when the choked man began to slide down again in collapse, gasping all the time pitifully.

'No, stand up; you're best standing up,' commanded Severn sharply, rearing his landlord up again. Thomas managed to obey, stupidly. His nose still bled, he still held his throat and gasped with a crowing sound. But his breathing was getting deeper.

'Water, Kate – and sponge – cold,' said Severn.

Kate was back in an instant. The young man bathed his landlord's face and temples and throat. The bleeding ceased directly, the stout man's breathing became a series of irregular, jerky gasps, like a child that has been sobbing hard. At last he took a long breath, and his breast settled into regular stroke, with little fluttering interruptions. Still holding his hand to his throat, he looked up with dazed, piteous brown eyes, mutely wretched and appealing. He moved his tongue as if to try it, put back his head a little, and moved the muscles of his throat. Then he replaced his hands on the place that ached.

Severn was grief-stricken. He would willingly, at that moment, have given his right hand for the man he had hurt.

Mrs Thomas, meanwhile, stood on the stairs, watching: for a long time she dared not move, knowing she would sink down. She watched. One of the crises of her life was passing. Full of remorse, she passed over into the bitter land of repentance. She must no longer allow herself to hope for anything for herself. The rest of her life must be spent in self-abnegation: she must seek for no sympathy, must ask for no grace in love, no grace and harmony in living. Henceforward, as far as her own desires went, she was dead. She took a fierce joy in the anguish of it.

'Do you feel better?' Severn asked of the sick man. Thomas looked at the questioner with tragic brown eyes, in which was no anger, only mute self-pity. He did not answer, but looked like a wounded animal, very pitiable. Mrs Thomas quickly repressed an impulse of impatient scorn, replacing it with a numb, abstract sense of duty, lofty and cold.

'Come,' said Severn, full of pity, and gentle as a woman, 'Let me help you to bed.'

Thomas, leaning heavily on the young man, whose white garments were dabbed with blood and water, stumbled forlornly into his room. There Severn unlaced his boots and got off the remnant of his collar. At this point Mrs Thomas came in. She had taken her part; she was weeping also.

'Thank you, Mr Severn,' she said coldly. Severn, dismissed, slunk out of the room. She went up to her husband, took his pathetic head upon her bosom, and pressed it there. As Severn went downstairs, he heard the few sobs of the husband, among the quick sniffing of the wife's tears. And he saw Kate, who had stood on the stairs to see all went well, climb up to her room with cold, calm face.

He locked up the house, put everything in order. Then he heated some water to bathe his face, which was swelling painfully. Having finished his fomentations, he sat thinking bitterly, with a good deal of shame.

As he sat, Mrs Thomas came down for something. Her bearing was cold and hostile. She glanced round to see all was safe. Then:

'You will put out the light when you go to bed, Mr Severn,' she said, more formally than a landlady at the seaside would speak. He was insulted: any ordinary being would turn off the light on retiring. Moreover, almost every night it was he who locked up the house, and came last to bed.

'I will, Mrs Thomas,' he answered. He bowed, his eyes flickering with irony, because he knew his face was swollen.

She returned again after having reached the landing.

'Perhaps you wouldn't mind helping *me* down with the box,' she said, quietly and coldly. He did not reply, as he would have done an hour before, that he certainly should not help her, because it was a man's job, and she must not do it. Now, he rose, bowed, and went upstairs with her. Taking the greater part of the weight, he came quickly downstairs with the load.

'Thank you; it's very good of you. Good night,' said Mrs Thomas, and she retired.

In the morning Severn rose late. His face was considerably swollen. He went in his dressing-gown across to Thomas's room. The other man lay in bed, looking much the same as ever, but mournful in aspect, though pleased within himself at being coddled.

'How are you this morning?' Severn asked.

Thomas smiled, looked almost with tenderness up at his friend.

'Oh, I'm all right, thanks,' he replied.

He looked at the other's swollen and bruised cheek, then again, affectionately, into Severn's eyes.

'I'm sorry' – with a glance of indication – 'for that,' he said simply. Severn smiled with his eyes, in his own winsome manner.

'I didn't know we were such essential brutes,' he said. 'I thought I was so civilized . . .'

Again he smiled, with a wry, stiff mouth. Thomas gave a deprecating little grunt of a laugh.

'Oh, I don't know,' he said. 'It shows a man's got some fight in him.'

He looked up in the other's face appealingly. Severn smiled, with a touch of bitterness. The two men grasped hands.

To the end of their acquaintance, Severn and Thomas were close friends, with a gentleness in their bearing, one towards the other. On the other hand, Mrs Thomas was only polite and formal with Severn, treating him as if he were a stranger.

Kate, her fate disposed of by her 'betters', passed out of their three lives.

The Witch à la Mode

WHEN Bernard Coutts alighted at East Croydon he knew he was tempting Providence.

'I may just as well,' he said to himself, 'stay the night here, where I am used to the place, as go to London. I can't get to Connie's forlorn spot tonight, and I'm tired to death, so why shouldn't I do what is easiest?'

He gave his luggage to a porter.

Again, as he faced the approaching tram-car: 'I don't see why I shouldn't go down to Purley. I shall just be in time for tea.'

Each of these concessions to his desires he made against his conscience. But beneath his sense of shame his spirit exulted.

It was an evening of March. In the dark hollow below Crown Hill the buildings accumulated, bearing the black bulk of the church tower up into the rolling and smoking sunset.

'I know it so well,' he thought. 'And love it,' he confessed secretly in his heart.

The car ran on familiarly. The young man listened for the swish, watched for the striking of the blue splash overhead, at the bracket. The sudden fervour of the spark, splashed out of the mere wire, pleased him.

'Where does it come from?' he asked himself, and a spark struck bright again. He smiled a little, roused.

The day was dying out. One by one the arc lamps fluttered or leaped alight, the strand of copper overhead glistened against the dark sky that now was deepening to the colour of monkshood. The tram-car dipped as it ran, seeming to exult. As it came clear of the houses, the young man, looking west, saw the evening star advance, a bright thing approaching from a long way off, as if it had been bathing in the surf of the daylight, and now was walking shorewards to the night. He greeted the naked star with a bow of the head, his heart surging as the car leaped.

'It seems to be greeting me across the sky – the star,' he said, amused by his own vanity.

Above the colouring of the afterglow the blade of the new moon hung sharp and keen. Something recoiled in him.

'It is like a knife to be used at a sacrifice,' he said to himself. Then, secretly: 'I wonder for whom?'

He refused to answer this question, but he had the sense of Constance, his betrothed, waiting for him in the Vicarage in the north. He closed his eyes.

Soon the car was running full-tilt from the shadow to the fume of yellow light at the terminus, where shop on shop and lamp beyond lamp heaped golden fire on the floor of the blue night. The car, like an eager dog, ran in home, sniffing with pleasure the fume of lights.

Coutts flung away uphill. He had forgotten he was tired. From the distance he could distinguish the house, by the broad white cloths of alyssum flowers that hung down the garden walls. He ran up the steep path to the door, smelling the hyacinths in the dark, watching for the pale fluttering of daffodils and the steadier show of white crocuses on the grassy banks.

Mrs Braithwaite herself opened the door to him.

'There!' she exclaimed. 'I expected you. I had your card saying you would cross from Dieppe today. You wouldn't make up your mind to come here, not till the last minute, would you? No – that's what I expected. You know where to put your things; I don't think we've altered anything in the last year.'

Mrs Braithwaite chattered on, laughing all the time. She was a young widow, whose husband had been dead two years. Of medium height, sanguine in complexion and temper, there was a rich oily glisten in her skin and in her black hair, suggesting the flesh of a nut. She was dressed for the evening in a long gown of soft, mole-coloured satin.

'Of course, I'm delighted you've come,' she said at last, lapsing into conventional politeness, and then, seeing his eyes, she began to laugh at her attempt at formality.

She let Coutts into a small, very warm room that had a dark, foreign sheen, owing to the black of the curtains and hangings covered thick with glistening Indian embroidery and to the sleekness of some Indian ware. A rosy old gentleman, with exquisite white hair and side-whiskers, got up shakily and stretched out his hand. His cordial expression of welcome was rendered strange by a puzzled, wondering look of old age, and by a certain stiffness of his countenance, which now would only render a few expressions. He wrung the newcomer's hand heartily, his manner contrasting pathetically with his bowed and trembling form.

'Oh, why – why, yes, it's Mr Coutts! H'm – ay. Well, and how are you – h'm? Sit down, sit down.' The old man rose again, bowing, waving the young man into a chair. 'Ay! well, and how are you? . . . What? Have some tea – come on, come along; here's the tray. Laura, ring for fresh tea for Mr Coutts. But I will do it.' He suddenly remembered his old gallantry, forgot his age and uncertainty. Fumbling, he rose to go to the bell-pull.

'It's done, Pater – the tea will be in a minute,' said his daughter in high, distinct tones. Mr Cleveland sank with relief into his chair.

'You know, I'm beginning to be troubled with rheumatism,' he explained in confidential tones. Mrs Braithwaite glanced at the young man and smiled. The old gentleman babbled and chattered. He had no knowledge of his guest beyond the fact of his presence; Coutts might have been any other young man, for all his host was aware.

'You didn't tell us you were going away. Why didn't you?' asked Laura, in her distinct tones, between laughing and reproach. Coutts looked at her ironically, so that she fidgeted with some crumbs on the cloth.

'I don't know,' he said. 'Why do we do things?'

'I'm sure I don't know. Why do we? Because we want to, I suppose,' and she ended again with a little run of laughter. Things were so amusing, and she was so healthy.

'Why *do* we do things, Pater?' she suddenly asked in a loud voice, glancing with a little chuckle of laughter at Coutts.

'Ay – why do we do things? What things?' said the old man, beginning to laugh with his daughter.

'Why, any of the things that we do.'

'Eh? Oh!' The old man was illuminated, and delighted. 'Well, now, that's a difficult question. I remember, when I was a little younger, we used to discuss Free Will – got very hot about it . . .' He laughed, and Laura laughed, then said, in a high voice:

'Oh! Free Will! We shall really think you're *passé*, if you revive that, Pater.'

Mr Cleveland looked puzzled for a moment. Then, as if answering a conundrum, he repeated:

'Why do we do things? Now, why *do* we do things?'

'I suppose,' he said, in all good faith, 'it's because we can't help it – eh? What?'

Laura laughed. Coutts showed his teeth in a smile.

'That's what I think, Pater,' she said, loudly.

'And are you still engaged to your Constance?' she asked of Coutts, with a touch of mockery this time. Coutts nodded.

'And how is she?' asked the widow.

'I believe she is very well – unless my delay has upset her,' said Coutts, his tongue between his teeth. It hurt him to give pain to his fiancée, and yet he did it wilfully.

'Do you know, she always reminds me of a Bunbury – I call her your Miss Bunbury,' Laura laughed.

Coutts did not answer.

'We missed you *so* much when you first went away,' Laura began, re-establishing the proprieties.

'Thank you,' he said. She began to laugh wickedly.

'On Friday evenings,' she said, adding quickly: 'Oh, and this is Friday evening, and Winifred is coming just as she used to – how long ago? – ten months?'

'Ten months,' Coutts corroborated.

'Did you quarrel with Winifred?' she asked suddenly.

'Winifred never quarrels,' he answered.

'I don't believe she does. Then why *did* you go away? You are such a puzzle to me, you know – and I shall never rest till I have had it out of you. Do you mind?'

'I like it,' he said, quietly, flashing a laugh at her.

She laughed, then settled herself in a dignified, serious way.

'No, I can't make you out at all – nor can I Winifred. You *are* a pair! But it's you who are the real wonder. When are you going to be married?'

'I don't know – When I am sufficiently well off.'

'I *asked* Winifred to come tonight,' Laura confessed. The eyes of the man and woman met.

'Why is she so ironic to me? – does she really like me?' Coutts asked of himself. But Laura looked too bonny and jolly to be fretted by love.

'And Winifred won't tell me a word,' she said.

'There is nothing to tell,' he replied.

Laura looked at him closely for a few moments. Then she rose and left the room.

Presently there arrived a German lady with whom Coutts was slightly acquainted. At about half past seven came Winifred Varley. Coutts heard the courtly old gentleman welcoming her in the hall, heard her low voice in answer. When she entered, and saw him, he knew it was a shock to her, though she hid it as well as she could. He suffered, too. After hesitating for a second in the doorway, she came forward, shook hands without speaking, only looking at him with rather frightened blue eyes. She was of medium height, sturdy in build. Her face was white and impassive, without the least trace of a smile. She was a blonde of twenty-eight, dressed in a white gown just short enough not to touch the ground. Her throat was solid and strong, her arms heavy and white and beautiful, her blue eyes heavy with unacknowledged passion. When she had turned away from Coutts, she flushed vividly. He could see the pink in her arms and throat, and he flushed in answer.

'That blush would hurt her,' he said to himself, wincing.

'I did not expect to see you,' she said, with a reedy *timbre* of voice, as if her throat were half-closed. It made his nerves tingle.

'No – nor I you. At least . . .' He ended indefinitely.

'You have come down from Yorkshire?' she asked. Apparently she was cold and self-possessed. Yorkshire meant the Rectory where his fiancée lived; he felt the sting of sarcasm.

'No,' he answered. 'I am on my way there.'

There was a moment's pause. Unable to resolve the situation, she turned abruptly to her hostess.

'Shall we play, then?'

They adjourned to the drawing-room. It was a large room upholstered in dull yellow. The chimney-piece took Coutt's attention. He knew it perfectly well, but this evening it had a new, lustrous fascination. Over the mellow marble of the mantel rose an immense mirror, very translucent and deep, like deep grey water. Before this mirror, shining white as moons on a soft grey sky, was a pair of statues in alabaster, two feet high. Both were nude figures. They glistened under the side lamps, rose clean and distinct from their pedestals. The Venus leaned slightly forward, as if anticipating someone's coming. Her attitude of suspense made the young man stiffen. He could see the clean suavity of her shoulders and waist reflected white on the deep mirror. She shone, catching, as she leaned forward, the glow of the lamp on her lustrous marble loins.

Laura played Brahms; the delicate, winsome German lady played Chopin; Winifred played on her violin a Grieg sonata, to Laura's accompaniment. After having sung twice, Coutts listened to the music. Unable to criticize, he listened till he was intoxicated. Winifred, as she played, swayed slightly. He watched the strong forward thrust of her neck, the powerful and angry striking of her arm. He could see the outline of her figure; she wore no corsets; and he found her of resolute independent build. Again he glanced at the Venus bending in suspense. Winifred was blonde with a solid whiteness, an isolated woman.

All the evening, little was said, save by Laura. Miss Syfurt exclaimed continually: 'Oh, that is fine! You play gra-and, Miss Varley, don't you know. If I could play the violin – ah! the violin!'

It was not later than ten o'clock when Winifred and Miss Syfurt rose to go, the former to Croydon, the latter to Ewell.

'We can go by car together to West Croydon,' said the German lady, gleefully, as if she were a child. She was a frail, excitable little woman of forty, naïve and innocent. She gazed with bright brown eyes of admiration on Coutts

'Yes, I am glad,' he answered.

He took up Winifred's violin, and the three proceeded downhill to the tram-terminus. There a car was on the point of departure. They hurried forward. Miss Syfurt mounted the step. Coutts waited for Winifred. The conductor called:

'Come along, please, if you're going.'

'No,' said Winifred. 'I prefer to walk this stage.'

'We can walk from West Croydon,' said Coutts.

The conductor rang the bell.

'Aren't you coming?' cried the frail, excitable little lady, from the footboard. 'Aren't you coming? – Oh!'

'I walk from West Croydon every day; I prefer to walk here, in the quiet,' said Winifred.

'Aw! aren't you coming with me?' cried the little lady, quite frightened. She stepped back, in supplication, towards the footboard. The conductor impatiently buzzed the bell. The car started forward, Miss Syfurt staggered, was caught by the conductor.

'Aw!' she cried, holding her hand out to the two who stood on the road, and breaking almost into tears of disappointment. As the tram darted forward she clutched at her hat. In a moment she was out of sight.

Coutts stood wounded to the quick by this pain given to the frail, child-like lady.

'We may as well,' said Winifred, 'walk over the hill to "The Swan".' Her note had that intense reedy quality which always set the man on edge; it was the note of her anger, or, more often, of her tortured sense of discord. The two turned away, to climb the hill again. He carried the violin; for a long time neither spoke.

'Ah, how I hate her, how I hate her!' he repeated in his heart. He winced repeatedly at the thought of Miss Syfurt's little cry of supplication. He was in a position where he was not himself, and he hated her for putting him there, forgetting that it was he who had come, like a moth to the candle. For half-a-mile he walked on, his head carried stiffly, his face set, his heart twisted with painful emotion. And all the time, as she plodded, head down, beside him, his blood beat with hate of her, drawn to her, repelled by her.

At last, on the high-up, naked down, they came upon those meaningless pavements that run through the grass, waiting for the houses to line them. The two were thrust up into the night above the little flowering of the lamps in the valley. In front was the daze of light from London, rising midway to the zenith, just fainter than the stars. Across the valley, on the blackness of the opposite hill, little groups of lights like gnats seemed to be floating in the darkness. Orion was heeled over the West. Below, in a cleft in the night, the long, low garland of arc lamps strung down the Brighton Road, where now and then the golden tram-cars flew low along the track, passing each other with a faint, angry sound.

'It is a year last Monday since we came over here,' said Winifred, as they stopped to look about them.

'I remember – but I didn't know it was then,' he said. There was a touch of hardness in his voice. 'I don't remember our dates.'

After a wait, she said in very low, passionate tones:

'It *is* a beautiful night.'

'The moon has set, and the evening star,' he answered; 'both were out as I came down.'

She glanced swiftly at him to see if this speech was a bit of symbolism. He was looking across the valley with a set face. Very slightly, by an inch or two, she nestled towards him.

'Yes,' she said, half-stubborn, half-pleading. 'But the night is a very fine one, for all that.'

'Yes,' he replied, unwillingly.

Thus, after months of separation, they dove-tailed into the same love and hate.

'You are staying down here?' she asked at length, in a forced voice. She never intruded a hair's-breadth on the most trifling privacy; in which she was Laura's antithesis; so that this question was almost an impertinence for her. He felt her shrink.

'Till the morning – then Yorkshire,' he said cruelly.

He hated it that she could not bear outspokenness.

At that moment a train across the valley threaded the opposite darkness with its gold thread. The valley re-echoed with vague threat. The two watched the express, like a gold-and-black snake, curve and dive seawards into the night. He turned, saw her full, fine face tilted up to him. It showed pale, distinct and firm, very near to him. He shut his eyes and shivered.

'I hate trains,' he said, impulsively.

'Why?' she asked, with a curious, tender little smile that caressed, as it were, his emotion towards her.

'I don't know; they pitch one about here and there...'

'I thought,' she said, with faint irony, 'that you preferred change.'

'I do like life. But now I should like to be nailed to something, if it were only a cross.'

She laughed sharply, and said, with keen sarcasm:

'Is it so difficult, then, to let yourself be nailed to a cross? I thought the difficulty lay in getting free.'

He ignored her sarcasm on his engagement.

'There is nothing now that matters,' he said, adding quickly, to forestall her, 'Of course I'm wild when dinner's late, and so on; but ... apart from those things ... nothing seems to matter.'

She was silent.

'One goes on – remains in office, so to speak; and life's all right – only, it doesn't seem to matter.'

'This does sound like complaining of trouble because you've got none,' she laughed.

'Trouble . . .' he repeated. 'No, I don't suppose I've got any. Vexation, which most folk call trouble; but something I really grieve about in my soul – no, nothing. I wish I had.'

She laughed again sharply; but he perceived in her laughter a little keen despair.

'I find a lucky pebble. I think, now I'll throw it over my left shoulder, and wish. So I spit over my little finger, and throw the white pebble behind me, and then, when I want to wish, I'm done. I say to myself: "Wish," and myself says back, "I don't want anything." I say again, "Wish, you fool," but I'm as dumb of wishes as a newt. And then, because it rather frightens me, I say in a hurry, "A million of money." Do *you* know what to wish for when you see the new moon?'

She laughed quickly.

'I think so,' she said. 'But my wish varies.'

'I wish mine did,' he said, whimsically lugubrious.

She took his hand in a little impulse of love.

They walked hand-in-hand on the ridge of the down, bunches of lights shining below, the big radiance of London advancing like a wonder in front.

'You know . . .' he began, then stopped.

'I don't . . .' she ironically urged.

'Do you want to?' he laughed.

'Yes; one is never at peace with oneself till one understands.'

'Understands what?' he asked brutally. He knew she meant that she wanted to understand the situation he and she were in.

'How to resolve the discord,' she said, balking the issue. He would have liked her to say: 'What you want of me?'

'Your foggy weather of symbolism, as usual,' he said.

'The fog is not of symbols,' she replied, in her metallic voice of displeasure. 'It may be symbols are candles in a fog.'

'I prefer my fog without candles. I'm the fog, eh? Then I'll blow out your candle, and you'll see me better. Your candles of speech, symbols and so forth, only lead you more wrong. I'm going to wander blind, and go by instinct, like a moth that flies and settles on the wooden box his mate is shut up in.'

'Isn't it an *ignis fatuus* you are flying after, at that rate?' she said.

'Maybe, for if I breathe outwards, in the positive movement towards you, you move off. If I draw in a vacant sigh of soulfulness, you flow nearly to my lips.'

'This is a very interesting symbol,' she said, with sharp sarcasm.

He hated her, truly. She hated him. Yet they held hands fast as they walked.

'We are just the same as we were a year ago,' he laughed. But he hated her, for all his laughter.

When, at the 'Swan and Sugar-Loaf', they mounted the car, she climbed to the top, in spite of the sharp night. They nestled side by side, shoulders caressing, and all the time that they ran under the round lamps neither spoke.

At the gate of a small house in a dark tree-lined street, both waited a moment. From her garden leaned an almond-tree whose buds, early this year, glistened in the light of the street lamp, with theatrical effect. He broke off a twig.

'I always remember this tree,' he said; 'how I used to feel sorry for it when it was full out, and so lively, at midnight in the lamplight. I thought it must be tired.'

'Will you come in?' she asked tenderly.

'I did get a room in town,' he answered, following her. She opened the door with her latch-key, showing him,

99

as usual, into the drawing-room. Everything was just the same; cold in colouring, warm in appointment; ivory-coloured walls, blond, polished floor, with thick ivory-coloured rugs; three deep armchairs in pale amber, with large cushions; a big black piano, a violin-stand beside it; and the room very warm with a clear red fire, the brass shining hot. Coutts, according to his habit, lit the piano-candles and lowered the blinds.

'I say,' he said; 'this is a variation from your line!'

He pointed to a bowl of magnificent scarlet anemones that stood on the piano.

'Why?' she asked, pausing in arranging her hair at the small mirror.

'On the *piano*!' he admonished.

'Only while the table was in use,' she smiled, glancing at the litter of papers that covered her table.

'And then – *red* flowers!' he said.

'Oh, I thought they were such a fine piece of colour,' she replied.

'I would have wagered you would buy freesias,' he said.

'Why?' she smiled. He pleased her thus.

'Well – for their cream and gold and restrained, bruised purple, and their scent. I can't believe you bought scent-less flowers!'

'What!' she went forward, bent over the flowers.

'I had not noticed,' she said, smiling curiously, 'that they were scentless.'

She touched the velvet black centres.

'Would you have bought them had you noticed?' he asked.

She thought for a moment, curiously.

'I don't know . . . probably I should not.'

'You would never buy scentless flowers,' he averred. 'Any more than you'd love a man because he was hand-some.'

'I did not know,' she smiled. She was pleased.

The housekeeper entered with a lamp, which she set on a stand.

'You will illuminate me?' he said to Winifred. It was her habit to talk to him by candle-light.

'I have thought about you – now I will look at you,' she said quietly, smiling.

'I see – to confirm your conclusions?' he asked.

Her eyes lifted quickly in acknowledgement of his guess.

'That is so,' she replied.

'Then,' he said, 'I'll wash my hands.'

He ran upstairs. The sense of freedom, of intimacy, was very fascinating. As he washed, the little everyday action of twining his hands in the lather set him suddenly considering his other love. At her house he was always polite and formal; gentlemanly, in short. With Connie he felt the old, manly superiority; he was the knight, strong and tender, she was the beautiful maiden with a touch of God on her brow. He kissed her, he softened and selected his speech for her, he forbore from being the greater part of himself. She was his betrothed, his wife, his queen, whom he loved to idealize, and for whom he carefully modified himself. She should rule him later on – that part of him which was hers. But he loved her, too, with a pitying, tender love. He thought of her tears upon her pillow in the northern Rectory, and he bit his lip, held his breath under the strain of the situation. Vaguely he knew she would bore him. And Winifred fascinated him. He and she really played with fire. In her house, he was roused and keen. But she was not, and never could be, frank. So he was not frank, even to himself. Saying nothing, betraying nothing, immediately they were together they began the same game. Each shuddered, each defenceless and exposed, hated the other by turns. Yet they came together again. Coutts felt a vague fear of Winifred. She was intense and unnatural – and he became unnatural and intense, beside her.

When he came downstairs she was fingering the piano from the score of 'Walküre'.

'First wash in England,' he announced, looking at his hands. She laughed swiftly. Impatient herself of the slightest soil, his indifference to temporary grubbiness amused her.

He was a tall, bony man, with small hands and feet. His features were rough and rather ugly, but his smile was taking. She was always fascinated by the changes in him. His eyes, particularly, seemed quite different at times; sometimes hard, insolent, blue; sometimes dark, full of warmth and tenderness; sometimes flaring like an animal's.

He sank wearily into a chair.

'My chair,' he said, as if to himself.

She bowed her head. Of compact physique, uncorsetted, her figure bowed richly to the piano. He watched the shallow concave between her shoulders, marvelling at its rich solidity. She let one arm fall loose; he looked at the shadows in the dimples of her elbow. Slowly, smiling a look of brooding affection, of acknowledgement upon him for a forgetful moment, she said:

'And what have you done lately?'

'Simply nothing,' he replied quietly. 'For all that these months have been so full of variety, I think they will sink out of my life; they will evaporate and leave no result; I shall forget them.'

Her blue eyes were dark and heavy upon him, watching. She did not answer. He smiled faintly at her.

'And you?' he said, at length.

'With me it is different,' she said quietly.

'You sit with your crystal,' he laughed.

'While you tilt . . .' She hung on her ending.

He laughed, sighed, and they were quiet awhile.

'I've got such a skinful of heavy visions, they come sweating through my dreams,' he said.

'Whom have you read?' she smiled.

'Meredith. Very healthy,' he laughed.

She laughed quickly at being caught.

'Now, have you found out all you want?' he asked.

'Oh, no,' she cried with full throat.

'Well, finish, at any rate. I'm not diseased. How are you?'

'But . . . but . . .' she stumbled on doggedly. 'What *do* you intend to do?'

He hardened the line of his mouth and eyes, only to retort with immediate lightness:

'Just go on.'

This was their battlefield: she could not understand how he could marry: it seemed almost monstrous to her; she fought against his marriage. She looked up at him, witch-like, from under bent brows. Her eyes were dark blue and heavy. He shivered, shrank with pain. She was so cruel to that other, common, everyday part of him.

'I wonder you dare go on like it,' she said.

'Why dare?' he replied. 'What's the odds?'

'I don't know,' she answered, in deep, bitter displeasure.

'And I don't care,' he said.

'But . . .' she continued, slowly, gravely pressing the point: 'You know what you intend to do.'

'Marry – settle – to be a good husband, good father, partner in the business; get fat, be an amiable gentleman – Q.E.F.'

'Very good,' she said, deep and final.

'Thank you.'

'I did not congratulate you,' she said.

'Ah!' His voice tailed off into sadness and self-mistrust.

Meanwhile she watched him heavily. He did not mind being scrutinized: it flattered him.

'Yes, it is, or may be, very good,' she began; 'but *why* all this? – *why*?'

'And why not? And why? – Because I want to.'

He could not leave it thus flippantly.

'You know, Winifred, we should only drive each other into insanity, you and I: become abnormal.'

'Well,' she said, 'and even so, why the other?'

'My marriage? – I don't know. Instinct.'

'One has so many instincts,' she laughed bitterly.

That was a new idea to him.

She raised her arms, stretched them above her head, in a weary gesture. They were fine, strong arms. They reminded Coutts of Euripides' 'Bacchae': white, round arms, long arms. The lifting of her arms lifted her breasts. She dropped suddenly as if inert, lolling her arms against the cushions.

'I really don't see why you should be,' she said drearily, though always with a touch of a sneer, 'why we should always be – fighting.'

'Oh, yes, you do,' he replied. It was a deadlock which he could not sustain.

'Besides,' he laughed, 'it's your fault.'

'Am I *so* bad', she sneered.

'Worse,' he said.

'But' – she moved irritably – 'is this to the point?'

'What point?' he answered; then, smiling: 'You know you only like a wild-goose chase.'

'I do,' she answered plaintively. 'I miss you very much. You snatch things from the Kobolds for me.'

'Exactly,' he said in a biting tone. 'Exactly! That's what you want me for. I am to be your crystal, your "genius". My length of blood and bone you don't care a rap for. Ah, yes, you like me for a crystal-glass, to see things in: to hold up to the light. I'm a blessed Lady-of-Shalott looking-glass for you.'

'You talk to *me*,' she said, dashing his fervour, 'of my fog of symbols!'

'Ah, well, if so, 'tis your own asking.'

'I did not know it.' She looked at him coldly. She was angry.

'No,' he said.

Again, they hated each other.

'The old ancients,' he laughed, 'gave the gods the suet and intestines: at least, I believe so. They ate the rest. You shouldn't be a goddess.'

'I wonder, among your rectory acquaintances, you haven't learned better manners,' she answered in cold contempt. He closed his eyes, lying back in his chair, his legs sprawled towards her.

'I suppose we're civilized savages,' he said sadly. All was silent.

At last, opening his eyes again, he said: 'I shall have to be going directly, Winifred; it is past eleven . . .' Then the appeal in his voice changed to laughter. 'Though I know I shall be winding through all the *Addios* in "Traviata" before you can set me travelling.' He smiled gently at her, then closed his eyes once more, conscious of deep, but vague, suffering. She lay in her chair, her face averted, rosily, towards the fire. Without glancing at her he was aware of the white approach of her throat towards her breast. He seemed to perceive her with another, unknown sense that acted all over his body. She lay perfectly still and warm in the fire-glow. He was dimly aware that he suffered.

'Yes,' she said at length: 'if we were linked together we should only destroy each other.'

He started, hearing her admit, for the first time, this point of which he was so sure.

'You should never *marry* anyone,' he said.

'And you,' she asked in irony, 'must offer your head to harness and be bridled and driven?'

'There's the makings of quite a good, respectable trotter in me,' he laughed. 'Don't you see it's what I *want* to be?'

'I'm not sure,' she laughed in return.

'I think so.'

'Ah! well, if you think so.'

They were silent for a time. The white lamp burned steadily as moonlight, the red fire like sunset; there was no stir or flicker.

'And what of you?' he asked.

She crooned a faint, tired laugh.

'If you are jetsam, as you say you are,' she answered, 'I am flotsam. I shall lie stranded.'

'Nay,' he pleaded. 'When were you wrecked?'

She laughed quickly, with a sound like a tinkle of tears.

'Oh, dear Winifred!' he cried despairingly.

She lifted her arms towards him, hiding her face between them, looking up through the white closure with dark, uncanny eyes, like an invocation. His breast lifted towards her uptilted arms. He shuddered, shut his eyes, held himself rigid. He heard her drop her arms heavily.

'I must go,' he said in a dull voice.

The rapidly-chasing quivers that ran in tremors down the front of his body and limbs made him stretch himself, stretch hard.

'Yes,' she assented gravely; 'you must go.'

He turned to her. Again looking up darkly, from under her lowered brows, she lifted her hands like small white orchids towards him. Without knowing, he gripped her wrists with a grasp that circled his blood-red nails with white rims.

'Good-bye,' he said, looking down at her. She made a small, moaning noise in her throat, lifting her face so that it came open and near to him like a suddenly-risen flower, borne on a strong white stalk. She seemed to extend, to fill the world, to become atmosphere and all. He did not know what he was doing. He was bending forward, his mouth on hers, her arms round his neck, and his own hands, still fastened on to her wrists, almost bursting the blood under his nails with the intensity of their grip. They remained for a few moments thus, rigid. Then, weary of the strain, she relaxed. She turned her face, offered him her throat, white hard, and rich, below the ear. Stooping still lower, so that he quivered in every fibre at the strain he laid his mouth to the kiss. In the intense silence, he heard the deep, dull pulsing of her blood, and a minute click of a spark within the lamp.

Then he drew her from the chair up to him. She came, arms always round his neck, till at last she lay along his breast as he stood, feet planted wide, clasping her tight, his mouth on her neck. She turned suddenly to meet his full, red mouth in a kiss. He felt his moustache prick back into his lips. It was the first kiss she had genuinely given. Dazed, he was conscious of the throb of one great pulse, as if his whole body were a heart that contracted in throbs. He felt, with an intolerable ache, as if he, the heart, were setting the pulse in her, in the very night, so that everything beat from the throb of his overstrained, bursting body.

The hurt became so great it brought him out of the reeling stage to distinct consciousness. She clipped her lips, drew them away, leaving him her throat. Already she had had enough. He opened his eyes as he bent with his mouth on her neck, and was startled; there stood the objects of the room, stark; there, close below his eyes, were the half-sunk lashes of the woman, swooning on her unnatural ebb of passion. He saw her thus, knew that she wanted no more of him than that kiss. And the heavy form of this woman hung upon him; his mouth was grown to her throat in a kiss; and, even so, as she lay in his arms, she was gradually dismissing him. His whole body ached like a swollen vein, with heavy intensity, while his heart grew dead with misery and despair. This woman gave him anguish and a cutting-short like death; to the other woman he was false. As he shivered with suffering, he opened his eyes again, and caught sight of the pure ivory of the lamp. His heart flashed with rage.

A sudden involuntary blow of his foot, and he sent the lamp-stand spinning. The lamp leaped off, fell with a smash on the fair, polished floor. Instantly a bluish hedge of flame quivered, leaped up before them. She had lightened her hold round his neck, and buried her face against his throat. The flame veered at her, blue, with a yellow tongue that licked her dress and her arm. Convulsive, she clutched him, almost strangled him, though she made no sound.

He gathered her up and bore her heavily out of the room. Slipping from her clasp, he brought his arms down her form, crushing the startling blaze of her dress. His face was singed. Staring at her, he could scarcely see her.

'I am not hurt,' she cried. 'But you?'

The housekeeper was coming; the flames were sinking and waving-up in the drawing-room. He broke away from Winifred, threw one of the great woollen rugs on to the flame, then stood a moment looking at the darkness.

Winifred caught at him as he passed her.

'No, no,' he answered, as he fumbled for the latch. 'I'm not hurt. Clumsy fool I am – clumsy fool!'

In another instant he was gone, running with burning-red hands held out blindly, down the street.

The Miner at Home

LIKE most colliers, Bower had his dinner before he washed himself. It did not surprise his wife that he said little. He seemed quite amiable, but evidently did not feel confidential. Gertie was busy with the three children, the youngest of whom lay kicking on the sofa, preparing to squeal; therefore she did not concern herself overmuch with her husband, once having ascertained by a few shrewd glances at his heavy brows and his blue eyes, which moved conspicuously in his black face, that he was only pondering.

He smoked a solemn pipe until six o'clock. Although he was really a good husband, he did not notice that Gertie was tired. She was irritable at the end of the long day.

'Don't you want to wash yourself?' she asked, grudgingly, at six o'clock. It was sickening to have a man sitting there in his pit-dirt, never saying a word, smoking like a Red Indian.

'I'm ready, when you are,' he replied.

She lay the baby on the sofa, barricaded it with pillows, and brought from the scullery a great panchion, a bowl of heavy earthenware like brick, glazed inside to a dark mahogany colour. Tall and thin and very pale, she stood before the fire holding the great bowl, her grey eyes flashing.

'Get up, our Jack, this minute, or I'll squash thee under the blessed panchion.'

The fat boy of six, who was rolling on the rug in the firelight, said broadly:

'Squash me, then.'

'Get up,' she cried, giving him a push with her foot.

'Gi'e ower,' he said, rolling jollily.

'I'll smack you,' she said grimly, preparing to put down the panchion.

'Get up, theer,' shouted the father.

Gertie ladled water from the boiler with a tin ladling can. Drops fell from her ladle hissing into the red fire, splashing on to the white hearth, blazing like drops of flame on the flat-topped fender. The father gazed at it all, unmoved.

'I've told you,' he said, 'to put cold water in the panchion first. If one o' th' children goes an' falls in ...'

'You can see as 'e doesn't then,' snapped she. She tempered the bowl with cold water, dropped in a flannel and a lump of soap, and spread the towel over the fender to warm.

Then, and only then, Bower rose. He wore no coat, and his arms were freckled black. He stripped to the waist, hitched his trousers into the strap, and kneeled on the rug to wash himself. There was a great splashing and sputtering. The red firelight shone on his cap of white soap, and on the muscles of his back, on the strange working of his red and white muscular arms, that flashed up and down like individual creatures.

Gertie sat with the baby clawing at her ears and hair and nose. Continually she drew back her face and head from the cruel little baby-clasp. Jack was hanging on to the kitchen door.

'Come away from that door,' cried the mother.

Jack did not come away, but neither did he open the door and run the risk of incurring his father's wrath. The room was very hot, but the thought of a draught is abhorrent to a miner.

With the baby on one arm, Gertie washed her husband's back. She sponged it carefully with the flannel, and then, still with one hand, began to dry it on the rough towel.

'Canna ter put th' childt down an' use both hands?' said her husband.

'Yes; an' then if th' childt screets, there's a bigger to-do than iver. There's no suitin' some folk.'

'The childt 'ud non screet.'

Gertie plumped it down. The baby began to cry. The wife rubbed her husband's back till it grew pink, while Bower quivered with pleasure. As soon as she threw the towel down:

'Shut that childt up,' he said.

He wrestled his way into his shirt. His head emerged, with black hair standing roughly on end. He was rather an ugly man, just above medium height, and stiffly built. He had a thin black moustache over a full mouth, and a very full chin that was marred by a blue seam, where a horse had kicked him when he was a lad in the pit.

With both hands on the mantelpiece above his head, he stood looking in the fire, his whitish shirt hanging like a smock over his pit trousers.

Presently, still looking absently in the fire, he said: 'Bill Andrews was standin' at th' pit top, an' give ivery man as 'e come up one o' these.'

He handed to his wife a small whity-blue paper, on which was printed simply:

February 14, 1912.

To the Manager –

I hereby give notice to leave your employment fourteen days from above date.

Signed —

Gertie read the paper, blindly dodging her head from the baby's grasp.

'An' what d'you reckon that's for?' she asked.

'I suppose it means as we come out.'

'I'm sure!' she cried in indignation. 'Well, *tha'rt* not goin' to sign it.'

'It'll ma'e no diff'rence whether I do or dunna – t'others will.'

'Then let 'em!' She made a small clicking sound in her mouth. 'This 'll ma'e th' third strike as we've had sin' we've been married; an' a fat lot th' better for it you are, arena you?'

He squirmed uneasily.

'No, but we mean to be,' he said.

'I'll tell you what, colliers is a discontented lot, as doesn't know what they *do* want. That's what they are.'

'Tha'd better not let some o' th' colliers as there is hear thee say so.'

'I don't care who hears me. An' there isn't a man in Eastwood but what'll say as th' last two strikes has ruined the place. There's that much bad blood now atween th' mesters an' th' men as there isn't a thing but what's askew. An' what *will* it be, I should like to know!'

'It's not on'y here; it's all ower th' country alike,' he gloated.

'Yes; it's them blessed Yorkshire an' Welsh colliers as does it. They're that bug nowadays, what wi' talkin' an' spoutin', they hardly know which side their back-side hangs. Here, take this childt!'

She thrust the baby into his arms, carried out the heavy bowlful of black suds, mended the fire, cleared round, and returned for the child.

'Ben Haseldine said, an' he's a union man – he told me when he come for th' union money yesterday, as th' men doesn't want to come out – not our men. It's th' union.'

'Tha knows nowt about it, woman. It's a' woman's jabber, from beginnin' to end.'

'You don't intend us to know. Who wants th' Minimum Wage? Butties doesn't. There th' butties'll be, havin' to pay seven shillin' a day to men as 'appen isn't worth a penny more than five.'

'But the butties is goin' to have eight shillin' accordin' to scale.'

'An' then th' men as can't work tip-top, an' is worth, 'appen, five shillin' a day, they get th' sack: an th' old men, an' so on.'

'Nowt o' th' sort, woman, nowt o' th' sort. Tha's got it off 'am-pat. There's goin' to be inspectors for all that, an' th' men'll get what they're worth, accordin' to age, an' so on.'

'An' accordin' to idleness an' – what somebody says about 'em. I'll back! There'll be a lot o' fairness!'

'Tha talks like a woman as knows nowt. What does thee know about it?'

'I know what you did at th' last strike. And I know this much, when Shipley men had *their* strike tickets, not one in three signed 'em – so there. An' *tha'rt* not goin' to!'

'We want a livin' wage,' he declared.

'Hanna you got one?' she cried.

'Han we?' he shouted. 'Han we? Who does more chaunterin' than thee when it's a short wik, an' tha gets 'appen a scroddy twenty-two shillin'? Tha goes at me 'ard enough.'

'Yi; but what better shall you be? What better *are* you for th' last two strikes – tell me that?'

'I'll tell thee this much, th' mesters doesna' mean us to ha'e owt. They promise, but they dunna keep it, not they. Up comes Friday night, an' nowt to draw, an' a woman fit to ha'e yer guts out for it.'

'It's nowt but th' day-men as wants the blessed Minimum Wage – it's not butties.'

'It's time as th' butties *did* ha'e ter let their men make a fair day's wage. Four an' sixpence a day is about as 'e's allowed to addle, whoiver he may be.'

'I wonder what you'll say next. You say owt as is put in your mouth, that's a fac'. What are thee, dost reckon? – are ter a butty, or day-man, or ostler, or are ter a mester? – for tha might be, ter hear thee talk.'

'I nedna neither. It ought to be fair a' round.'

'It ought, hang my rags, it ought! Tha'rt very fair to me, for instance.'

'An' arena I?'

'Tha thinks 'cause tha gi'es me a lousy thirty shillin' reg'lar th'art th' best man i' th' Almighty world. Tha mun be waited on han' an' foot, an' sided wi' whativer tha says. But I'm *not*! No, an' I'm not, not when it comes to strikes. I've seen enough on 'em.'

'Then niver open thy mouth again if it's a short wik, an' we're pinched.'

'We're niver pinched that much. An' a short wik isn't no shorter than a strike wik; put that i' thy pipe an' smoke it. It's th' idle men as wants th' strikes.'

'Shut thy mouth, woman. If every man worked as hard as I do ...'

'He wouldn't ha'e as much to do as me; an' 'e wouldna. But *I've* nowt to do, as tha'rt flig ter tell me. No, it's th' idle men as wants th' strike. It's a union strike, this is, not a men's strike. You're sharpenin' th' knife for your own throats.'

'Am I not sick of a woman as listens to every tale as is poured into her ears? No, I'm not takin' th' kid. I'm goin' out.'

He put on his boots determinedly.

She rocked herself with vexation and weariness.

Her Turn

SHE was his second wife, and so there was between them that truce which is never held between a man and his first woman.

He was one for the women, and as such, an exception among the colliers. In spite of their prudery, the neighbour women liked him; he was big, naïve, and very courteous with them; he was so, even to his second wife.

Being a large man of considerable strength and perfect health, he earned good money in the pit. His natural courtesy saved him from enemies, while his fresh interest in life made his presence always agreeable. So he went his own way, had always plenty of friends, always a good job down pit.

He gave his wife thirty-five shillings a week. He had two grown-up sons at home, and they paid twelve shillings each. There was only one child by the second marriage, so Radford considered his wife did well.

Eighteen months ago, Bryan and Wentworth's men were out on strike for eleven weeks. During that time, Mrs Radford could neither cajole nor entreat nor nag the ten shillings strike-pay from her husband. So that when the second strike came on, she was prepared for action.

Radford was going, quite inconspicuously, to the publican's wife at the 'Golden Horn'. She is a large, easy-going lady of forty, and her husband is sixty-three, more-over crippled with rheumatism. She sits in the little bar-parlour of the wayside public-house, knitting for dear life, and sipping a very moderate glass of Scotch. When a decent man arrives at the three-foot width of bar, she rises, serves him, surveys him over, and, if she likes his looks, says:

'Won't you step inside sir?'

If he steps inside, he will find not more than one or two men present. The room is warm, quite small. The landlady knits. She gives a few polite words to the stranger, then resumes her conversation with the man who interests her most. She is straight, highly-coloured, with indifferent brown eyes.

'What was that you asked me, Mr Radford?'

'What is the difference between a donkey's tail and a rainbow?' asked Radford, who had a consuming passion for conundrums.

'All the difference in the world,' replied the landlady.

'Yes, but what special difference?'

'I s'll have to give it up again. You'll think me a donkey's head, I'm afraid.'

'Not likely. But just you consider now, wheer . . .'

The conundrum was still under weigh, when a girl entered. She was swarthy, a fine animal. After she had gone out:

'Do you know who that is?' asked the landlady.

'I can't say as I do,' replied Radford.

'She's Frederick Pinnock's daughter, from Stony Ford. She's courting our Willy.'

'And a fine lass, too.'

'Yes, fine enough, as far as that goes. What sort of a wife'll she make him, think you?'

'You just let me consider a bit,' said the man. He took out a pocket-book and a pencil. The landlady continued to talk to the other guests.

Radford was a big fellow, black-haired, with a brown moustache, and darkish blue eyes. His voice, naturally deep, was pitched in his throat, and had a peculiar, tenor quality, rather husky, and disturbing. He modulated it a good deal as he spoke, as men do who talk much with women. Always, there was a certain indolence in his carriage.

'Our mester's lazy,' his wife said. 'There's many a bit of a job wants doin', but get him to do it if you can.'

But she knew he was merely indifferent to the little jobs, and not lazy.

He sat writing for about ten minutes, at the end of which time, he read:

'I see a fine girl full of life.
I see her just ready for wedlock,
But there's jealousy between her eyebrows
And jealousy on her mouth.
I see trouble ahead.
Willy is delicate.
She would do him no good.
She would never see when he wasn't well,
She would only see what she wanted –'

So, in phrases, he got down his thoughts. He had to fumble for expression, and therefore anything serious he wanted to say he wrote in 'poetry', as he called it.

Presently, the landlady rose, saying:

'Well, I s'll have to be looking after our mester. I s'll be in again before we close.'

Radford sat quite comfortably on. In a while, he too bade the company good night.

When he got home, at a quarter-past eleven, his sons were in bed, and his wife sat awaiting him. She was a woman of medium height, fat and sleek, a dumpling. Her black hair was parted smooth, her narrow-opened eyes were sly and satirical, she had a peculiar twang in her rather sleering voice.

'Our missis is a puss-puss,' he said easily, of her. Her extraordinarily smooth, sleek face was remarkable. She was very healthy.

He never came in drunk. Having taken off his coat and his cap, he sat down to supper in his shirt-sleeves. Do as he might, she was fascinated by him. He had a strong neck, with the crisp hair growing low. Let her be angry as she would, yet she had a passion for that neck of his, particularly when she saw the great vein rib under the skin.

'I think, Missis,' he said, 'I'd rather ha'e a smite o' cheese than this meat.'

'Well, can't you get it yourself?'

'Yi, surely I can,' he said, and went out to the pantry.

'I think, if yer comin' in at this time of night, you can wait on yourself,' she justified herself.

She moved uneasily in her chair. There were several jam-tarts alongside the cheese on the dish he brought.

'Yi, Missis, them tan-tafflins'll go down very nicely,' he said.

'Oh, will they! Then you'd better help to pay for them,' she said, amiably, but determined.

'Now what art after?'

'What am I after? Why, can't you think?' she said sarcastically.

'I'm not for thinkin', Missis.'

'No, I know you're not. But wheer's my money? You've been paid the Union today. Wheer do I come in?'

'Tha's got money, an' tha mun use it.'

'Thank yer. An' 'aven't you none, as well?'

'I hadna, not till we was paid, not a ha'p'ny.'

'Then you ought to be ashamed of yourself to say so.'

' 'Appen so.'

'We'll go shares wi' th' Union money,' she said. 'That's nothing but what's right.'

'We shonna. Tha's got plenty o' money as tha can use.'

'Oh, all right,' she said. 'I will do.'

She went to bed. It made her feel sharp that she could not get at him.

The next day, she was just as usual. But at eleven o'clock she took her purse and went up town. Trade was very slack. Men stood about in gangs, men were playing marbles everywhere in the streets. It was a sunny morning. Mrs Radford went into the furnisher-and-upholsterer's shop.

'There's a few things,' she said to Mr Allcock, 'as I'm wantin' for the house, and I might as well get them now, while the men's at home, and can shift me the furniture.'

She put her fat purse on to the counter with a click. The man should know she was not wanting 'strap'. She bought linoleum for the kitchen, a new wringer, a breakfast-service, a spring mattress, and various other things, keeping a mere thirty shillings, which she tied in a corner of her handkerchief. In her purse was some loose silver.

Her husband was gardening in a desultory fashion when she got back home. The daffodils were out. The colts in the field at the end of the garden were tossing their velvety brown necks.

'Sithee here, Missis,' called Radford, from the shed which stood half-way down the path. Two doves in a cage were cooing.

'What have you got?' asked the woman, as she approached. He held out to her in his big, earthy hand, a tortoise. The reptile was very, very slowly issuing its head again to the warmth.

'He's wakened up betimes,' said Radford.

'He's like th' men, wakened up for a holiday,' said the wife. Radford scratched the little beast's scaly head.

'We pleased to see him out,' he said.

They had just finished dinner, when a man knocked at the door.

'From Allcock's!' he said.

The plump woman took up the clothes-basket containing the crockery she had bought.

'Whativer hast got theer?' asked her husband.

'We've been wantin' some breakfast-cups for ages, so I went up town an' got 'em this mornin',' she replied.

He watched her taking out the crockery.

'Hm!' he said. 'Tha's been on th' spend, seemly.'

Again there was a thud at the door. The man had put down a roll of linoleum. Mr Radford went to look at it.

'They come rolling in!' he exclaimed.

'Who's grumbled more than you about the raggy oil-cloth of this kitchen?' said the insidious, cat-like voice of the wife.

'It's all right, it's all right,' said Radford.

The carter came up the entry with another roll, which he deposited with a grunt at the door.

'An' how much do you reckon this lot is?' he asked.

'Oh, they're all paid for, don't worry,' replied the wife.

'Shall yer gi'e me a hand, Mester?' asked the carter.

Radford followed him down the entry, in his easy, slouching way. His wife went after. His waistcoat was hanging loose over his shirt. She watched his easy movement of well-being as she followed him, and she laughed to herself.

The carter took hold of one end of the wire mattress, dragged it forth.

'Well, this is a corker!' said Radford, as he received the burden.

'Now the mangle!' said the carter.

'What dost reckon tha's been up to, Missis?' asked the husband.

'I said to myself last wash-day, if I had to turn that mangle again, tha'd ha'e ter wash the clothes thyself.'

Radford followed the carter down the entry again. In the street, women were standing watching, and dozens of men were lounging round the cart. One officiously helped with the wringer.

'Gi'e him thrippence,' said Mrs Radford.

'Gi'e 't him thysen,' replied her husband.

'I've no change under half-a-crown.'

Radford tipped the carter, and returned indoors. He surveyed the array of crockery, linoleum, mattress, mangle, and other goods crowding the house and the yard.

'Well, this is a winder!' he repeated.

'We stood in need of 'em enough,' she replied.

'I hope tha's got plenty more from wheer they came from,' he replied dangerously.

'That's just what I haven't.' She opened her purse. 'Two half-crowns, that's every copper I've got i' th' world.'

He stood very still as he looked.

'It's right,' she said.

There was a certain smug sense of satisfaction about her. A wave of anger came over him, blinding him. But he waited and waited. Suddenly his arm leapt up, the fist clenched, and his eyes blazed at her. She shrank away, pale and frightened. But he dropped his fist to his side, turned, and went out, muttering. He went down to the shed that stood in the middle of the garden. There he picked up the tortoise, and stood with bent head, rubbing its horny head.

She stood hesitating, watching him. Her heart was heavy, and yet there was a curious, cat-like look of satisfaction round her eyes. Then she went indoors and gazed at her new cups, admiringly.

The next week he handed her his half-sovereign without a word.

'You'll want some for yourself,' she said, and she gave him a shilling. He accepted it.

Delilah and Mr Bircumshaw

'HE looked,' said Mrs Bircumshaw to Mrs Gillatt, 'he looked like a positive saint: one of the noble sort, you know, that will suffer with head up and with dreamy eyes. I nearly died of laughing.'

She spoke of Mr Bircumshaw, who darted a look at his wife's friend. Mrs Gillatt broke into an almost derisive laugh. Bircumshaw shut tight his mouth, and set his large, square jaw. Frowning, he lowered his face out of sight.

Mrs Bircumshaw seemed to glitter in the twilight. She was like a little, uncanny machine, working unheard and unknown, but occasionally snapping a spark. A small woman, very quiet in her manner, it was surprising that people should so often say of her, 'She's *very* vivacious.' It was her eyes: they were brown, very wide-open, very swift and ironic. As a rule she said little. This evening, her words and her looks were quick and brilliant. She had been married four years.

'I was thankful, I can tell you, that you didn't go,' she continued to Mrs Gillatt. 'For a church pageant, it was the most astonishing show. People blossomed out so differently. *I* never knew what a fine apostle was lost in Harry. When I saw him, I thought I should scream.'

'You looked sober enough every time I noticed you,' blurted Harry, in deep bass.

'You were much too rapt to notice *me*,' his wife laughed gaily. Nevertheless, her small head was lifted and alert, like a fighting bird's. Mrs Gillat fell instinctively into rank with her, unconscious of the thrill of battle that moved her.

Mr Bircumshaw, bowing forward, rested his arms on his knees, and whistled silently as he contemplated his feet. Also, he listened acutely to the women. He was a large-limbed, clean, powerful man, and a bank clerk. Son of a country clergyman, he had a good deal of vague, sensuous, religious feeling, but he lacked a Faith. He would have been a fine man to support a cause, but he had no cause. Even had he been forced to work hard and unremittingly, he would have remained healthy in spirit. As it was, he was a bank clerk, with a quantity of unspent energy turning sour in his veins, and a fair amount of barren leisure torturing his soul. He was degenerating: and now his wife turned upon him.

She had been a schoolteacher. He had had the money and the position. He was inclined to bully her, when he was not suited: which was fairly often.

'Harry was one of the "Three Wise men". You should have seen him, Mrs Gillatt. With his face coming out of that white forehead band, and the cloth that hung over his ears, he looked a picture. Imagine him – !'

Mrs Gillatt looked at Bircumshaw, imagining him. Then she threw up her hands and laughed aloud. It *was* ludicrous to think of Bircumshaw, a hulking, frequently churlish man, as one of the Magi. Mrs Gillatt was a rather beautiful woman of forty, almost too full in blossom. Better off than the Bircumshaws, she assumed the manner of patron and protector.

'Oh,' she cried, 'I can *see* him – I can see him looking great and grand – Abraham! Oh, he's got that grand cut of face, and plenty of size.'

She laughed rather derisively. She was a man's woman, by instinct serving flattery with mockery.

'That's it!' cried the little wife, deferentially. 'Abraham setting out to sacrifice. He marched – his march was splendid.'

The two women laughed together. Mrs Gillatt drew herself up superbly, laughing, then coming to rest.

'And usually, you know,' the wife broke off, 'there's a good deal of the whipped schoolboy about his walk.'

'There is, Harry,' laughed Mrs Gillatt, shaking her white and jewelled hand at him. 'You just remember that for the next time, my lad.' She was his senior by some eight years. He grinned sickly.

'But now,' Mrs Bircumshaw continued, 'he marched like a young Magi. You could see a look of the Star in his eyes.'

'Oh,' cried Mrs Gillatt. 'Oh! the look of the Star –!'

'Oftener the look of the Great Bear, isn't it?' queried Mrs Bircumshaw.

'That is quite true, Harry,' said the elder woman, laughing.

Bircumshaw cracked his strong fingers, brutally.

'Well, he came on,' continued the wife, 'with the light of the Star in his eyes, his mouth fairly sweet with Christian resignation –'

'Oh!' cried Mrs Gillatt, 'oh – and he beats the baby. Christian resignation!' She laughed aloud. 'Let me hear of you beating that child again, Harry Bircumshaw, and I'll Christian-resignation you –'

Suddenly she remembered that this might implicate her friend. 'I came in yesterday,' she explained, 'at dinner. "What's the matter, baby?" I said, "what are you crying for?" "Dadda beat baby – naughty baby." It was a good thing you had gone back to business, my lad, I can tell you. . . .'

Mrs Bircumshaw glanced swiftly at her husband. He had ducked his head and was breaking his knuckles tensely. She turned her head with a quick, thrilled movement, more than ever like a fighting bird.

'And you know his nose,' she said, blithely resuming her narrative, as if it were some bit of gossip. 'You know it usually looks a sort of "Mind your own business or you'll get a hit in the jaw" nose?'

'Yes,' cried Mrs Gillatt, 'it does –' and she seemed unable to contain her laughter. Then she dropped her fine head, pretending to be an angry buffalo glaring under bent brows, seeking whom he shall devour, in imitation of Harry's nose.

Mrs Bircumshaw bubbled with laughter.

'Ah!' said Mrs Gillatt, and she winked at her friend as she sweetened Harry's pill, 'I know him – I know him.' Then: 'And what *did* his nose look like?' she asked of the wife.

'Like Sir Galahad on horseback,' said Ethel Bircumshaw, spending her last shot.

Mrs Gillatt drew her hand down her own nose, which was straight, with thin, flexible nostrils.

'How does it feel, Harry,' she asked, 'to stroke Galahad on horseback?'

'I don't know, I'm sure,' he said icily.

'Then stroke it, man, and tell me,' cried the elder woman: with which *her* last shot was sped. There was a moment of painful silence.

'And the way the others acted – it was screamingly funny,' the wife started. Then the two women, with one accord, began to make mock of the other actors in the pageant, people they knew, ridiculing them, however, only for blemishes that Harry had not, pulling the others to pieces in places where Harry was solid, thus leaving their man erect like a hero among the litter of his acquaintances.

This did not mollify him: it only persuaded him he was a fine figure, not to be carped at.

Suddenly, before the women had gone far, Bircumshaw jumped up. Mrs Gillatt started. She got a glimpse of his strict form, in its blue serge, passing before her, then the door banged behind him.

Mrs Gillatt was really astonished. She had helped in clipping this ignoble Samson, all unawares, from instinct. She had no idea of what she had been doing. She sat erect and superb, the picture of astonishment that is merging towards contempt.

'Is it someone at the door?' she asked, listening.

Mrs Bircumshaw, with alert, listening eyes, shook her head quickly, with a meaning look of contempt.

'Is he mad?' whispered the elder woman. Her friend nodded. Then Mrs Gillatt's eyes dilated, and her face hardened with scorn. Mrs Bircumshaw had not ceased to listen. She bent forward.

'Praise him,' she whispered, making a quick gesture that they should play a bit of fiction. They rose with zest to the game. 'Praise him,' whispered the wife. Then she herself began. Every woman is a first-rate actress in private. She leaned forward, and in a slightly lowered yet very distinct voice, screened as if for privacy, yet penetrating clearly to the ears of her husband – he had lingered in the hall, she could hear – she said:

'You know Harry really acted splendidly.'

'I know,' said Mrs Gillatt eagerly. 'I know. I know he's a really good actor.'

'He is. The others did look paltry beside him, I have to confess.'

Harry's pride was soothed, but his wrath was not appeased.

'Yes,' he heard the screened voice of his wife say. 'But for all that, I don't care to see him on the stage. It's not manly, somehow. It seems unworthy of a man with any character, somehow. Of course it's all right for strangers – but for anyone you care for – anyone *very* near to you –'

Mrs Gillatt chuckled to herself: this was a thing well done. The two women, however, had not praised very long – and the wife's praise was sincere by the time she had finished her first sentence – before they were startled by a loud 'Thud!' on the floor above their heads. Both started. It was dark, nearly nine o'clock. They listened in silence. Then came another 'Thud!'

Mrs Bircumshaw gave a little spurt of bitter-contemptuous laughter.

'He's not –?' began Mrs Gillatt.

'He's gone to bed, and announces the fact by dropping his boots as he takes them off,' said the young wife bitterly.

Mrs Gillatt was wide-eyed with amazement. 'You don't mean it!' she exclaimed.

Childless, married to an uxorious man whom she loved, this state of affairs was monstrous to her. Neither of the women spoke for a while. It was dark in the room. Then Mrs Gillatt began, sotto voce:

'Well, I could never have believed it, no, not if you'd told me for ever. He's always so fussy –'

So she went on. Mrs Bircumshaw let her continue. A restrained woman herself, the other's outburst relieved her own tension. When she had sufficiently overcome her own emotion, and when she knew her husband to be in bed, she rose.

'Come into the kitchen, we can talk there,' she said. There was a new hardness in her voice. She had not 'talked' before to anyone, had never mentioned her husband in blame.

The kitchen was bare, with drab walls glistening to the naked gas-jet. The tiled floor was uncovered, cold and damp. Everything was clean, stark and cheerless. The large stove, littered with old paper, was black, black-cold. There was a baby's high chair in one corner, and a teddy-bear, and a tin pigeon. Mrs Bircumshaw threw a cloth on the table that was pushed up under the drab-blinded window, against the great, black stove, which radiated coldness since it could not radiate warmth.

'Will you stay to supper?' asked Mrs Bircumshaw.

'What have you got?' was the frank reply.

'I'm afraid there's only bread and cheese.'

'No thanks then. I don't eat bread and cheese for supper, Ethel, and you ought not.'

They talked – or rather Mrs Gillatt held forth for a few minutes, on suppers. Then there was a silence.

'I never knew such a thing in my life,' began Mrs Gillatt, rather awkwardly, as a tentative: she wanted her friend to unbosom. 'Is he often like it?' she persisted.

'Oh yes.'

'Well, I can see now,' Mrs Gillatt declared, 'I can understand now. Often have I come in and seen you with your eyes all red: but you've not said anything, so I haven't liked to. But I know now. Just fancy – the brute! – and will he be all right when you go to bed?'

'Oh no.'

'Will he keep it up tomorrow?' Mrs Gillatt's tone expressed nothing short of amazed horror.

'Oh yes, and very likely for two or three days.'

'Oh the brute! the brute!! Well, this *has* opened my eyes. I've been watching a few of these men lately, and I tell you –. You'll not sleep with him tonight, shall you?'

'It would only make it worse.'

'Worse or not worse, I wouldn't. You've got another bed aired – you had visitors till yesterday – there's the bed – take baby and sleep there.'

'It would only make it worse,' said Mrs Bircumshaw, weariedly. Mrs Gillatt was silent a moment.

'Well – you're better to him than I should be, I can tell you,' she said. 'Ah, the brute, to think he should always be so fair and fussy to my face, and I think him so nice. But let him touch that child again –! Haven't I seen her with her little arms red? "Gentlemanly" – so fond of quoting his "gentlemanly"! Eh, but this has opened my eyes,

Ethel. Only let him touch that child again, to my knowledge. I only wish he would.'

Mrs Bircumshaw listened to this threat in silence. Yet she did wish she could see the mean bully in her husband matched by this spoiled, arrogant, generous woman.

'But tell him, Ethel,' said Mrs Gillatt, bending from her handsome height, and speaking in considerate tones, 'tell him that I saw nothing – nothing. Tell him I thought he had suddenly been called to the door: tell him that – and that I thought he'd gone down the "Drive" with a caller – say that – you can do it, it's perfectly true – I did think so. So tell him – the brute!'

Mrs Bircumshaw listened patiently, occasionally smiling to herself. She would tell her husband nothing, would never mention the affair to him. Moreover, she intended her husband to think he had made a fool of himself before this handsome woman whom he admired so much.

Bircumshaw heard his wife's friend take her leave. He had been in torment while the two women were together in the far-off kitchen. Now the brute in him felt more sure, more triumphant. He was afraid of *two* women: he could cow one. He felt he had something to punish: that he had his own dignity and authority to assert: and he was going to punish, was going to assert.

'I should think,' said Mrs Gillatt in departing, 'that you won't take him any supper.'

Mrs Bircumshaw felt a sudden blaze of anger against him. But she laughed deprecatingly.

'You *are* a silly thing if you do,' cried the other. 'My word, I'd starve him if I had him.'

'But you see you haven't got him,' said the wife quietly.

'No, I'm thankful to say. But if I had – the brute!'

He heard her go, and was relieved. Now he could lie in bed and sulk to his heart's content, and inflict the penalties of ill-humour on his insolent wife. He was such a lusty, emotional man – and he had nothing to do. What was his work to him? Scarcely more than nothing. And what was to fill the rest of his life – nothing. He wanted something to do, and he thought he wanted more done for him. So he got into this irritable, sore state of moral debility. A man cannot respect himself unless he does something. But he can do without his own positive self-respect, so long as his wife respects him. But when the man who has no foothold for self-esteem sees his wife and his wife's friend despise him, it is hell: he fights for very life. So Bircumshaw lay in bed in this state of ignoble misery. His wife had striven for a long time to pretend he was still her hero: but he had tried her patience too far. Now he was confounding heroism, mastery, with brute tyranny. He would be a tyrant, if not a hero.

She, downstairs, occasionally smiled to herself. This time she had given him his dues. Though her heart was pained and anxious, still she smiled: she had clipped a large lock from her Samson. Her smile rose from the deep of her woman's nature.

After having eaten a very little supper, she worked about the house till ten o'clock. Her face had regained that close impassivity which many women wear when alone. Still impassive, at the end of her little tasks she fetched the dinner joint and made him four sandwiches, carefully seasoned and trimmed. Pouring him a glass of milk, she went upstairs with the tray, which looked fresh and tempting.

He had been listening acutely to her last movements. As she entered, however, he lay well under the bedclothes, breathing steadily, pretending to sleep. She came in quite calmly.

'Here is your supper,' she said, in a quiet, indifferent tone, ignoring the fact that he was supposed to be asleep. Another lock fell from his strength. He felt virtue depart from him, felt weak and watery in spirit, and he hated her. He made no reply, but kept up his pretence of sleep.

She bent over the cot of the sleeping baby, a bonny child of three. The little one was flushed in her sleep. Her fist was clenched in a tangle of hair over her small round ear, whilst even in sleep she pouted in her wilful, imperious way. With very gentle fingers the mother loosened the bright hair and put it back from the full, small brow, that reminded one of the brow of a little Virgin by Memling. The father felt that he was left out, ignored. He would have wished to whisper a word to his wife, and so bring himself into the trinity, had he not been so wroth. He retired further into his manly bulk, felt weaker and more miserably insignificant, at the same time more enraged.

Mrs Bircumshaw slipped into bed quietly, settling to rest at once, as far as possible from the broad form of her husband. Both lay quite still, although, as each knew, neither slept. The man felt he wanted to move, but his will was so weak and shrinking, he could not rouse his muscles. He lay tense, paralyzed with self-conscious shrinking, yet bursting to move. She nestled herself down quite at ease. She did not care, this evening, how he felt or thought: for once she let herself rest in indifference.

Towards one o'clock in the morning, just as she was drifting into sleep, her eyes flew open. She did not start or stir; she was merely wide awake. A match had been struck.

Her husband was sitting up in bed, leaning forward to the plate on the chair. Very carefully, she turned her head just enough to see him. His big back bulked above her. He was leaning forward to the chair. The candle, which he had set on the floor, so that its light should not penetrate the sleep of his wife, threw strange shadows on the ceiling, and lighted his throat and underneath his strong chin. Through the arch of his arm, she could see his jaw and his throat working. For some strange reason, he felt that he could not eat in the dark. Occasionally she could see his cheek bulged with food. He ate rapidly, almost voraciously, leaning over the edge of the bed and taking care of the crumbs. She noticed the weight of his shoulder muscles at rest upon the arm on which he leaned.

'The strange animal!' she said to herself, and she laughed, laughed heartily within herself.

'Are they nice?' she longed to say, slyly.

'Are they nice?' – she must say it – 'are they nice?' The temptation was almost too great. But she was afraid of this lusty animal startled at his feeding. She dared not twit him.

He took the milk, leaned back, almost arching backwards over her as he drank. She shrank with a little fear, a little repulsion, which was nevertheless half pleasurable. Cowering under his shadow, she shrugged with contempt, yet her eyes widened with a small, excited smile. This vanished, and a real scorn hardened her lips: when he was sulky his blood was cold as water, nothing could rouse it to passion; he resisted caresses as if he had thin acid in his veins. 'Mean in the blood,' she said to herself.

He finished the food and milk, licked his lips, nipped out the candle, then stealthily lay down. He seemed to sink right into a grateful sleep.

'Nothing on earth is so vital to him as a meal,' she thought.

She lay a long time thinking, before she fell asleep.

A Chapel and A Hay Hut
among the Mountains

I

IT is all very well trying to wander romantically in the Tyrol. Sadly I sit on the bed, my head and shoulders emerging from the enormous overbolster like a cherub from a cloud, writing out of sheer exasperation, while Anita lies on the other bed and is amused.

Two days ago it began to rain. When I think of it I wonder. The gutter of the heavens hangs over the Tyrolese Alps.

We set off with the iridescent cloud of romance ahead, leading us southwards from the Isar towards Italy. We haven't got far. And the iridescent cloud, turned into a column of endless water, still endures around the house.

I omit the pathos of our setting forth, in the dimmery-glimmery light of the Isar Valley, before breakfast-time, with blue chicory flowers open like wonder on either side the road. Neither will I describe our crawling at dinner-time along the foot of the mountains, the rain running down our necks from the flabby straw hats, and dripping cruelly into one's boots from the pent-house of our ruck-sacks. We entered ashamed into a wayside inn, where seven ruddy, joyous peasants, three of them handsome, made a bonfire of their hearts in honour of Anita, whilst I sat in a corner and dripped. . .

Yesterday I admit it was fine in the afternoon and evening. We made tea by a waterfall among yellow-dangling noli-me-tangere flowers, while an inquisitive lot of mountains poked their heads up to look, and a great green grasshopper, armoured like Ivanhoe, took a flying leap into eternity over a lovely, black-blue gentian. At least, I saw him no more.

They had told us there was a footpath over the mountain, three and a half hours to Glashütte. There *was* a faint track, and a myriad of strawberries like ruddy stars below, and a few dark bilberries. We climbed one great steep slope, and scrambled down beyond, into a pine wood. There it was damp and dark and depressing. But one makes the best of things, when one sets out on foot. So we toiled on for an hour, traversing the side of a slope, black, wet, gloomy, looking through the fir-trees across the gulf at another slope, black and gloomy and forbidding, shutting us back. For two hours we slipped and struggled, and still there we were, clamped between these two black slopes, listening to the water that ran uncannily, noisily along the bottom of the trap.

We grew silent and hot with exertion and the dark monotony of the struggle. A rucksack also has its moments of treachery, close friend though it seems. You are quite certain of a delicate and beautiful balance on a slippery tree-root; you take the leap; then the ironic rucksack gives you a pull from behind, and you are grovelling.

And the path *had* been a path. The side of the dark slope, steep as a roof, had innumerable little bogs where waters tried to ooze out and call themselves streams, and could not. Across these bogs went an old bed of fir-boughs, dancy and treacherous. So, there was a path! Suddenly there were no more fir-boughs, and one stood lost before the squalor of the slope. I wiped my brow.

'You so soon lose your temper,' said Anita. So I stood aside, and yielded her the lead.

She blundered into another little track lower down.

'You *see*!' she said, turning round.

I did not answer. She began to hum a little tune, because her path descended. We slipped and struggled. Then her path vanished into the loudly-snorting, chuckling stream, and did not emerge.

'Well?' I said.

'But where is it?' she said with vehemence and pathos.

'You see even *your* road ends in nowhere,' I said.

'I *hate* you when you preach,' she flashed. 'Besides it *doesn't* end in nowhere.'

'At any rate,' I said, 'we can't sleep on the end of it.'

I found another track, but I entered on it delicately, without triumph. We went in silence. And it vanished into the same loudly-snorting stream.

'Oh, don't look like that!' cried Anita. So I followed the bedraggled tail of her skirts once more up the wet, dark opposition of the slope. We found another path, and once more we lost the scent in the overjoyed stream.

'Perhaps we're supposed to go across,' I said meekly, as we stood beside the waters.

'I – *why* did I take a damp match of a man like you!' she cried. 'One could scratch you for ever and you wouldn't strike.'

I looked at her, wondering, and turned to the stream, which was cunningly bethinking itself. There were chunks of rock, and spouts and combs and rattles of sly water. So I put my raincoat over my rucksack and ventured over.

The opposite bank was very steep and high. We were swallowed in this black gorge, swallowed to the bottom, and gazing upwards I set off on all fours, climbing with my raincoat over my rucksack, cloakwise, to leave me free. I scrambled and hauled and struggled.

And from below came shriek upon shriek of laughter. I reached the top, and looked down. I could see nothing, only the whirring of laughter came up.

'What is it?' I called, but the sound was lost amid the

cackle of the waters. So I crawled over the edge and sat in the gloomy solitude, extinguished.

Directly I heard a shrill, frightened call:

'Where are you?'

My heart exulted and melted at the same moment.

'Come along,' I cried, satisfied that there was one spot in this gloomy solitude to call to.

She arrived, scared with the steep climb, and the fear of loneliness in this place.

'I might never have found you again,' she said.

'I don't intend you should lose me,' I said. So she sat down, and presently her head began to nod with laughter, and her bosom shook with laughter, and she was laughing wildly without me.

'Well, what?' I said.

'You – you looked like a camel – with a hump – climbing up,' she shrieked.

'We'd better be moving,' I said. She slipped and laughed and struggled. At last we came to a beautiful savage road. It was the bed of some stream that came no more this way, a mass of clear boulders leading up the slope through the gloom.

'We are coming out now,' said Anita, looking ahead. I also was quite sure of it. But after an hour of climbing, we were still in the bed of clear boulders, between dark trees, among the toes of the mountains.

Anita spied a hunter's hut, made of bark, and she went to investigate. Night was coming on.

'I can't get in,' she called to me, obscurely.

'Then come,' I said.

It was too wet and cold to sleep out of doors in the woods. But instead of coming, she stooped in the dark twilight for strawberries. I waited like the shadow of wrath. But she, unconcerned, careless and happy in her contrariety, gathered strawberries among the shadows.

'We *must* find a place to sleep in,' I said. And my utter

insistence took effect.

She realized that I was lost among the mountains, as well as she, that night and the cold and the great dark slopes were close upon us, and we were of no avail, even being two, against the coldness and desolation of the mountains.

So in silence we scrambled upwards, hand in hand. Anita was sure a dozen times that we were coming out. At last even she got disheartened.

Then, in the darkness, we spied a hut beside a path among the thinning fir-trees.

'It will be a woodman's hut,' she said.

'A shrine,' I answered.

I was right for once. It was a wooden hut just like a model, with a black old wreath hanging on the door. There was a click of the latch in the cold, watchful silence of the upper mountains, and we entered.

By the grey darkness coming in from outside we made out the tiny chapel, candles on the altar and a whole covering of ex-voto pictures on the walls, and four little praying-benches. It was all close and snug as a box.

Feeling quite safe, and exalted in this rare, upper shadow, I lit the candles, all. Point after point of flame flowed out on the night. There were six. Then I took off my hat and my rucksack, and rejoiced, my heart at home.

The walls of the chapel were covered close with naked little pictures, all coloured, painted by the peasants on wood, and framed with little frames. I glanced round, saw the cows and the horses on the green meadows, the men on their knees in their houses, and I was happy as if I had found myself among the angels.

'What wonderful luck!' I said to Anita.

'But what are we going to do?' she asked.

'Sleep on the floor – between the praying-desks. There's just room.'

'But we can't sleep on a wooden floor,' she said.

'What better can you find?'

'A hay hut. There must be a hay hut somewhere near. We *can't* sleep here.'

'Oh yes,' I said.

But I was bound to look at the little pictures. I climbed on to a bench. Anita stood in the open doorway like a disconsolate, eternal angel. The light of the six dusky tapers glimmered on her discontended mouth. Behind her, I could see tips of fir branches just illuminated, and then the night.

She turned and was gone like darkness into the darkness. I heard her boots upon the stones. Then I turned to the little pictures I loved. Perched upon the praying-desks, I looked at one, and then another. They were picture-writings that seemed like my own soul talking to me. They were really little pictures for God, because horses and cows and men and women and mountains, they are His own language. How should He read German and English and Russian, like a schoolmaster? The peasants could trust Him to understand their pictures: they were not so sure that He would concern Himself with their written script.

I was looking at a pale blue picture. That was a bedroom, where a woman lay in bed, and a baby lay in a cradle not far away. The bed was blue, and it seemed to be falling out of the picture, so it gave me a feeling of fear and insecurity. Also, as the distance receded, the bedstead got wider, uneasily. The woman lay looking straight at me, from under the huge, blue-striped overbolster. Her pink face was round like a penny doll's, with the same round stare. And the baby, like a pink-faced farthing doll, also stared roundly.

'Maria hat geholfen E.G. – 1777.'

I looked at them. And I knew that I was the husband looking and wondering. G., the husband, did not appear himself. It was from the little picture on his retina that this picture was reproduced. He could not sum it up, and explain it, this vision of his wife suffering in child-birth, and then lying still and at peace with the baby in the cradle. He could not make head or tail of it. But at least he could represent it, and hang it up like a mirror before the eyes of God, giving the statement even if he could get no explanation. And he was satisfied. And so, perforce, was I, though my heart began to knock for knowledge.

The men never actually saw themselves unless in precarious conditions. When their lives were threatened, then they had a fearful flash of self-consciousness, which haunted them till they had represented it. They represented themselves in all kinds of ridiculous postures, at the moment when the accident occurred.

Joseph Rieck, for example, was in a toppling-backward attitude rather like a footballer giving a very high kick and losing his balance. But on his left ankle had fallen a great grey stone, that might have killed him, squashing out much blood, orange-coloured – or so it looked by the candle-light – whilst the Holy Mary stood above in a bolster-frame of clouds, holding up her hands in mild surprise.

> 'Joseph Rieck
> Gott sey Danck gasagt 1834.'

It was curious that he thanked God because a stone had fallen on his ankle. But perhaps the thanks were because it had not fallen on his head. Or perhaps because the ankle had got better, though it looked a nasty smash, according to the picture. It didn't occur to him to thank God that all the mountains of the Tyrol had not tumbled on him the first day he was born. It doesn't occur to any of us. We wait till a big stone falls on our ankle. Then we paint a vivid picture and say: 'In the midst of life we are in death,' and we thank God that we've escaped. All kinds of men were saying: 'Gott sey Danck'; either because big stones had squashed them, or because trees had come down on them whilst they were felling, or else because they'd tumbled over cliffs, or got carried away in streams: all little events which caused them to ejaculate: 'God be thanked, I'm still alive'.

Then some of the women had picture prayers that were touching, because they were prayers for other people, for their children and not for themselves. In a sort of cell kneeled a woman, wearing a Catherine of Russia kind of dress, opposite a kneeling man in Vicar of Wakefield attire. Between them, on the stone wall, hung two long iron chains with iron rings dangling at the end. Above these, framed in an oval of bolster-clouds, Christ on the Cross, and above Him, a little Maria, short in stature, something like Queen Victoria, with a very blue cloth over her head, falling down her dumpy figure. She, the Holy Mother of heaven, looked distressed. The woman kneeling in the cell put up her hands, saying:

'O Mutter Gottes von Rerelmos, Ich bitte mach mir mein Kind von Gefangenschaft los mach im von Eissen und Bandten frey wansz des Gottliche Willen sey.
Susanna Grillen 1783.'

I suppose Herr Grillen knew that it was not the affair of the Mutter Gottes. Poor Susanna Grillen! It was natural and womanly in her to identify the powers that be with the eternal powers. What I can't see, is whether the boy had really done anything wrong, or whether he had merely transgressed some law of some duke or king or community. I suppose the poor thing did not know herself how to make the distinction. But evidently the father, knowing he was in temporal difficulty, was not very active in asking help of the eternal.

One must look up the history of the Tyrol for the 1783 period.

A few pictures were family utterances, but the voice which spoke was always the voice of the mother. Marie Schneeberger thanked God for healing her son. She kneeled on one side of the bedroom, with her three daughters behind her; Schneeberger kneeled facing her, with a space between them, and his one son behind him. The Holy Mary floated above the space of their thanks. The whole family united this time to bless the heavenly powers that the bad had not been worse. And, in the face of the divine power, the man was separate from the woman, the daughter from the son, the sister from the brother – one set on one side, one set on the other, separate before the eternal grace, or the eternal fear.

The last set of pictures thanked God for the salvation of property. One lady had six cows – all red ones – painted feeding on a meadow with rocks behind. All the cows I have seen in these parts have been dun or buff coloured. But these are red. And the goodwife thanks God very sincerely for restoring to her that which was lost for five days, viz. her six cows and the little cow-girl Kate. The little girl did not appear in the picture nor in the thanks: she was only mentioned as having been lost along with the cows. I do not know what became of her. Cows can always eat grass. I suppose she milked her beasts, and perhaps cranberries were ripe. But five days was a long time for poor Kathel.

There were hundreds of cattle painted standing on meadows like a child's Noah's Ark toys arranged in groups: a group of red cows, a group of brown horses, a group of brown goats, a few grey sheep; as if they had all been summoned into their classes. Then Maria in her cloud-frame blessed them. But standing there so hiero-glyphic, the animals had a symbolic power. They did not merely represent property. They were the wonderful animal life which man must take for food. Arrayed there in their numbers, they were almost frightening, as if they might overthrow us, like an army.

Only one woman had had an accident. She was seen falling downstairs, just landing at the bottom into her peaceful kitchen where the kitten lay asleep by the stove. The kitten slept on, but Mary in a blue mantle appeared through the ceiling, mildly shocked and deprecating.

Alone among all the women, the women who had suffered childbirth or had suffered through some child of their own, was this housewife who had fallen downstairs into the kitchen where the cat slept peacefully. Perhaps she had not any children. However that may be, her position was ignoble, as she bumped on the bottom stair.

There they all were, in their ex-voto pictures that I think the women had ordered and paid for, these peasants of the valley below, pictured in their fear. They lived under the mountains where always was fear. Sometimes they knew it to close on a man or a woman. Then there was no peace in the heart of this man till the fear had been pictured, till he was represented in the grip of terror, and till the picture had been offered to the Deity, the dread, unnamed Deity; whose might must be acknowledged, whilst in the same picture the milder divine succour was represented and named and thanked. Deepest of all things, among the mountain darknesses, was the ever-felt fear. First of all gods was the unknown god who crushed life at any moment, and threatened it always. His shadow was over the valleys. And a tacit acknowledgement and propitiation of Him were the ex-voto pictures, painted out of fear and offered to Him unnamed. Whilst upon the face of them all was Mary the divine Succour, She, who had suffered, and knew. And that which had suffered and known, had prevailed, and was openly thanked. But that which had neither known nor suffered, the dread unnamed, which had aimed and missed by a little, this must be acknowledged covertly. For his own soul's sake, man must acknowledge his own fear, acknowledge the power beyond him.

Whilst I was reading the inscriptions high up on the wall, Anita came back. She stood below me in her weather-beaten panama hat, looking up dissatisfied. The light fell warm on her face. She was discontented and excited.

'There's a gorgeous hay hut a little farther on,' she said.

'Hold me a candle a minute, will you?' I said.

'A great hay hut full of hay, in an open space. I climbed in –'

'Do you mind giving me a candle for a moment?'

'But no – come along –'

'I just want to read this – give me a candle.' In a silence of impatience, she handed me one of the tapers. I was reading a little inscription.

'Won't you come?' she said.

'We could sleep well here,' I said. 'It is so dry and secure.'

'Why!' she cried irritably. 'Come to the hay hut and see.'

'In one moment,' I said.

She turned away.

'Isn't this altar adorable!' she cried. 'Lovely little paper roses, and ornaments.'

She was fingering some artificial flowers, thinking to put them in her hair. I jumped down, saying I must finish reading my pictures in the morning. So I gathered the rucksack and examined the cash-box by the door. It was open and contained six kreutzers. I put in forty pfennigs, out of my poor pocket, to pay for the candles. Then I called Anita away from the altar trinkets, and we closed the door, and were out in the darkness of the mountains.

2

I resented being dragged out of my kapelle into the black and dismal night. In the chapel were candles and a boarded floor. And the streams in the mountains refuse to run anywhere but down the paths made by man. Anita said: 'You cannot imagine how lovely your chapel looked, as I came on it from the dark, its row of candles shining, and all the inside warm!'

'Then why on earth didn't you stay there?' I said.

'But think of sleeping in a hay hut,' she cried.

'I think a kapelle is much more soul stirring,' I insisted.

'But much harder to the bones,' she replied.

We struggled out on to a small meadow, between the mountain tops. Anita called it a kettle. I presumed then that we had come in by the spout and should have to get out by the lid. At any rate, the black heads of the mountains poked up all round, and I felt tiny, like a beetle in a basin.

The hay hut stood big and dark and solid, on the clear grass.

'I know just how to get in,' said Anita, who was full of joy now we were going to be uncomfortably situated. 'And now we must eat and drink tea.'

'Where's your water?' I asked.

She listened intently. There was a light swishing of pine-trees on the mountain side.

'I hear it,' she said.

'Somewhere down some horrid chasm,' I answered.

'I will go and look,' she said.

'Well,' I answered, 'you needn't go hunting on a hill-side where there isn't the faintest sign of a rut or water-course.'

We spoke *sotto voce*, because of the darkness and the stillness. I led down the meadow, nearly breaking my neck over the steepest places. Now I was very thirsty, and we had only a very little schnapps.

'There is sure to be water in the lowest place,' I said.

She followed me stealthily and with glee. Soon we squelched in a soft place.

'A confounded marsh,' I said.

'But,' she answered, 'I hear it trickling.'

'What's the good of its trickling, if it's nasty.'

'You *are* consoling,' she mocked.

'I suppose,' I said, 'it rises here. So if we can get at the Quelle –'

I don't know why 'Quelle' was necessary, instead of 'source', but it was. We paddled up the wet place, and in the darkness found where the water welled out. Having filled our can, and our boots by the way, we trudged back. I slipped and spilled half the water.

'This,' said Anita, 'makes me perfectly happy.'

'I wish it did me,' I replied.

'Don't you like it, dear?' she said, grieved.

My feet were soddened and stone cold. Everywhere was wet, and very dark.

'It's all right,' I said. 'But the chapel –'

So we sat at the back of the hut, where the wind didn't blow so badly, and we made tea and ate sausage. The wind wafted the flame of the spirit lamp about, drops of rain began to fall. In the pitch dark, we lost our sausage and the packet of tea among the logs.

'At last I'm perfectly happy,' Anita repeated.

I found it irritating to hear her. I was looking for the tea.

Before we had finished this precious meal, the rain came pelting down. We hurried the things into our rucksacks and bundled into the hut. There was one little bread left for morning.

The hut was as big as a small cottage. It was made of logs laid on top of one another, but they had not been properly notched, so there were stripes of light all round the Egyptian darkness. And in a hay hut one dares not strike a light.

'There's the ladder to the big part,' said Anita.

The front compartment was only one-quarter occupied with hay: the back compartment was full nearly to the ceiling. I climbed up the ladder, and felt the hay, putting my hand straight into a nasty messy place where the water had leaked in among the hay from the roof.

'That's all puddly, and the man'll have his whole crop rotten if he doesn't watch it,' I said. 'It's a stinkingly badly-made hay hut.'

'Listen to the rain,' whispered Anita.

It was rattling on the roof furiously. Then, although there were slots of light, and a hundred horse-power draught tearing across the hut, I was glad to be inside the place.

'Hay,' I remarked after a while, 'has two disadvantages. It tickles like all the creeping insects, and it is porous to the wind.'

' "Porous to the wind",' mocked Anita.

'It is,' I said.

There was a great preparation. All valuables, such as hair-pins and garters and pfennigs and hellers and trinkets and collar studs, I carefully collected in my hat. It was pitch dark. I laid the hat somewhere. We took off our soddened shoes and stockings. Imagining they would somehow generate heat and dry better, I pushed the boots into the wall of hay. Then I hung up various draggled garments, hoping they would dry.

'I insist on your tying up your head in a hanky, and on my spreading my waistcoat for a pillow-cloth,' I said.

Anita humbly submitted. She was too full of joy to

refuse. We had no blankets, nothing but a Burberry each.

'A good large hole,' I said, 'as large as a double grave. And I only hope it won't be one.'

'If you catch cold,' said Anita, 'I shall hate you.'

'And if *you* catch cold,' I answered, 'I s'll nurse you tenderly.'

'You dear!' she exclaimed, affectionately.

We dug like two moles at the grave.

'But see the mountains of hay that come out,' she said.

'All right,' I said, 'you can amuse your German fancy by putting them back again, and sleeping underneath them.'

'How lovely!' she cried.

'And how much lovelier a German fat bolster would be.'

'Don't!' she implored. 'Don't spoil it.'

'I'd sleep in a lobster-pot to please you,' I said.

'I don't want you to please me, I want you to be pleased,' she insisted.

'God help me, I *will* be pleased,' I promised.

At first it was pretty warm in the trough, but every minute I had to rub my nose or my neck. This hay was the most insidious, persistent stuff. However much I tried to fend it off, one blade tickled my nostrils, a seed fell on my eyelid, a great stalk went down my neck. I wrestled with it like a Hercules, to keep it at bay, but in vain. And Anita merely laughed at my puffs and snorts.

'Evidently,' I said, 'you have not so sensitive a skin as I.'

'Oh no – not so delicate and fine,' she mocked.

'In fact, you can't have,' I said, sighing. But presently, she also sighed.

'Why,' she said, 'did you choose a waistcoat for a pillow? I've always got my face in one of the armholes.'

'You should arrange it better,' I said.

We sighed, and suffered the fiendish ticklings of the hay. Then I suppose we slept, in a sort of fitful fever.

I was awakened by the cracks of thunder. Anita clutched me. It was fearfully dark. Like a great whip clacking, the thunder cracked and spattered over our hut, seemed to rattle backwards and forwards from the mountain peaks.

'Something more for your money,' I groaned, too sleepy to live.

'Does thunder strike hay huts?' Anita asked.

'Yes, it makes a dead set at them – simply preys on hay huts, does thunder,' I declared.

'Now you needn't frighten me,' she reproached.

'Go to sleep,' I commanded.

But she wouldn't. There was Anita, there was thunder, and lightning, then a raging wind and cataracts of rain, and the slow, persistent, evil tickling of the hay seeds, all warring on my sleepiness. Occasionally I got a wink. Then it began to get cold, with the icy wind rushing in through the wide slots between the logs of the walls. The miserable hay couldn't even keep us warm. Through the chinks of it penetrated the vicious wind. And Anita would not consent to be buried, she would have her shoulders and head clear. So of course we had little protection. It grew colder and colder, miserably cold. I burrowed deeper and deeper. Then I felt Anita's bare feet, and they were icy.

'Woman,' I said, 'poke your wretched head in, and be covered up, and save what modicum of animal heat you can generate.'

'I must breathe,' she answered crossly.

'The hay is quite well aerated,' I assured her.

At last it began to get dawn. Slots of grey came in place of slots of blue-black, all round the walls. There was twilight in the crate of a hay hut. I could distinguish the ladder and the rucksacks. Somewhere outside, I thought, drowsily, a boy was kicking a salmon tin down the street; till it struck me as curious, and I remembered it was only the sound of a cow-bell, or a goat-bell.

'It's morning,' said Anita.

'Call this morning?' I groaned.

'Are you warm, dear?'

'Baked.'

'Shall we get up?'

'Yes. At all events we can be one degree more wretched and cold.'

'I'm perfectly happy,' she persisted.

'You look it,' I said.

Immediately she was full of fear.

'Do I look horrid?' she asked.

She was huddled in her coat: her tousled hair was full of hay.

I pulled on my boots and clambered through the square opening.

'But come and look!' I exclaimed.

It had snowed terrifically during the night; not down at our level, but a little higher up. We were on a grassy place, about half a mile across, and all round us was the blackness of pine-woods, rising up. Then suddenly in the middle air, it changed, and great peaks of snow balanced, intensely white, in the pallid dawn. All the upper world around us belonged to the sky; it was wonderfully white, and fresh, and awake with joy. I felt I had only to run upwards through the pine-trees, then I could tread the slopes that were really sky-slopes, could walk up the sky.

'No!' cried Anita, in protest, her eyes filling with tears. 'No!'

We had quite a solemn moment together, all because of that snow. And the fearfully gentle way we talked and moved, as if we were the only two people God had made, touches me to remember.

'Look!' cried Anita.

I thought at least the Archangel Gabriel was standing beside me. But she only meant my breath, that froze while on the air. It reminded me.

'And the cold!' I groaned. 'It fairly reduces one to an ash.'

'Yes, my dear – we must drink tea,' she replied solicitously. I took the can for water. Everything looked so different in the morning. I could find the marsh, but not the water bubbling up. Anita came to look for me. She was barefoot, because her boots were wet. Over the icy mown meadow she came, took the can from me, and found the spring. I went back and prepared breakfast. There was one little roll, some tea, and some schnapps. Anita came with water, balancing it gingerly. She had a distracted look.

'Oh, how it hurts!' she cried. 'The ice-cold stubbles, like blunt icy needles, they did hurt!'

I looked at her bare feet and was furious with her.

'No one,' I cried, 'but a lunatic, would dream of going down there *barefoot* under these conditions –'

' "Under these conditions",' she mocked.

'It ought to have hurt you *more*,' I cried. 'There is no crime but stupidity.'

' "Crime but stupidity",' she echoed, laughing at me. Then I went to look at her feet.

We ate the miserable knob of bread, and swallowed the tea. Then I bullied Anita into coming away. She performed a beautiful toilet that I called the 'brave Tyrolese', and at last we set out. The snow all above us was laughing with brightness. But the earth, and our boots, were soddened.

'Isn't it wonderful!' cried Anita.

'Yes – with feet of clay,' I answered. 'Wet, raw clay!'

Sobered, we squelched along an indefinite track. Then we spied a little, dirty farm-house, and saw an uncouth-looking man go into the cow-sheds.

'This,' I said, 'is where the villains and robbers live.'

Then we saw the woman. She was wearing the blue linen trousers that peasant women wear at work.

'Go carefully,' said Anita. 'Perhaps she hasn't performed her toilet.'

'I shouldn't think she's got one to perform,' I replied.

It was a deadly lonely place, high up, cold, and dirty. Even in such a frost, it stank bravely beneath the snow peaks. But I went softly.

Seeing Anita, the woman came to the door. She was dressed in blue overalls, trousers and bodice, the trousers tight round the ankles, nearly like the old-fashioned leg-of-mutton sleeves. She was pale, seemed rather deadened, as if this continuous silence acted on her like a deadening drug. Anita asked her the way. She came out to show us, as there was no track, walking before us with strides like a man, but in a tired, deadened sort of way. Her figure was not ugly, and the nape of her neck was a woman's, with soft wisps of hair. She pointed us the way down.

'How old was she?' I asked Anita, when she had gone back.

'How old do you think?' replied Anita.

'Forty to forty-five.'

'Thirty-two or three,' answered Anita.

'How do you know, any more than I?'

'I am sure.'

I looked back. The woman was going up the steep path in a mechanical, lifeless way. The brilliant snow glistened up above, in peaks. The hollow green cup that formed the farm was utterly still. And the woman seemed infected with all this immobility and silence. It was as if she were gradually going dead, because she had no place there. And

I saw the man at the cow-shed door. He was thin, with sandy moustaches; and there was about him the same look of distance, as if silence, loneliness, and the mountains deadened him too.

We went down between the rocks, in a cleft where a river rushed. On every side, streams fell and bounded down. Some, coming over the sheer wall of a cliff, drifted dreamily down like a roving rope of mist. All round, so white and candid, were the flowers they call Grass of Parnassus, looking up at us, and the regal black-blue gentian reared themselves here and there.

(*The following ending was erased.*)

We ran ourselves warm, but I felt as if the fires had gone out inside me. Down and down we raced the streams, that fell into beautiful green pools, and fell out again with a roar. Anita actually wanted to bathe, but I forbade it. So, after two hours' running downhill, we came out in the level valley at Glashütte. It was raining now, a thick dree rain. We pushed on to a little Gasthaus, that was really the home of a forester. There the stove was going, so we drank quantities of coffee, ale, and went to bed.

'You spent the night in a hay hut,' said I to Anita. 'And the next day in bed.'

'But I've done it, and I loved it,' said she. 'And besides, it's raining.'

And it continued to pour. So we stayed in the house of the Jäger, who had a good, hard wife. She made us comfortable. But she kept her children in hand. They sat still and good, with their backs against the stove, and watched.

'Your children are good,' I said.

'They are wild ones,' she answered, shaking her head sternly. And I saw the boy's black eyes sparkle.

'The boy is like his father,' I said.

She looked at him.

'Yes – yes! perhaps,' she said shortly.

But there was a proud stiffness in her neck, nevertheless. The father was a mark-worthy man, evidently. He was away in the forests now for a day or two. But he had photos of himself everywhere, a good-looking, well-made, conceited Jäger, who was photographed standing with his right foot on the shoulder of a slaughtered chamois. And soon his wife had thawed sufficiently to tell me: 'Yes, he had accompanied the Crown Prince to shoot his first chamois.' And finally, she recited to us this letter, from the same Crown Prince:

'Lieber Karl, Ich möchte wissen wie und wann die letzte Gemse geschossen worden —'

Once

THE morning was very beautiful. White packets of mist hung over the river, as if a great train had gone by leaving its steam idle, in a trail down the valley. The mountains were just faint grey-blue, with the slightest glitter of snow high up in the sunshine. They seemed to be standing a long way off, watching me, and wondering. As I bathed in the shaft of sunshine that came through the wide-opened window, letting the water slip swiftly down my sides, my mind went wandering through the hazy morning, very sweet and far-off and still, so that I had hardly wit enough to dry myself. And as soon as I had got on my dressing-gown, I lay down again idly on the bed, looking out at the morning that still was greenish from the dawn, and thinking of Anita.

I had loved her when I was a boy. She was an aristocrat's daughter, but she was not rich. I was simply middle-class, then. I was much too green and humble-minded to think of making love to her. No sooner had she come home from school than she married an officer. He was rather handsome, something in the Kaiser's fashion, but stupid as an ass. And Anita was only eighteen. When at last she accepted me as a lover, she told me about it.

'The night I was married,' she said, 'I lay counting the flowers on the wall-paper, how many on a string; he bored me so.'

He was of good family, and of great repute in the Army, being a worker. He had the tenacity of a bulldog, and rode like a centaur. These things look well from a distance, but to live with they weary one beyond endurance, so Anita says.

She had her first child just before she was twenty: two

years afterwards, another. Then no more. Her husband was something of a brute. He neglected her, though not outrageously, treated her as if she were a fine animal. To complete matters, he more than ruined himself owing to debts, gambling and otherwise, then utterly disgraced himself by using Government money and being caught.

'You have found a hair in your soup,' I wrote to Anita.

'Not a hair, a whole plait,' she replied.

After that, she began to have lovers. She was a splendid young creature, and was not going to sit down in her rather elegant flat in Berlin, to run to seed. Her husband was officer in a crack regiment. Anita was superb to look at. He was proud to introduce her to his friends. Then, moreover, she had her own relatives in Berlin, aristocratic but also rich, and moving in the first society. So she began to take lovers.

Anita shows her breeding: erect, rather haughty, with a good-humoured kind of scorn. She is tall and strong, her brown eyes are full of scorn, and she has a downy, warm-coloured skin, brownish to match her black hair.

At last she came to love me a little. Her soul is unspoiled. I think she has almost the soul of a virgin. I think, perhaps, it frets her that she has never really loved. She has never had the real respect – *Ehrfurcht* – for a man. And she has been here with me in the Tyrol these last ten days. I love her, and I am not satisfied with myself. Perhaps I too shall fall short.

'You have never *loved* your men?' I asked her.

'I loved them – but I have put them all in my pocket,' she said, with just the faintest disappointment in her good humour. She shrugged her shoulders at my serious gaze.

I lay wondering if I too were going into Anita's pocket, along with her purse and her perfume and the little sweets she loved. It would almost have been delicious to do so. A kind of voluptuousness urged me to let her have me, to let her put me in her pocket. It would be so nice. But I loved her: it would not be fair to her. I wanted to do more than give her pleasure.

Suddenly the door opened on my musing, and Anita came into my bedroom. Startled, I laughed in my very soul, and I adored her. She was so natural! She was dressed in a transparent lacy chemise, that was slipping over her shoulder, high boots, upon one of which her string-coloured stocking had fallen. And she wore an enormous hat, black, lined with white, and covered with a tremendous creamy-brown feather, that streamed like a flood of brownish foam, swaying lightly. It was an immense hat on top of her shamelessness, and the great, soft feather seemed to spill over, fall with a sudden gush, as she put back her head.

She looked at me, then went straight to the mirror.

'How do you like my hat?' she said.

She stood before the panel of looking-glass, conscious only of her hat, whose great feather-strands swung in a tide. Her bare shoulder glistened, and through the fine web of her chemise I could see all her body in warm silhouette, with golden reflections under the breasts and arms. The light ran in silver up her lifted arms, and the gold shadow stirred as she arranged her hat.

'How do you like my hat?' she repeated.

Then, as I did not answer, she turned to look at me. I was still lying on the bed. She must have seen that I had looked at her, instead of at her hat, for a quick darkness and a frown came into her eyes, cleared instantly, as she asked, in a slightly hard tone:

'Don't you like it?'

'It's rather splendid,' I answered. 'Where did it come from?'

'From Berlin this morning – or last evening,' she replied.

'It's a bit huge,' I ventured.

She drew herself up.

'Indeed not!' she said, turning to the mirror.

I got up, dropped off my dressing-gown, put a silk hat quite correctly on my head, and then, naked save for a hat and a pair of gloves, I went forward to her.

'How do you like my hat?' I asked her.

She looked at me and went off into a fit of laughter. She dropped her hat on to a chair, and sank on to the bed, shaking with laughter. Every now and then she lifted her head, gave one look from her dark eyes, then buried her face in the pillows. I stood before her clad in my hat, feeling a good bit of a fool. She peeped up again.

'You are lovely, you are lovely!' she cried.

With a grave and dignified movement I prepared to remove the hat, saying:

'And even then, I lack high-laced boots and one stocking.'

But she flew at me, kept the hat on my head, and kissed me.

'Don't take it off,' she implored. 'I love you for it.'

So I sat down gravely and unembarrassed on the bed.

'But don't you like my hat?' I said in injured tones. 'I bought it in London last month.'

She looked up at me comically, and went into peals of laughter.

'Think,' she cried, 'if all those Englishmen in Piccadilly went like that!'

That amused even me.

At last I assured her her hat was adorable, and, much to my relief, I got rid of my silk and into a dressing-gown.

'You *will* cover yourself up,' she said reproachfully. 'And you look so nice with nothing on – but a hat.'

'It's that old Apple I can't digest,' I said.

She was quite happy in her shift and her high boots. I lay looking at her beautiful legs.

'How many more men have you done that to?' I asked.

'What?' she answered.

'Gone into their bedrooms clad in a wisp of mist, trying a new hat on?'

She leaned over to me and kissed me.

'Not many,' she said. 'I've not been *quite* so familiar before, I don't think.'

'I suppose you've forgotten,' said I. 'However, it doesn't matter.' Perhaps the slight bitterness in my voice touched her. She said almost indignantly:

'Do you think I want to flatter you and make you believe you are the first that ever I really – *really* –'

'I don't know,' I replied. 'Neither you nor I are so easily deluded.'

She looked at me peculiarly and steadily.

'I know all the time,' said I, 'that I am *pro tem.*, and that I shan't even last as long as most.'

'You are sorry for yourself?' she mocked.

I shrugged my shoulders, looking into her eyes. She caused me a good deal of agony, but I didn't give in to her.

'I shan't commit suicide,' I replied.

'*On est mort pour si longtemps,*' she said, suddenly dancing on the bed. I loved her. She had the courage to live, almost joyously.

'When you think back over your affairs – they are numerous, though you are only thirty-one –'

'Not numerous – only several – and you *do* underline the thirty-one –,' she laughed.

'But how do you feel, when you think of them?' I asked.

She knitted her eyebrows quaintly, and there was a shadow, more puzzled than anything, on her face.

'There is something nice in all of them,' she said. 'Men are really fearfully good,' she sighed.

'If only they weren't all pocket-editions,' I mocked.

She laughed, then began drawing the silk cord through the lace of her chemise, pensively. The round caps of her shoulders gleamed like old ivory: there was a faint brown stain towards the arm-pit.

'No,' she said, suddenly lifting her head and looking me calmly into the eyes, 'I have nothing to be ashamed of – that is, – no, I have nothing to be ashamed of!'

'I believe you,' I said. 'And I don't suppose you've done anything that even *I* shouldn't be able to swallow – have you?'

I felt rather plaintive with my question. She looked at me and shrugged her shoulders.

'I know you haven't,' I preached. 'All your affairs have been rather decent. They've meant more to the men than they have to you.'

The shadows of her breasts, fine globes, shone warm through the linen veil. She was thinking.

'Shall I tell you,' she asked, 'one thing I did?'

'If you like,' I answered. 'But let me get you a wrap.' I kissed her shoulder. It had the same fine, delicious coldness of ivory.

'No – yes, you may,' she replied.

I brought her a Chinese thing of black silk with gorgeous embroidered dragons, green as flame, writhing upon it.

'How white against that black silk you are,' I said, kissing the half globe of her breast, through the linen.

'Lie there,' she commanded me. She sat in the middle of the bed, whilst I lay looking at her. She picked up the black silk tassel of my dressing-gown and began flattening it out like a daisy.

'Gretchen!' I said.

'"Marguerite with one petal",' she answered in French, laughing. 'I am ashamed of it, so you must be nice with me –'

'Have a cigarette!' I said.

She puffed wistfully for a few moments.

'You've got to hear it,' she said.

'Go on!'

'I was staying in Dresden in quite a grand hotel; which I rather enjoy: ringing bells, dressing three times a day, feeling half a great lady, half a cocotte. Don't be cross with me for saying it: look at me! The man was at a garrison a little way off. I'd have married him if I could –'

She shrugged her brown, handsome shoulders, and puffed out a plume of smoke.

'It began to bore me after three days. I was always alone, looking at shops alone, going to the opera alone – where the beastly men got behind their wives' backs to look at me. In the end I got cross with my poor man, though of course it wasn't his fault, that he couldn't come.'

She gave a little laugh as she took a draw at her cigarette.

'The fourth morning I came downstairs – I was feeling fearfully good-looking and proud of myself. I know I had a sort of *café au lait* coat and skirt, very pale – and its fit was a *joy!*'

After a pause, she continued: 'And a big black hat with a cloud of white ospreys. I nearly jumped when a man almost ran into me. O jeh! it was a young officer, just bursting with life, a splendid creature: the German aristocrat at his best. He wasn't over tall, in his dark blue uniform, but simply firm with life. An electric shock went through me, it slipped down me like fire, when I looked into his eyes. O jeh! they just flamed with consciousness of me – and they were just the same colour as the soft-blue reveres of his uniform. He looked at me – ha! – and then, he bowed, the sort of bow a woman enjoys like a caress.

' " *Verzeihung, gnädiges Fräulein!* "

'I just inclined my head, and we went our ways. It felt as if something mechanical shifted us, not our wills.

'I was restless that day, I could stay nowhere. Something stirred inside my veins. I was drinking tea on the Brühler Terasse, watching the people go by like a sort of mechanical procession, and the broad Elbe as a stiller background, when he stood before me, saluting, and taking a seat, half apologetically, half devil-may-care. I was not nearly so much surprised at him, as at the mechanical parading people. And I could see he thought me a cocotte –'

She looked thoughtfully across the room, the past roused dangerously in her dark eyes.

'But the game amused and excited me. He told me he had to go to a Court ball tonight – and then he said, in his nonchalant yet pleadingly passionate way:

' "And afterwards –?"

' "And afterwards –!" I repeated.

' "May I –?" he asked.

'Then I told him the number of my room.

'I dawdled to the hotel, and dressed for dinner, and talked to somebody sitting next to me, but I was an hour or two ahead, when he would come. I arranged my silver and brushes and things, and I had ordered a great bunch of lilies of the valley; they were in a black bowl. There were delicate pink silk curtains, and the carpet was a cold colour, nearly white, with a tawny pink and turquoise ravelled border, a Persian thing, I should imagine. I know I liked it. And didn't that room feel fresh, full of expectation, like myself!

'That last half-hour of waiting – so funny – I seemed to have no feeling, no consciousness. I lay in the dark, holding my nice pale blue gown of *crêpe de Chine* against my body for comfort. There was a fumble at the door, and I caught my breath! Quickly he came in, locked the door, and switched on all the lights. There he stood, the centre of everything, the light shining on his bright brown hair. He was holding something under his cloak. Now he came to me, and threw on me from out of his cloak a whole armful of red and pink roses. It was delicious! Some of them were cold, when they fell on me. He took off his cloak. I loved his figure in its blue uniform; and then, oh jeh! he picked me off the bed, the roses and all, and kissed me – *how* he kissed me!'

She paused at the recollection.

'I could feel his mouth through my thin gown. Then, he went still and intense. He pulled off my *saut-de-lit*, and looked at me. He held me away from him, his mouth parted with wonder, and yet, as if the gods would envy him – wonder and adoration and pride! I liked his worship. Then he laid me on the bed again, and covered me up gently, and put my roses on the other side of me, a heap just near my hair, on the pillow.

'Quite unashamed and not the least conscious of himself, he got out of his clothes. And he *was* adorable – so young, and rather spare, but with a *rich* body, that simply glowed with love of me. He stood looking at me, quite humbly; and I held out my hands to him.

'All that night we loved each other. There were crushed, crumpled little rose-leaves on him when he sat up, almost like crimson blood! Oh, and he was fierce, and at the same time, tender!'

Anita's lips trembled slightly, and she paused. Then, very slowly, she went on:

'When I woke in the morning he was gone, and just a few passionate words on his dancing-card with a gold crown, on the little table beside me, imploring me to see him again in the Brühler Terasse in the afternoon. But I took the morning express to Berlin –'

We both were still. The river rustled far off in the morning.

'And –?' I said.

'And I never saw him again.'

We were both still. She put her arms round her bright knee, and caressed it, lovingly, rather plaintively, with her mouth. The brilliant green dragons on her wrap seemed to be snarling at me.

'And you regret him?' I said at length.

'No,' she answered, scarcely heeding me. 'I remember the way he unfastened his sword-belt and trappings from his loins, flung the whole with a jingle on the other bed –'

I was burning now with rage against Anita. Why should she love a man for the way he unbuckled his belt!

'With him,' she mused, 'everything felt so inevitable.'

'Even your never seeing him again,' I retorted.

'Yes!' she said, quietly.

Still musing, dreaming, she continued to caress her own knees.

'He said to me: "We are like the two halves of a walnut".' And she laughed slightly. 'He said some lovely things to me – "Tonight, you're an Answer". And then: "Whichever bit of you I touch seems to startle me afresh with joy". And he said he should never forget the velvety feel of my skin. – Lots of beautiful things he told me.'

Anita cast them over pathetically in her mind. I sat biting my finger with rage.

'– And I made him have roses in his hair. He sat so still and good while I trimmed him up, and was quite shy. He had a figure nearly like yours –'

Which compliment was a last insult to me.

'And he had a long gold chain, threaded with little emeralds, that he wound round and round my knees, binding me like a prisoner, never thinking.'

'And you wish he had kept you prisoner,' I said.

'No,' she answered. 'He couldn't!'

'I see! You just preserve him as the standard by which you measure the amount of satisfaction you get from the rest of us.'

'Yes,' she said, quietly.

Then I knew she was liking to make me furious.

'But I thought you were rather ashamed of the adventure?' I said.

'No,' she answered, perversely.

She made me tired. One could never be on firm ground with her. Always, one was slipping and plunging on uncertainly. I lay still, watching the sunshine streaming white outside.

'What are you thinking?' she asked.

'The waiter will smile when we go down for coffee.'

'No – tell me!'

'It is half past nine.'

She fingered the string of her shift.

'What were you thinking?' she asked, very low.

'I was thinking, all you want, you get.'

'In what way?'

'In love.'

'And what do I want?'

'Sensation.'

'Do I?'

'Yes.'

She sat with her head drooped down.

'Have a cigarette,' I said. 'And are you going to that place for sleighing today?'

'Why do you say I only want sensation?' she asked quietly.

'Because it's all you'll take from a man. – You *won't* have a cigarette?'

'No thanks – and what else could I take –?'

I shrugged my shoulders.

'Nothing, I suppose,' I replied.

Still she picked pensively at her chemise string.

'Up to now, you've missed nothing – you haven't felt the lack of anything – in love,' I said.

She waited awhile.

'Oh yes, I have,' she said gravely.

Hearing her say it, my heart stood still.

New Eve and Old Adam

I

'After all,' she said, with a little laugh, 'I can't see it was so wonderful of you to hurry home to me, if you are so cross when you do come.'

'You would rather I stayed away?' he asked.

'I wouldn't mind.'

'You would rather I had stayed a day or two in Paris – or a night or two.'

She burst into a jeering 'pouf!' of laughter.

'You!' she cried. 'You and Parisian Nights' Entertainment! What a fool you would look.'

'Still,' he said, 'I could try.'

'You *would*!' she mocked. 'You would go dribbling up to a woman. "Please take me – my wife is so unkind to me!"'

He drank his tea in silence. They had been married a year. They had married quickly, for love. And during the last three months there had gone on almost continuously that battle between them which so many married people fight, without knowing why. Now it had begun again. He felt the physical sickness rising in him. Somewhere down in his belly the big, feverish pulse began to beat, where was the inflamed place caused by the conflict between them.

She was a beautiful woman of about thirty, fair, luxuriant, with proud shoulders and a face borne up by a fierce, native vitality. Her green eyes had a curiously puzzled contraction just now. She sat leaning on the table against the tea-tray, absorbed. It was as if she battled with herself in him. Her green dress reflected in the silver, against the red of the firelight. Leaning abstractedly forward, she pulled some primroses from the bowl, and threaded them at intervals in the plait which bound round her head in the peasant fashion. So, with her little starred fillet of flowers, there was something of the Gretchen about her. But her eyes retained the curious half-smile.

Suddenly her face lowered gloomily. She sank her beautiful arms, laying them on the table. Then she sat almost sullenly, as if she would not give in. He was looking away out of the window. With a quick movement she glanced down at her hands. She took off her wedding-ring, reached to the bowl for a long flower-stalk, and shook the ring glittering round and round upon it, regarding the spinning gold, and spinning it as if she would spurn it. Yet there was something about her of a fretful, naughty child as she did so.

The man sat by the fire, tired, but tense. His body seemed so utterly still because of the tension in which it was held. His limbs, thin and vigorous, lay braced like a listening thing, always vivid for action, yet held perfectly still. His face was set and expressionless. The wife was all the time, in spite of herself, conscious of him, as if the cheek that was turned towards him had a sense which perceived him. They were both rendered elemental, like impersonal forces, by the battle and the suffering.

She rose and went to the window. Their flat was the fourth, the top storey of a large house. Above the high-ridged, handsome red roof opposite was an assembly of telegraph wires, a square, squat framework, towards which hosts of wires sped from four directions, arriving in darkly-stretched lines out of the white sky. High up, at a great height, a seagull sailed. There was a noise of traffic from the town beyond.

Then, from behind the ridge of the house-roof opposite a man climbed up into the tower of wires, belted himself amid the netted sky, and began to work, absorbedly. Another man, half-hidden by the roof-ridge, stretched up to him with a wire. The man in the sky reached down to receive it. The other, having delivered, sank out of sight. The solitary man worked absorbedly. Then he seemed drawn away from his task. He looked round almost furtively, from his lonely height, the space pressing on him. His eyes met those of the beautiful woman who stood in her afternoon gown, with flowers in her hair, at the window.

'I like you,' she said, in her normal voice.

Her husband, in the room with her, looked round slowly and asked:

'Whom do you like?'

Receiving no answer, he resumed his tense stillness.

She remained watching at the window, above the small, quiet street of large houses. The man, suspended there in the sky, looked across at her and she at him. The city was far below. Her eyes and his met across the lofty space. Then, crouching together again into his forgetfulness, he hid himself in his work. He would not look again. Presently he climbed down, and the tower of wires was empty against the sky.

The woman glanced at the little park at the end of the clear, grey street. The diminished, dark-blue form of a soldier was seen passing between the green stretches of grass, his spurs giving the faintest glitter to his walk.

Then she turned hesitating from the window, as if drawn by her husband. He was sitting still motionless, and detached from her, hard; held absolutely away from her by his will. She wavered, then went and crouched on the hearthrug at his feet, laying her head on his knee.

'Don't be horrid with me!' she pleaded, in a caressing, languid, impersonal voice. He shut his teeth hard, and his lips parted slightly with pain.

'You know you love me,' she continued, in the same heavy, sing-song way. He breathed hard, but kept still.

'Don't you?' she said, slowly, and she put her arms round his waist, under his coat, drawing him to her. It was as if flames of fire were running under his skin.

'I have never denied it,' he said, woodenly.

'Yes,' she pleaded, in the same heavy, toneless voice. 'Yes. You are always trying to deny it.' She was rubbing her cheek against his knee, softly. Then she gave a little laugh, and shook her head. 'But it's no good.' She looked up at him. There was a curious light in his eyes, of subtle victory. 'It's no good, my love, is it?'

His heart ran hot. He knew it was no good trying to deny he loved her. But he saw her eyes, and his will remained set and hard. She looked away into the fire.

'You hate it that you have to love me,' she said, in a pensive voice through which the triumph flickered faintly. 'You hate it that you love me – and it is petty and mean of you. You hate it that you had to hurry back to me from Paris.'

Her voice had become again quite impersonal, as if she were talking to herself.

'At any rate,' he said, 'it is your triumph.'

She gave a sudden, bitter-contemptuous laugh.

'Ha!' she said. 'What is triumph to me, you fool? You can have your triumph. I should be only too glad to give it you.'

'And I to take it.'

'Then take it,' she cried, in hostility. 'I offer it you often enough.'

'But you never mean to part with it.'

'It is a lie. It is you, you, who are too paltry to take a woman. How often do I fling myself at you –'

'Then don't – don't.'

'Ha! – and if I don't – I get nothing out of you. Self! self! – that is all you are.'

His face remained set and expressionless. She looked up at him. Suddenly she drew him to her again, and hid her face against him.

'Don't kick me off, Pietro, when I come to you,' she pleaded.

'You *don't* come to me,' he answered stubbornly.

She lifted her head a few inches away from him and seemed to listen, or to think.

'What do I do, then?' she asked, for the first time quietly.

'You treat me as if I were a piece of cake, for you to eat when you wanted.'

She rose from him with a mocking cry of scorn, that yet had something hollow in its sound.

'Treat you like a piece of cake, do I!' she cried. 'I, who have done all I have for you!'

There was a knock, and the maid entered with a telegram. He tore it open.

'No answer,' he said, and the maid softly closed the door.

'I suppose it is for you,' he said, bitingly, rising and handing her the slip of paper. She read it, laughed, then read it again, aloud:

' "Meet me Marble Arch 7.30 – theatre – Richard." Who is Richard?' she asked, looking at her husband rather interested. He shook his head.

'Nobody of mine,' he said. 'Who is he?'

'I haven't the faintest notion,' she said, flippantly.

'But,' and his eyes went bullying, 'you *must* know.'

She suddenly became quiet, and jeering, took up his challenge.

'Why must I know?' she asked.

'Because it isn't for me, therefore it must be for you.'

'And couldn't it be for anybody else?' she sneered.

' "Moest, 14 Merrilies Street," ' he read, decisively.

For a second she was puzzled into earnestness.

'Pah, you fool,' she said, turning aside. 'Think of your own friends,' and she flung the telegram away.

'It is not for me,' he said, stiffly and finally.

'Then it is for the man in the moon – I should think *his* name is Moest,' she added, with a pouf of laughter against him.

'Do you mean to say you know nothing about it?' he asked.

'Do you mean to say,' she mocked, mouthing the words, and sneering; 'Yes, I do mean to say, poor little man.'

He suddenly went hard with disgust.

'Then I simply don't believe you,' he said coldly.

'Oh – don't you believe me!' she jeered, mocking the touch of sententiousness in his voice. 'What a calamity. The poor man doesn't believe!'

'It can't possibly be any acquaintance of mine,' he said slowly.

'Then hold your tongue!' she cried harshly. 'I've heard enough of it.'

He was silent, and soon she went out of the room. In a few minutes he heard her in the drawing-room, improvising furiously. It was a sound that maddened him: something yearning, yearning, striving, and something perverse, that counteracted the yearning. Her music was always working up towards a certain culmination, but never reaching it, falling away in a jangle. How he hated it. He lit a cigarette, and went across to the sideboard for a whisky-and-soda. Then she began to sing. She had a good voice, but she could not keep time. As a rule it made his heart warm with tenderness for her, hearing her ramble through the songs in her own fashion, making Brahms sound so different by altering his time. But today he hated her for it. Why the devil couldn't she submit to the natural laws of the stuff!

In about fifteen minutes she entered, laughing. She laughed as she closed the door, and as she came to him where he sat.

'Oh,' she said, 'you silly thing, you silly thing! Aren't you a stupid clown?'

She crouched between his knees and put her arms round him. She was smiling into his face, her green eyes looking into his, were bright and wide. But somewhere in them, as he looked back, was a little twist that could not come loose to him, a little cast, that was like an aversion from him, a strain of hate for him. The hot waves of blood flushed over his body, and his heart seemed to dissolve under her caresses. But at last, after many months, he knew her well enough. He knew that curious little strain in her eyes, which was waiting for him to submit to her, and then would spurn him again. He resisted her while ever it was there.

'Why don't you let yourself love me?' she asked, pleading, but a touch of mockery in her voice. His jaw set hard.

'Is it because you are afraid?'

He heard the slight sneer.

'Of what?' he asked.

'Afraid to trust yourself?'

There was silence. It made him furious that she could sit there caressing him and yet sneer at him.

'What *have* I done with myself?' he asked.

'Carefully saved yourself from giving all to me, for fear you might lose something.'

'Why should I lose anything?' he asked.

And they were both silent. She rose at last and went away from him to get a cigarette. The silver box flashed red with firelight in her hands. She struck a match, bungled, threw the stick aside, lit another.

'What did you come running back for?' she asked, insolently, talking with half-shut lips because of the cigarette. 'I told you I wanted peace. I've had none for a year. And for the last three months you've done nothing but try to destroy me.'

'You have not gone frail on it,' he answered sarcastically.

'Nevertheless,' she said, 'I am ill inside me. I am sick of you – sick. You make an eternal demand, and you give nothing back. You leave one empty.' She puffed the cigarette in feminine fashion, then suddenly she struck her forehead with a wild gesture. 'I have a ghastly, empty feeling in my head,' she said. 'I feel I simply *must* have rest – I must.'

The rage went through his veins like flame.

'From your labours?' he asked, sarcastically, suppressing himself.

'From you – from *you*?' she cried, thrusting forward her head at him. 'You, who use a woman's soul up, with your rotten life. I suppose it is partly your health, and you can't help it,' she added, more mildly. 'But I simply can't stick it – I simply can't, and that is all.'

She shook her cigarette carelessly in the direction of the fire. The ash fell on the beautiful Asiatic rug. She glanced at it, but did not trouble. He sat, hard with rage.

'May I ask how I use you up, as you say?' he asked.

She was silent a moment, trying to get her feeling into words. Then she shook her hand at him passionately, and took the cigarette from her mouth.

'By – by following me about – by not leaving me *alone*. You give me no peace – *I* don't know what you do, but it is something ghastly.'

Again the hard stroke of rage went down his mind.

'It is very vague,' he said.

'I know,' she cried. 'I can't put it into words – but there

it is. You – you don't love. I pour myself out to you, and then – there's nothing there – you simply aren't there.'

He was silent for some time. His jaw had set hard with fury and hate.

'We have come to the incomprehensible,' he said. 'And now, what about Richard?'

It had grown nearly dark in the room. She sat silent for a moment. Then she took the cigarette from her mouth and looked at it.

'I'm going to meet him,' her voice, mocking, answered out of the twilight.

His head went molten, and he could scarcely breathe.

'Who is he?' he asked, though he did not believe the affair to be anything at all, even if there were a Richard.

'I'll introduce him to you when I know him a little better,' she said. He waited.

'But who is he?'

'I tell you, I'll introduce him to you later.'

There was a pause.

'Shall I come with you?'

'It would be like you,' she answered, with a sneer.

The maid came in, softly, to draw the curtains and turn on the light. The husband and wife sat silent.

'I suppose,' he said, when the door was closed again, 'you are wanting a Richard for a rest?'

She took his sarcasm simply as a statement.

'I am,' she said. 'A simple, warm man who would love me without all these reservations and difficulties. That is just what I do want.'

'Well, you have your own independence,' he said.

'Ha,' she laughed. 'You needn't tell me that. It would take more than you to rob me of my independence.'

'I meant your own income,' he answered quietly, while his heart was plunging with bitterness and rage.

'Well,' she said, 'I will go and dress.'

He remained without moving, in his chair. The pain of this was almost too much. For some moments the great, inflamed pulse struck through his body. It died gradually down, and he went dull. He had not wanted to separate from her at this point of their union; they would probably, if they parted in such a crisis, never come together again. But if she insisted, well then, it would have to be. He would go away for a month. He could easily make business in Italy. And when he came back, they could patch up some sort of domestic arrangement, as most other folk had to do.

He felt dull and heavy inside, and without the energy for anything. The thought of having to pack and take a train to Milan appalled him; it would mean such an effort of will. But it would have to be done, and so he must do it. It was no use his waiting at home. He might stay in town a night, at his brother-in-law's, and go away the next day. It were better to give her a little time to come to herself. She was really impulsive. And he did not really want to go away from her.

He was still sitting thinking, when she came downstairs. She was in costume and furs and toque. There was a radiant, half-wistful, half-perverse look about her. She was a beautiful woman, her bright, fair face set among the black furs.

'Will you give me some money?' she said. 'There isn't any.'

He took two sovereigns, which she put in her little black purse. She would go without a word of reconciliation. It made his heart set hard again.

'You would like me to go away for a month?' he said, calmly.

'Yes,' she answered, stubbornly.

'All right, then, I will. I must stop in town for to-morrow, but I will sleep at Edmund's.'

'You could do that, couldn't you?' she said, accepting his suggestion, a little bit hesitating.

'If you want me to.'

'I'm so *tired!*' she lamented.

But there was exasperation and hate in the last word, too.

'Very well,' he answered.

She finished buttoning her glove.

'You'll go, then?' she said suddenly, brightly, turning to depart. 'Good-bye.'

He hated her for the flippant insult of her leavetaking.

'I shall be at Edmund's tomorrow,' he said.

'You will write to me from Italy, won't you?'

He would not answer the unnecessary question.

'Have you taken the dead primroses out of your hair?' he asked.

'I haven't,' she said.

And she unpinned her hat.

'Richard *would* think me cracked,' she said, picking out the crumpled, creamy fragments. She strewed the withered flowers carelessly on the table, set her hat straight.

'Do you *want* me to go?' he asked, again, rather yearning.

She knitted her brows. It irked her to resist the appeal. Yet she had in her breast a hard, repellent feeling for him. She had loved him, too. She had loved him dearly. And – he had not seemed to realize her. So that now she *did* want to be free of him for a while. Yet the love, the passion she had had for him clung about her. But she did want, first and primarily, to be free of him again.

'Yes,' she said, half pleading.

'Very well,' he answered.

She came across to him, and put her arms round his neck. Her hat-pin caught his head, but he moved, and she did not notice.

'You don't mind very much, do you, my love?' she said caressingly.

'I mind all the world, and all I am,' he said.

She rose from him, fretted, miserable, and yet determined.

'I *must* have some rest,' she repeated.

He knew that cry. She had had it, on occasions, for two months now. He had cursed her, and refused either to go away or to let her go. Now he knew it was no use.

'All right,' he said. 'Go and get it from Richard.'

'Yes.' She hesitated. 'Good-bye,' she called, and was gone.

He heard her cab whirr away. He had no idea whither she was gone – but probably to Madge, her friend.

He went upstairs to pack. Their bedroom made him suffer. She used to say, at first, that she would give up anything rather than her sleeping with him. And still they were always together. A kind of blind helplessness drove them to one another, even when, after he had taken her, they only felt more apart than ever. It had seemed to her that he had been mechanical and barren with her. She felt a horrible feeling of aversion from him, inside her, even while physically she still desired him. His body had always a kind of fascination for her. But had hers for him? He seemed, often, just to have served her, or to have obeyed some impersonal instinct for which she was the only outlet, in his loving her. So at last she rose against him, to cast him off. He seemed to follow her so, to draw her life into his. It made her feel she would go mad. For he seemed to do it just blindly, without having any notion of her herself. It was as if she were sucked out of herself by some non-human force. As for him, he seemed only like an instrument for his work, his business, not like a person at all. Sometimes she thought he was a big fountain-pen which was always sucking at her blood for ink.

He could not understand anything of this. He loved her
– he could not bear to be away from her. He tried to realize
her and to give her what she wanted. But he could not
understand. He could not understand her accusations
against him. Physically, he knew, she loved him, or had
loved him, and was satisfied by him. He also knew that she
would have loved another man nearly as well. And for the
rest, he was only himself. He could not understand what
she said about his using her and giving her nothing in
return. Perhaps he did not think of her, as a separate person from himself, sufficiently. But then he did not see, he
could not see that she had any real personal life, separate
from himself. He tried to think of her in every possible
way, and to give her what she wanted. But it was no good;
she was never at peace. And lately there had been growing
a breach between them. They had never come together
without his realizing it, afterwards. Now he must submit,
and go away.

And her quilted dressing-gown – it was a little bit torn,
like most of her things – and her pearl-backed mirror,
with one of the pieces of pearl missing – all her untidy,
flimsy, lovable things hurt him as he went about the bedroom, and made his heart go hard with hate, in the midst
of his love.

2

Instead of going to his brother-in-law's, he went to an
hotel for the night. It was not till he stood in the lift, with
the attendant at his side, that he began to realize that he
was only a mile or so away from his own home, and yet
further away than any miles could make him. It was about
nine o'clock. He hated his bedroom. It was comfortable,
and not ostentatious; its only fault was the neutrality
necessary to an hotel apartment. He looked round. There

was one semi-erotic Florentine picture of a lady with cat's
eyes, over the bed. It was not bad. The only other ornament on the walls was the notice of hours and prices of
meals and rooms. The couch sat correctly before the
correct little table, on which the writing-sachet and ink-
stand stood mechanically. Down below, the quiet street
was half illuminated, the people passed sparsely, like
stunted shadows. And of all times of the night, it was a
quarter-past nine. He thought he would go to bed. Then
he looked at the white-and-glazed doors which shut him
off from the bath. He would bath, to pass the time away.
In the bath-closet everything was so comfortable and
white and warm – too warm; the level, unvarying heat of
the atmosphere, from which there was no escape anywhere,
seemed so hideously hotel-like; this central-heating forced
a unity into the great building, making it more than ever
like an enormous box with incubating cells. He loathed it.
But at any rate the bath-closet was human, white and business-like and luxurious.

He was trying, with the voluptuous warm water, and
the exciting thrill of the shower-bath, to bring back the
life into his dazed body. Since she had begun to hate him,
he had gradually lost that physical pride and pleasure in
his own physique which the first months of married life
had given him. His body had gone meaningless to him
again, almost as if it were not there. It had wakened up,
there had been the physical glow and satisfaction about his
movements of a creature which rejoices in itself; a glow
which comes on a man who loves and is loved passionately and successfully. Now this was going again. All the
life was accumulating in his mental consciousness, and his
body felt like a piece of waste. He was not aware of this.
It was instinct which made him want to bathe. But that,
too, was a failure. He went under the shower-spray with
his mind occupied by business, or some care of affairs,

taking the tingling water almost without knowing it, stepping out mechanically, as a man going through a barren routine. He was dry again, and looking out of the window, without having experienced anything during the last hour.

Then he remembered that she did not know his address. He scribbled a note and rang to have it posted.

As soon as he had turned out the light, and there was nothing left for his mental consciousness to flourish amongst, it dropped, and it was dark inside him as without. It was his blood, and the elemental male in it, that now rose from him; unknown instincts suffocated him, and he could not bear it, that he was shut in this great, warm building. He wanted to be outside, with space springing from him. But, again, the reasonable being in him knew it was ridiculous, and he remained staring at the dark, having the horrible sensation of a roof low down over him; whilst that dark, unknown being, which lived below all his consciousness in the eternal gloom of his blood, heaved and raged blindly against him.

It was not his thoughts that represented him. They spun like straws or the iridescence of oil on a dark stream. He thought of her, sketchily, spending an evening of light amusement with the symbolical Richard. That did not mean much to him. He did not really speculate about Richard. He had the dark, powerful sense of her, how she wanted to get away from him and from the deep, underneath intimacy which had gradually come between them, back to the easy, everyday life where one knows nothing of the underneath, so that it takes its way apart from the consciousness. She did not want to have the deeper part of herself in direct contact with or under the influence of any other intrinsic being. She wanted, in the deepest sense, to be free of him. She could not bear the close, basic intimacy into which she had been drawn. She wanted her life for herself. It was true, her strongest desire had been previously to know the contact through the whole of her being, down to the very bottom. Now it troubled her. She wanted to disengage his roots. Above, in the open, she would give. But she must live perfectly free of herself, and not, at her source, be connected with anybody. She was using this symbolic Richard as a spade to dig him away from her. And he felt like a thing whose roots are all straining on their hold, and whose elemental life, that blind source, surges backwards and forwards darkly, in a chaos, like something which is threatened with spilling out of its own vessel.

This tremendous swaying of the most elemental part of him continued through the hours, accomplishing his being, whilst superficially he thought of the journey, of the Italian he would speak, how he had left his coat in the train, and the rascally official interpreter had tried to give him twenty lire for a sovereign – how the man in the hat-shop in the Strand had given him the wrong change – of the new shape in hats, and the new felt – and so on. Underneath it all, like the sea under a pleasure pier, his elemental, physical soul was heaving in great waves through his blood and his tissue, the sob, the silent lift, the slightly-washing fall away again. So his blood, out of whose darkness everything rose, being moved to its depths by her revulsion, heaved and swung towards its own rest, surging blindly to its own re-settling.

Without knowing it, he suffered that night almost more than he had ever suffered during his life. But it was all below his consciousness. It was his life itself at storm, not his mind and his will engaged at all.

In the morning he got up, thin and quiet, without much movement anywhere, only with some of the clearing after-storm. His body felt like a clean, empty shell. His mind was limpidly clear. He went through the business of the toilet with a certain accuracy, and at breakfast, in the restaurant, there was about him that air of neutral correctness which makes men seem so unreal.

At lunch, there was a telegram for him. It was like her to telegraph.

'Come to tea, my dear love.'

As he read it, there was a great heave of resistance in him. But then he faltered. With his consciousness, he remembered how impulsive and eager she was when she dashed off her telegram, and he relaxed. It went without saying that he would go.

3

When he stood in the lift going up to his own flat, he was almost blind with the hurt of it all. They had loved each other so much in his first home. The parlour-maid opened to him, and he smiled at her affectionately. In the golden-brown and cream-coloured hall – Paula would have nothing heavy or sombre about her – a bush of rose-coloured azaleas shone, and a little tub of lilies twinkled naïvely.

She did not come out to meet him.

'Tea is in the drawing-room,' the maid said, and he went in while she was hanging up his coat. It was a big room, with a sense of space, and a spread of whitey carpet almost the colour of unpolished marble – and grey and pink border; of pink roses on big white cushions, pretty Dresden china, and deep chintz-covered chairs and sofas which looked as if they were used freely. It was a room where one could roll in soft, fresh comfort, a room which had not much breakable in it, and which seemed, in the dusky spring evening, fuller of light than the streets outside.

Paula rose, looking queenly and rather radiant, as she

held out her hand. A young man whom Peter scarcely noticed rose on the other side of the hearth.

'I expected you an hour ago,' she said, looking into her husband's eyes. But though she looked at him, she did not see him. And he sank his head.

'This is another Moest,' she said, presenting the stranger. 'He knows Richard, too.'

The young man, a German of about thirty, with a clean-shaven aesthetic face, long black hair brushed back a little wearily or bewildered from his brow, and inclined to fall in an odd loose strand again, so that he nervously put it back with his fine hand, looked at Moest and bowed. He had a finely-cut face, but his dark-blue eyes were strained, as if he did not quite know where he was. He sat down again, and his pleasant figure took a self-conscious attitude, of a man whose business it was to say things that should be listened to. He was not conceited or affected – naturally sensitive and rather naïve; but he could only move in an atmosphere of literature and literary ideas; yet he seemed to know there was something else, vaguely, and he felt rather at a loss. He waited for the conversation to move his way, as, inert, an insect waits for the sun to set it flying.

'Another Moest,' Paula was pronouncing emphatically. 'Actually another Moest, of whom we have never heard, and under the same roof with us.'

The stranger laughed, his lips moving nervously over his teeth.

'You are in this house?' Peter asked, surprised.

The young man shifted in his chair, dropped his head, looked up again.

'Yes,' he said, meeting Moest's eyes as if he were somewhat dazzled. 'I am staying with the Lauriers, on the second floor.'

He spoke English slowly, with a quaint, musical

quality in his voice, and a certain rhythmic enunciation.

'I see; and the telegram was for you?' said the host.

'Yes,' replied the stranger, with a nervous little laugh.

'My husband,' broke in Paula, evidently repeating to the German what she had said before, for Peter's benefit this time, 'was quite convinced I had an *affaire*' – she pronounced it in the French fashion – 'with this terrible Richard.'

The German gave his little laugh, and moved, painfully self-conscious, in his chair.

'Yes,' he said, glancing at Moest.

'Did you spend a night of virtuous indignation?' Paula laughed to her husband, 'imagining my perfidy?'

'I did not,' said her husband. 'Were you at Madge's?'

'No,' she said. Then, turning to her guest: 'Who is Richard, Mr Moest?'

'Richard,' began the German, word by word, 'is my cousin.' He glanced quickly at Paula, to see if he were understood. She rustled her skirts, and arranged herself comfortably, lying, or almost squatting, on the sofa by the fire. 'He lives in Hampstead.'

'And what is he like?' she asked, with eager interest.

The German gave his little laugh. Then he moved his fingers across his brow, in his dazed fashion. Then he looked, with his beautiful blue eyes, at his beautiful hostess.

'I –' He laughed again nervously. 'He is a man whose parts – are not very much – very well known to me. You see,' he broke forth, and it was evident he was now conversing to an imaginary audience – 'I cannot easily express myself in English. I – I never have talked it. I shall speak, because I know nothing of modern England, a kind of Renaissance English.'

'How lovely!' cried Paula. 'But if you would rather, speak German. We shall understand sufficiently.'

'I would rather hear some Renaissance English,' said Moest.

Paula was quite happy with the new stranger. She listened to descriptions of Richard, shifting animatedly on her sofa. She wore a new dress, of a rich red-tile colour, glossy and long and soft, and she had threaded daisies, like buttons, in the braided plait of her hair. Her husband hated her for these familiarities. But she was beautiful too, and warm-hearted. Only, through all her warmth and kindliness, lay, he said, at the bottom, an almost feline selfishness, a coldness.

She was playing to the stranger – nay, she was not playing, she was really occupied by him. The young man was the favourite disciple of the most famous present-day German poet and *Meister*. He himself was occupied in translating Shakespeare. Having been always a poetic disciple, he had never come into touch with life save through literature, and for him, since he was a rather fine-hearted young man, with a human need to live, this was a tragedy. Paula was not long in discovering what ailed him, and she was eager to come to his rescue.

It pleased her, nevertheless, to have her husband sitting by, watching her. She forgot to give tea to anyone. Moest and the German both helped themselves, and the former attended also to his wife's cup. He sat rather in the background, listening, and waiting. She had made a fool of him with her talk to this stranger of 'Richard'; lightly and flippantly she had made a fool of him. He minded, but was used to it. Now she had absorbed herself in this dazed, starved, literature-bewildered young German, who was, moreover, really lovable, evidently a gentleman. And she was seeing in him her mission – 'just as,' said Moest bitterly to himself, 'she saw her mission in me, a year ago. She is no woman. She's got a big heart for everybody, but it must be like a common-room; she's got no private, sacred heart, except perhaps for herself, where there's no room for a man in it.'

At length the stranger rose to go, promising to come again.

'Isn't he adorable?' cried Paula, as her husband returned to the drawing-room. 'I think he is simply adorable.'

'Yes!' said Moest.

'He called this morning to ask about the telegram. But, poor devil, isn't it a shame, what they've done to him?'

'What who have done to him?' her husband asked, coldly, jealous.

'Those literary creatures. They take a young fellow like that, and stick him up among the literary gods, like a mantelpiece ornament, and there he has to sit, being a minor ornament, while all his youth is gone. It is criminal.'

'He should get off the mantelpiece, then,' said Moest.

But inside him his heart was black with rage against her. What had she, after all, to do with this young man, when he himself was being smashed up by her? He loathed her pity and her kindliness, which was like a charitable institution. There was no core to the woman. She was full of generosity and bigness and kindness, but there was no heart in her, no security, no place for one single man. He began to understand now sirens and sphinxes and the other Greek fabulous female things. They had not been created by fancy, but out of bitter necessity of the man's human heart to express itself.

'Ha!' she laughed, half contemptuous. 'Did *you* get off your miserable, starved isolation by yourself? – you didn't. You had to be fetched down, and I had to do it.'

'Out of your usual charity,' he said.

'But you can sneer at another man's difficulties,' she said.

'Your name ought to be Panacea, not Paula,' he replied.

He felt furious and dead against her. He could even look at her without the tenderness coming. And he was glad. He hated her. She seemed unaware. Very well; let her be so.

'Oh, but he makes me so miserable, to see him!' she cried. 'Self-conscious, can't get into contact with anybody, living a false literary life like a man who takes poetry as a drug. – One *ought* to help him.'

She was really earnest and distressed.

'Out of the frying-pan into the fire,' he said.

'I'd rather be in the fire any day, than in a frying-pan,' she said, abstractedly, with a little shudder. She never troubled to see the meaning of her husband's sarcasms.

They remained silent. The maid came in for the tray, and to ask him if he would be in to dinner. He waited for his wife to answer. She sat with her chin in her hands, brooding over the young German, and did not hear. The rage flashed up in his heart. He would have liked to smash her out of this false absorption.

'No,' he said to the maid. 'I think not. Are you at home for dinner, Paula?'

'Yes,' she said.

And he knew by her tone, easy and abstracted, that she intended him to stay, too. But she did not trouble to say anything.

At last, after some time, she asked:

'What did you do?'

'Nothing – went to bed early,' he replied.

'Did you sleep well?'

'Yes, thank you.'

And he recognized the ludicrous civilities of married

people, and he wanted to go. She was silent for a time. Then she asked, and her voice had gone still and grave:

'Why don't you ask me what I did?'

'Because I don't care – you just went to somebody's for dinner.'

'Why don't you care what I do? Isn't it your place to care?'

'About the things you do to spite me? – no!'

'Ha!' she mocked. 'I did nothing to spite you. I was in deadly earnest.'

'Even with your Richard?'

'Yes,' she cried. 'There *might* have been a Richard. What did you care!'

'In that case you'd have been a liar and worse, so why should I care about you then?'

'You *don't* care about me,' she said, sullenly.

'You say what you please,' he answered.

She was silent for some time.

'And did you do absolutely nothing last night?' she asked.

'I had a bath and went to bed.'

Then she pondered.

'No,' she said, 'you don't care for me.'

He did not trouble to answer. Softly, a little china clock rang six.

'I shall go to Italy in the morning,' he said.

'Yes.'

'And,' he said, slowly, forcing the words out, 'I shall stay at the Aquila Nera at Milan – you know my address.'

'Yes,' she answered.

'I shall be away about a month. Meanwhile you can rest.'

'Yes,' she said, in her throat, with a little contempt of him and his stiffness. He, in spite of himself, was breathing heavily. He knew that his parting was the real separation of their souls, marked the point beyond which they could go no further, but accepted the marriage as a comparative failure. And he had built all his life on his marriage. She accused him of not loving her. He gripped the arms of his chair. Was there something in it? Did he only want the attributes which went along with her, the peace of heart which a man has in giving to one woman, even if the love between them be not complete; the singleness and unity in his life that made it easy; the fixed establishment of himself as a married man with a home; the feeling that he belonged somewhere, that one woman existed – not was paid but *existed* – really to take care of him; was it these things he wanted, and not her? But he wanted her for these purposes – her, and nobody else. But was that not enough for her? Perhaps he wronged her – it was possible. What she said against him was in earnest. And what she said in earnest he had to believe, in the long run, since it was the utterance of her being. He felt miserable and tired.

When he looked at her, across the gathering twilight of the room, she was staring into the fire and biting her finger-nail, restlessly, restlessly, without knowing. And all his limbs went suddenly weak, as he realised that she suffered too, that something was gnawing at her. Something in the look of her, the crouching, dogged, wondering look made him faint with tenderness for her.

'Don't bite your finger-nails,' he said quietly, and, obediently, she took her hand from her mouth. His heart was beating quickly. He could feel the atmosphere of the room changing. It had stood aloof, the room, like something placed round him, like a great box. Now everything got softer, as if it partook of the atmosphere, of which he partook himself, and they were all one.

His mind reverted to her accusations, and his heart beat like a caged thing against what he could not understand.

She said he did not love her. But he knew that in his way, he did. In his way – but was his way wrong? His way was himself, he thought, struggling. Was there something wrong, something missing in his nature, that he could not love? He struggled madly, as if he were in a mesh, and could not get out. He did not want to believe that he was deficient in his nature. Wherein was he deficient? It was nothing physical. She said he would not come out of himself, that he was no good to her, because he could not get outside himself. What did she mean? Not outside himself! It seemed like some acrobatic feat, some slippery, contortionist trick. No, he could not understand. His heart flashed hot with resentment. She did nothing but find fault with him. What did she care about him, really, when she could taunt him with not being able to take a light woman when he was in Paris? Though his heart, forced to do her justice, knew that for this she loved him, really.

But it was too complicated and difficult, and already, as they sat thinking, it had gone wrong between them, and things felt twisted, horribly twisted, so that he could not breathe. He must go. He could dine at the hotel and go to the theatre.

'Well,' he said casually, 'I must go. I think I shall go and see "The Black Sheep".'

She did not answer. Then she turned and looked at him with a queer, half-bewildered, half-perverse smile that seemed conscious of pain. Her eyes, shining rather dilated and triumphant, and yet with something heavily yearning behind them, looked at him. He could not understand, and, between her appeal and her defiant triumph, he felt as if his chest was crushed so that he could not breathe.

'My love,' she said, in a little singing, abstract fashion, her lips somehow sipping towards him, her eyes shining dilated; and yet he felt as if he were not in it, himself.

His heart was a flame that prevented his breathing. He gripped the chair like a man who is going to be put under torture.

'What?' he said, staring back at her.

'Oh, my love!' she said softly, with a little, intense laugh on her face, that made him pant. And she slipped from her sofa and came across to him, quickly, and put her hand hesitating on his hair. The blood struck like flame across his consciousness, and the hurt was keen like joy, like the releasing of something that hurts as the pressure is relaxed and the movement comes, before the peace. Afraid, his fingers touched her hand, and she sank swiftly between his knees, and put her face on his breast. He held her head hard against his chest, and again and again the flame went down his blood, as he felt her round, small, nut of a head between his hands pressing into his chest where the hurt had been bruised in so deep. His wrists quivered as he pressed her head to him, as he felt the deadness going out of him; the real life, released, flowing into his body again. How hard he had shut it off, against her, when she hated him. He was breathing heavily with relief, blindly pressing her head against him. He believed in her again.

She looked up, laughing, childish, inviting him with her lips. He bent to kiss her, and as his eyes closed, he saw hers were shut. The feeling of restoration was almost unbearable.

'Do you love me?' she whispered, in a little ecstasy.

He did not answer, except with the quick tightening of his arms, clutching her a little closer against him. And he loved the silkiness of her hair, and its natural scent. And it hurt him that the daisies she had threaded in should begin to wither. He resented their hurting her by their dying.

He had not understood. But the trouble had gone off. He was quiet, and he watched her from out of his sensitive stillness, a little bit dimly, unable to recover. She was loving to him, protective, and bright, laughing like a glad child too.

'We must tell Maud I shall be in to dinner,' he said.

That was like him – always aware of the practical side of the case, and the appearances. She laughed a little bit ironically. Why should she have to take her arms from round him, just to tell Maud he would be in to dinner?

'I'll go,' she said.

He drew the curtains and turned on the light in the big lamp that stood in a corner. The room was dim, and palely warm. He loved it dearly.

His wife, when she came back, as soon as she had closed the door, lifted her arms to him in a little ecstasy, coming to him. They clasped each other closer, body to body. And the intensity of his feeling was so fierce, he felt himself going dim, fusing into something soft and plastic between her hands. And this connection with her was bigger than life or death. And at the bottom of his heart was a sob.

She was gay and winsome at the dinner. Like lovers, they were just deliciously waiting for the night to come up. But there remained in him always the slightly broken feeling which the night before had left.

'And you won't go to Italy,' she said, as if it were an understood thing.

She gave him the best things to eat, and was solicitous for his welfare – which was not usual with her. It gave him deep, shy pleasure. He remembered a verse she was often quoting as one she loved. He did not know it for himself:

> 'On my breasts I warm thy foot-soles;
> Wine I pour, and dress thy meats;
> Humbly, when my lord disposes,
> Lie with him on perfumed sheets.'

She said it to him sometimes, looking up at him from the pillow. But it never seemed real to him. She might, in her sudden passion, put his feet between her breasts. But he never felt like a lord, never more pained and insignificant than at those times. As a little girl, she must have subjected herself before her dolls. And he was something like her lordliest plaything. He liked that too. If only . . .

Then, seeing some frightened little way of looking at him which she had, the pure pain came back. He loved her, and it would never be peace between them; she would never belong to him, as a wife. She would take him and reject him, like a mistress. And perhaps for that reason he would love her all the more; it might be so.

But then, he forgot. Whatever was or was not, now she loved him. And whatever came after, this evening he was the lord. What matter if he were deposed tomorrow, and she hated him!

Her eyes, wide and candid, were staring at him a little bit wondering, a little bit forlorn. She knew he had not quite come back. He held her close to him.

'My love,' she murmured consolingly. 'My love.'

And she put her fingers through his hair, arranging it in little, loose curves, playing with it and forgetting everything else. He loved her dearly, to feel the light lift and touch – touch of her finger-tips making his hair, as she said, like an Apollo's. She lifted his face to see how he looked, and, with a little laugh of love, kissed him. And he loved to be made much of by her. But he had the dim, hurting sense that she would not love him tomorrow, that it was only her great need to love that exalted him tonight. He *knew* he was no king; he did not feel a king, even when she was crowning and kissing him.

'Do you love me?' she asked, playfully whispering.

He held her fast and kissed her, while the blood hurt in his heart-chambers.

'You know,' he answered, with a struggle.

Later, when he lay holding her with a passion intense like pain, the words blurted from him:

'Flesh of my flesh. Paula! – Will you –?'

'Yes, my love,' she answered consolingly.

He bit his mouth with pain. For him it was almost an agony of appeal.

'But, Paula – I mean it – flesh of my flesh – a wife?'

She tightened her arms round him without answering. And he knew, and she knew, that she put him off like that.

4

Two months later, she was writing to him in Italy: 'Your idea of your woman is that she is an expansion, no, a *rib* of yourself, without any existence of her own. That I am a being by myself is more than you can grasp. I wish I could absolutely submerge myself in a man – and *so I do*. I *always* loved you ...

'You will say "I was patient." Do you call that patient, hanging on for your needs, as you have done? The innermost life you have *always* had of me, and you held yourself aloof because you were afraid.

'The unpardonable thing was you told me you loved me. – Your *feelings* have hated me these three months, which did not prevent you from taking my love and every breath from me. – Underneath you undermined me, in some subtle, corrupt way that I did not see because I believed you, when you told me you loved me ...

'The insult of the way you took me these last three months I shall never forgive you. I honestly *did* give myself, and always in vain and rebuffed. The strain of it all has driven me quite mad.

'You say I am a tragédienne, but I don't do any of your perverse undermining tricks. You are always luring one into the open like a clever enemy, but you keep safely under cover all the time.

'This practically means, for me, that life is over, my belief in life – I hope it will recover, but it never could do so with you ...'

To which he answered; 'If you kept under cover it is funny, for there isn't any cover now. – And you can hope, pretty easily, for your own recovery apart from me. For my side, without you, I am done ... But you lie to yourself. You *wouldn't* love *me*, and you won't be able to love anybody else – except yourself.'

The Thimble

SHE had not seen her husband for ten months, not since her fortnight's honeymoon with him, and his departure for France. Then, in those excited days of the early war, he was her comrade, her counterpart in a sort of Bacchic revel before death. Now all that was shut off from her mind, as by a great rent in her life.

Since then, since the honeymoon, she had lived and died and come to life again. There had been his departure to the front. She had loved him then.

'If you want to love your husband,' she had said to her friends, with splendid recklessness, 'you should see him in khaki.' And she had really loved him, he was so handsome in uniform, well-built, yet with a sort of reserve and remoteness that suited the neutral khaki perfectly.

Before, as a barrister with nothing to do, he had been slack and unconvincing, a sort of hanger-on, and she had never come to the point of marrying him. For one thing they neither of them had enough money.

Then came the great shock of the war, his coming to her in a new light, as lieutenant in the artillery. And she had been carried away by his perfect calm manliness and significance, now he was a soldier. He seemed to have gained a fascinating importance that made her seem quite unimportant. It was she who was insignificant and subservient, he who was dignified, with a sort of indifferent lordliness.

So she had married him, all considerations flung to the wind, and had known the bewildering experience of their fortnight's honeymoon, before he left her for the front.

And she had never got over the bewilderment. She had, since then, never thought at all, she seemed to have rushed on in a storm of activity and sensation. There was a home to make, and no money to make it with: none to speak of. So, with the swift, business-like aptitude of a startled woman, she had found a small flat in Mayfair, had attended sales and bought suitable furniture, had made the place complete and perfect. She was satisfied. It was small and insignificant, but it was a complete unity.

Then she had had a certain amount of war-work to do, and she had kept up all her social activities. She had not had a moment which was not urgently occupied.

All the while came his letters from France, and she was writing her replies. They both sent a good deal of news to each other, they both expressed their mutual passion.

Then suddenly, amid all this activity, she fell ill with pneumonia and everything lapsed into delirium. And whilst she was ill, he was wounded, his jaw smashed and his face cut up by the bursting of a shell. So they were both laid by.

Now, they were both better, and she was waiting to see him. Since she had been ill, while she had lain or sat in her room in the castle in Scotland, she had thought, thought very much. For she was a woman who was always trying to grasp the whole of her context, always trying to make a complete thing of her own life.

Her illness lay between her and her previous life like a dark night, like a great separation. She looked back, she remembered all she had done, and she was bewildered, she had no key to the puzzle. Suddenly she realized that she knew nothing of this man she had married, he knew nothing of her. What she had of him, vividly, was the visual image. She could *see* him, the whole of him, in her mind's eye. She could remember him with peculiar distinctness, as if the whole of his body were lit up by an intense light, and the image fixed on her mind.

But he was an impression, only a vivid impression.

What her own impression was, she knew most vividly. But what *he* was *himself*: the very thought startled her, it was like looking into a perilous darkness. All that she knew of him was her own affair, purely personal to her, a subjective impression. But there must be a *man*, another being, somewhere in the darkness which she had never broached.

The thought frightened her exceedingly, and her soul, weak from illness, seemed to weep. Here was a new peril, a new terror. And she seemed to have no hope.

She could scarcely bear to think of him as she knew him. She could scarcely bear to conjure up that vivid image of him which remained from the days of her honeymoon. It was something false, it was something which had only to do with herself. The man himself was something quite other, something in the dark, something she dreaded, whose coming she dreaded, as if it were a mitigation of her own being, something set over against her, something that would annul her own image of herself.

Nervously she twisted her long white fingers. She was a beautiful woman, tall and loose and rather thin, with swinging limbs, one for whom the modern fashions were perfect. Her skin was pure and clear, like a Christmas rose, her hair was fair and heavy. She had large, slow, unswerving eyes, that sometimes looked blue and open with a childish candour, sometimes greenish and intent with thought, sometimes hard, sea-like, cruel, sometimes grey and pathetic.

Now she sat in her own room, in the flat in Mayfair, and he was coming to see her. She was well again: just well enough to see him. But she was tired as she sat in the chair whilst her maid arranged her heavy, fair hair.

She knew she was a beauty, she knew it was expected of her that she should create an impression of modern beauty. And it pleased her, it made her soul rather hard and proud: but also, at the bottom, it bored her. Still, she would have her hair built high, in the fashionable mode, she would have it modelled to the whole form of her head, her figure. She lifted her eyes to look. They were slow, greenish, and cold like the sea at this moment, because she was so perplexed, so heavy with trying, all alone, always quite coldly alone, to understand, to understand and to adjust herself. It never occurred to her to expect anything of the other person: she was utterly self-responsible.

'No,' she said to her maid, in her slow, laconic, plangent voice, 'don't let it swell out over the ears, lift it straight up, then twist it under – like that – so it goes clean from the side of the face. Do you see?'

'Yes, my lady.'

And the maid went on with the hair-dressing, and she with her slow, cold musing.

She was getting dressed now to see her bridegroom. The phrase, with its association in all the romances of the world, made her snigger involuntarily to herself. She was still like a schoolgirl, always seeing herself in her part. She got curious satisfaction from it, too. But also she was always humorously ironical when she found herself in these romantic situations. If brigands and robbers had carried her off, she would have played up to the event perfectly. In life, however, there was always a certain painful, laborious heaviness, a weight of self-responsibility. The event never carried her along, a helpless protagonist. She was always responsible, in whatever situation.

Now, this morning, her husband was coming to see her, and she was dressing to receive him. She felt heavy and inert as stone, yet inwardly trembling convulsively. The known man, he did not affect her. Heavy and inert in her soul, yet amused, she would play her part in his reception.

But the unknown man, what was he? Her dark, unknown soul trembled apprehensively.

At any rate he would be different. She shuddered. The vision she had of him, of the good-looking, clean, slightly tanned, attractive man, ordinary and yet with odd streaks of understanding that made her ponder, this she must put away. They said his face was rather horribly cut up. She shivered. How she hated it, coldly hated and loathed it, the thought of disfigurement. Her fingers trembled, she rose to go downstairs. If he came he must not come into her bedroom.

So, in her fashionable but inexpensive black silk dress, wearing her jewels, her string of opals, her big, ruby brooch, she went downstairs. She knew how to walk, how to hold her body according to the mode. She did it almost instinctively, so deep was her consciousness of the impression her own appearance must create.

Entering the small drawing-room she lifted her eyes slowly and looked at herself: a tall, loose woman in black, with fair hair raised up, and with slow, greenish, cold eyes looking into the mirror. She turned away with a cold, pungent sort of satisfaction. She was aware also of the traces of weariness and illness and age, in her face. She was twenty-seven years old.

So she sat on the little sofa by the fire. The room she had made was satisfactory to her, with its neutral, brown-grey walls, its deep brown, plain, velvety carpet, and the old furniture done in worn rose brocade, which she had bought from Countess Ambersyth's sale. She looked at her own large feet, upon the rose-red Persian rug.

Then nervously, yet quite calm, almost static, she sat still to wait. It was one of the moments of deepest suffering and suspense which she had ever known. She did not want to think of his disfigurement, she did not want to have any preconception of it. Let it come upon her. And the man, the unknown strange man who was coming now to take up his position over against her soul, her soul so naked and exposed from illness, the man to whose access her soul was to be delivered up! She could not bear it. Her face set pale, she began to lose her consciousness.

Then something whispered in her:

'If I am like this, I shall be quite impervious to him, quite oblivious of anything but the surface of him.' And an anxious sort of hope sent her hands down onto the sofa at her side, pressed upon the worn brocade, spread flat. And she remained in suspense.

But could she bear it, could she bear it? She was weak and ill in a sort of after-death. Now what was this that she must confront, this other being? Her hands began to move slowly backwards and forwards on the sofa bed, slowly, as if the friction of the silk gave her some ease.

She was unaware of what she was doing. She was always so calm, so self-contained, so static; she was much too stoically well-bred to allow these outward nervous agitations. But now she sat still in suspense in the silent drawing-room, where the fire flickered over the dark brown carpet and over the pale rose furniture and over the pale face and the black dress and the white, sliding hands of the woman, and her hands slid backwards and forwards, backwards and forwards like a pleading, a hope, a tension of madness.

Her right hand came to the end of the sofa and pressed a little into the crack, the meeting between the arm and the sofa bed. Her long white fingers pressed into the fissure, pressed and entered rhythmically, pressed and pressed further and further into the tight depths of the fissure, between the silken, firm upholstery of the old sofa, whilst her mind was in a trance of suspense, and the firelight flickered on the yellow chrysanthemums that stood in a jar in the window.

The working, slow, intent fingers pressed deeper and deeper in the fissure of the sofa, pressed and worked their way intently, to the bottom. It was the bottom. They were there, they made sure. Making sure, they worked all along, very gradually, along the tight depth of the fissure.

Then they touched a little extraneous object, and a consciousness awoke in the woman's mind. Was it something? She touched again. It was something hard and rough. The fingers began to ply upon it. How firmly it was embedded in the depths of the sofa-crack. It had a thin rim, like a ring, but it was not a ring. The fingers worked more insistently. What was this little hard object?

The fingers pressed determinedly, they moved the little object. They began to work it up to the light. It was coming, there was success. The woman's heart relaxed from its tension, now her aim was being achieved. Her long, strong, white fingers brought out the little find.

It was a thimble set with brilliants; it was an old, rather heavy thimble of tarnished gold, set round the base with little diamonds or rubies. Perhaps it was not gold, perhaps they were only paste.

She put it on her sewing finger. The brilliants sparkled in the firelight. She was pleased. It was a vulgar thing, a gold thimble with ordinary pin-head dents, and a belt of jewels around the base. It was large too, big enough for her. It must have been some woman's embroidery thimble, some bygone woman's, perhaps some Lady Ambersyth's. At any rate, it belonged to the days when women did stitching as a usual thing. But it was heavy, it would make one's hand ache.

She began to rub the gold with her handkerchief. There was an engraved monogram, an Earl's, and then Z, Z, and a date, 15 Oct., 1801. She was very pleased, trembling with the thought of the old romance. What did Z. stand for? She thought of her acquaintances, and could only think of Zouche. But he was not an Earl. Who would give the gift of a gold thimble set with jewels, in the year 1801? Perhaps it was a man come home from the wars: there were wars then.

The maid noiselessly opened the door and saw her mistress sitting in the soft light of the winter day, polishing something with her handkerchief.

'Mr Hepburn has come, my lady.'

'Has he!' answered the laconic, slightly wounded voice of the woman.

She collected herself and rose. Her husband was coming through the doorway, past the maid. He came without hat or coat or gloves, like an inmate of the house. He was an inmate of the house.

'How do you do?' she said, with stoic, plangent helplessness. And she held out her hand.

'How are *you*?' he replied, rather mumbling, with a sort of muffled voice.

'All right now, thanks,' and she sat down again, her heart beating violently. She had not yet looked at his face. The muffled voice terrified her so much. It mumbled rather mouthlessly.

Abstractedly, she put the thimble on her middle finger, and continued to rub it with her handkerchief. The man sat in silence opposite, in an armchair. She was aware of his khaki trousers and his brown shoes. But she was intent on burnishing the thimble.

Her mind was in a trance, but as if she were on the point of waking, for the first time in her life, waking up.

'What are you doing? What have you got?' asked the mumbling, muffled voice. A pang went through her. She looked up at the mouth that produced the sound. It was broken in, the bottom teeth all gone, the side of the chin battered small, while a deep seam, a deep, horrible groove ran right into the middle of the cheek. But the mouth was the worst, sunk in at the bottom, with half the lip cut away.

'It is treasure-trove,' answered the plangent, cold-sounding voice. And she held out the thimble.

He reached to take it. His hand was white, and it trembled. His nerves were broken. He took the thimble between his fingers.

She sat obsessed, as if his disfigurement were photographed upon her mind, as if she were some sensitive medium to which the thing had been transferred. There it was, her whole consciousness was photographed into an image of his disfigurement, the dreadful sunken mouth that was not a mouth, which mumbled in talking to her, in a disfigurement of speech.

It was all accident, accident had taken possession of her very being. All she was, was purely accidental. It was like a sleep, a thin, taut, overfilming sleep in which the wakefulness struggles like a thing as yet unborn. She was sick in the thin, transparent membrane of her sleep, her overlying dream-consciousness, something actual but too unreal.

'How treasure-trove?' he mumbled. She could not understand.

She felt his moment's hesitation before he tried again, and a hot pain pierced through her, the pain of his maimed, crippled effort.

'Treasure-trove, you said,' he repeated, with a sickening struggle to speak distinctly.

Her mind hovered, then grasped, then caught the threads of the conversation.

'I found it,' she said. Her voice was clear and vibrating as bronze, but cold. 'I found it just before you came in.'

There was a silence. She was aware of the purely accidental condition of her whole being. She was framed and constructed of accident, accidental association. It was like being made up of dream-stuff, without sequence or adherence to any plan or purpose. Yet within the imprisoning film of the dream was herself, struggling unborn, struggling to come to life.

It was difficult to break the inert silence that had succeeded between them. She was afraid it would go on for ever. With a strange, convulsive struggle, she broke into communication with him.

'I found it here, in the sofa,' she said, and she lifted her eyes for the first time to him.

His forehead was white, and his hair brushed smooth, like a sick man's. And his eyes were like the eyes of a child that has been ill, blue and abstract, as if they only listened from a long way off, and did not see any more. So far-off he looked, like a child that belongs almost more to death than to life. And her soul divined that he was waiting vaguely where the dark and the light divide, whether he should come in to life, or hesitate, and pass back.

She lowered her eyelids, and for a second she sat erect like a mask, with closed eyes, while a spasm of pure unconsciousness passed over her. It departed again, and she opened her eyes. She was awake.

She looked at him. His eyes were still abstract and without answer, changing only to the dream-psychology of his being. She contracted as if she were cold and afraid. They lit up now with a superficial over-flicker of interest.

'Did you really? Why, how did it come there?'

It was the same voice, the same stupid interest in accidental things, the same man as before. Only the enunciation of the words was all mumbled and muffled, as if the speech itself were disintegrating.

Her heart shrank, to close again like an over-sensitive

newborn thing, that is not yet strong enough in its own being. Yet once more she lifted her eyes, and looked at him.

He was flickering with his old, easily roused, spurious interest in the accidents of life. The film of separateness seemed to be coming over her. Yet his white forehead was somewhat deathly, with its smoothly brushed hair. He was like one dead. He was within the realm of death. His over-flicker of interest was only extraneous.

'I suppose it had got pushed down by accident,' she said, answering from her mechanical mind.

But her eyes were watching him who was dead, who was there like Lazarus before her, as yet unrisen.

'How did it happen?' she said, and her voice was changed, penetrating with sadness and approach. He knew what she meant.

'Well, you see I was knocked clean senseless, and that was all I knew for three days. But it seems that it was a shell fired by one of our own fellows, and it hit me because it was faultily made.'

Her face was very still as she watched.

'And how did you feel when you came round?'

'I felt pretty bad, as you can imagine; there was a crack on the skull as well as this on the jaw.'

'Did you think you were going to die?'

There was a long pause, whilst the man laughed self-consciously. But he laughed only with the upper part of his face: the maimed part remained still. And though the eyes seemed to laugh, just as of old, yet underneath them was a black, challenging darkness. She waited while this superficial smile of reserve passed away.

Then came the mumbling speech, simple, in confession.

'Yes, I lay and looked at it.'

The darkness of his eyes was now watching her, her soul was exposed and new-born. The triviality was gone, the dream-psychology, the self-dependence. They were naked and new-born in soul, and depended on each other.

It was on the tip of her tongue to say: 'And why didn't you die?' But instead, her soul, weak and new-born, looked helplessly at him.

'I couldn't while you were alive,' he said.

'What?'

'Die.'

She seemed to pass away into unconsciousness. Then, as she came to, she said, as if in protest:

'What difference should *I* make to you! You can't live off me.'

He was watching her with unlighted, sightless eyes. There was a long silence. She was thinking, it was not her consciousness of him which had kept *her* alive. It was her own will.

'What did you hope for, from me?' she asked.

His eyes darkened, his face seemed very white, he really looked like a dead man as he sat silent and with open, sightless eyes. Between his slightly-trembling fingers was balanced the thimble, that sparkled sometimes in the firelight. Watching him, a darkness seemed to come over her. She could not see, he was only a presence near her in the dark.

'We are both of us helpless,' she said, into the silence.

'Helpless for what?' answered his sightless voice.

'To live,' she said.

They seemed to be talking to each other's souls, their eyes and minds were sightless.

'We are helpless to live,' he repeated.

'Yes,' she said.

There was still a silence.

'I know,' he said, 'we are helpless to live. I knew that when I came round.'

'I am as helpless as you are,' she said.

'Yes,' came his slow, half-articulate voice. 'I know that. You're as helpless as I am.'

'Well then?'

'Well then, we are helpless. We are as helpless as babies,' he said.

'And how do you like being a helpless baby,' came the ironic voice.

'And how do *you* like being a helpless baby?' he replied.

There was a long pause. Then she laughed brokenly.

'I don't know,' she said. 'A helpless baby can't know whether it likes being a helpless baby.'

'That's just the same. But I feel *hope*, don't you?'

Again there was an unwilling pause on her part.

'Hope of what?'

'If I am a helpless baby now, that I shall grow into a man.'

She gave a slight, amused laugh.

'And I ought to hope that I shall grow into a woman,' she said.

'Yes, of course.'

'Then what am I now?' she asked, humorously.

'Now, you're a helpless baby, as you said.'

It piqued her slightly. Then again, she knew it was true.

'And what was I before – when I married you?' she asked, challenging.

'Why, then – I don't know what you were. I've had my head cracked and some dark let in, since then. So I don't know what you were, because it's all gone, don't you see.'

'I see.'

There was a pause. She became aware of the room about her, of the fire burning low and red.

'And what are we doing together?' she said.

'We're going to love each other,' he said.

'Didn't we love each other before?' challenged her voice.

'No, we couldn't. We weren't born.'

'Neither were we dead,' she answered.

He seemed struck.

'Are we dead now?' he asked in fear.

'Yes, we are.'

There was a suspense of anguish, it was so true.

'Then we must be born again,' he said.

'Must we?' said her deliberate, laconic voice.

'Yes, we must – otherwise –.' He did not finish.

'And do you think we've got the power to come to life again, now we're dead?' she asked.

'I think we have,' he said.

There was a long pause.

'Resurrection?' she said, almost as if mocking. They looked slowly and darkly into each other's eyes. He rose unthinking, went over and touched her hand.

'"Touch me not, for I am not yet ascended unto the Father,"' she quoted, in her level, cold-sounding voice.

'No,' he answered; 'it takes time.'

The incongruous plainness of his statement made her jerk with laughter. At the same instant her face contracted and she said in a loud voice, as if her soul was being torn from her:

'Am I going to love you?'

Again he stretched forward and touched her hand, with the tips of his fingers. And the touch lay still, completed there.

Then at length he noticed that the thimble was stuck on his little finger. In the same instant she also looked at it.

'I want to throw it away,' he said.

Again she gave a little jerk of laughter.

He rose, went to the window, and raised the sash. Then, suddenly with a strong movement of the arm and shoulder, he threw the thimble out into the murky street. It bounded on the pavement opposite. Then a taxi-cab went by, and he could not see it any more.

The Mortal Coil

I

SHE stood motionless in the middle of the room, some-thing tense in her reckless bearing. Her gown of reddish stuff fell silkily about her feet; she looked tall and splendid in the candle-light. Her dark-blond hair was gathered loosely in a fold on top of her head, her young, blossom-fresh face was lifted. From her throat to her feet she was clothed in the elegantly-made dress of silky red stuff, the colour of red earth. She looked complete and lovely, only love could make her such a strange, complete blossom. Her cloak and hat were thrown across a table just in front of her.

Quite alone, abstracted, she stood there arrested in a conflict of emotions. Her hand, down against her skirt, worked irritably, the ball of the thumb rubbing, rubbing across the tips of the fingers. There was a slight tension between her lifted brows.

About her the room glowed softly, reflecting the candle-light from its whitewashed walls, and from the great, bowed, whitewashed ceiling. It was a large attic, with two windows, and the ceiling curving down on either side, so that both the far walls were low. Against one, on one side, was a single bed, opened for the night, the white over-bolster piled back. Not far from this was the iron stove. Near the window closest to the bed was a table with writing materials, and a handsome cactus-plant with clear scarlet blossoms threw its bizarre shadow on the wall. There was another table near the second window, and opposite was the door on which hung a military cloak. Along the far wall, were guns and fishing-tackle, and some clothes too, hung on pegs – all men's clothes, all military. It was evidently the room of a man, probably a young lieutenant.

The girl, in her pure red dress that fell about her feet, so that she looked a woman, not a girl, at last broke from her abstraction and went aimlessly to the writing-table. Her mouth was closed down stubbornly, perhaps in anger, perhaps in pain. She picked up a large seal made of agate, looked at the ingraven coat of arms, then stood rubbing her finger across the cut-out stone, time after time. At last she put the seal down, and looked at the other things – a beautiful old beer-mug used as a tobacco-jar, a silver box like an urn, old and of exquisite shape, a bowl of sealing wax. She fingered the pieces of wax. This, the dark-green, had sealed her last letter. Ah, well! She carelessly turned over the blotting book, which again had his arms stamped on the cover. Then she went away to the window. There, in the window-recess, she stood and looked out. She opened the casement and took a deep breath of the cold night air. Ah, it was good! Far below was the street, a vague golden milky way beneath her, its tiny black figures moving and crossing and recrossing with marion-ette, insect-like intentness. A small horse-car rumbled along the lines, so belittled, it was an absurdity. So much for the world! . . . he did not come.

She looked overhead. The stars were white and flashing, they looked nearer than the street, more kin to her, more real. She stood pressing her breast on her arms, her face lifted to the stars, in the long, anguished suspense of waiting. Noises came up small from the street, as from some insect-world. But the great stars overhead struck white and invincible, infallible. Her heart felt cold like the stars.

At last she started. There was a noisy knocking at the door, and a female voice calling:

'Anybody there?'

'Come in,' replied the girl.

She turned round, shrinking from this intrusion, unable to bear it, after the flashing stars.

There entered a thin, handsome dark girl dressed in an extravagantly-made gown of dark purple silk and dark blue velvet. She was followed by a small swarthy, inconspicuous lieutenant in pale-blue uniform.

'Ah *you!* ... alone?' cried Teresa, the newcomer, advancing into the room. 'Where's the Fritz, then?'

The girl in red raised her shoulders in a shrug, and turned her face aside, but did not speak.

'Not here! You don't know where he is? Ach, the dummy, the lout!' Teresa swung round on her companion.

'Where is he?' she demanded.

He also lifted his shoulders in a shrug.

'He said he was coming in half an hour,' the young lieutenant replied.

'Ha! – half an hour! Looks like it! How long is that ago – two hours?'

Again the young man only shrugged. He had beautiful black eye-lashes, and steady eyes. He stood rather deprecatingly, while his girl, golden like a young panther, hung over him.

'One knows where he is,' said Teresa, going and sitting on the opened bed. A dangerous contraction came between the brows of Marta, the girl in red, at this act.

'Wine, Women and Cards!' said Teresa, in her loud voice. 'But they prefer the women on the cards.

> ' "My love he has four Queenies,
> Four Queenies has my lo-o-ove".'

she sang. Then she broke off, and turned to Podewils. 'Was he winning when you left him, Karl?'

Again the young baron raised his shoulders.

'Tant pis que mal,' he replied, cryptically.

'Ah, *you!*' cried Teresa, 'with your *tant pis que mal!* Are *you* tant pis que mal?' She laughed her deep, strange laugh. 'Well,' she added, 'he'll be coming in with a fortune for you, Marta –'

There was a vague, unhappy silence.

'I know his fortunes,' said Marta.

'Yes,' said Teresa, in sudden sober irony, 'he's a horseshoe round your neck, is that young jockey. – But what are you going to do, Matzen dearest? You're not going to wait for him any longer? – Don't dream of it! The idea, waiting for that young gentleman as if you were married to him! – Put your hat on, dearest, and come along with us . . . Where are we going, Karl, you pillar of salt? – Eh? – Geier's? – To Geier's, Marta, my dear. Come, quick, up – you've been martyred enough, Marta, my martyr – haw! – haw!! – put your hat on. Up – away!'

Teresa sprang up like an explosion, anxious to be off.

'No, I'll wait for him,' said Marta, sullenly.

'Don't be such a fool!' cried Teresa, in her deep voice. 'Wait for him! *I'd* give him wait for him. Catch this little bird waiting.' She lifted her hand and blew a little puff across the fingers. 'Choo-fly!' she sang, as if a bird had just flown.

The young lieutenant stood silent with smiling dark eyes. Teresa was quick, and golden as a panther.

'No, but really, Marta, you're not going to wait any more – really! It's stupid for you to play Gretchen – your eyes are much to green. Put your hat on, there's a darling.'

'No,' said Marta, her flower-like face strangely stubborn. 'I'll wait for him. He'll have to come some time.'

There was a moment's uneasy pause.

'Well,' said Teresa, holding her shoulders for her cloak,

'so long as you don't wait as long as Lenora-fuhr-ums-Morgenrot –! Adieu, my dear, God be with you.'

The young lieutenant bowed a solicitous bow, and the two went out, leaving the girl in red once more alone.

She went to the writing-table, and on a sheet of paper began writing her name in stiff Gothic characters, time after time:

Marta Hohenest
Marta Hohenest
Marta Hohenest.

The vague sounds from the street below continued. The wind was cold. She rose and shut the window. Then she sat down again.

At last the door opened, and a young officer entered. He was buttoned up in a dark-blue great-coat, with large silver buttons going down on either side of the breast. He entered quickly, glancing over the room, at Marta, as she sat with her back to him. She was marking with a pencil on paper. He closed the door. Then with fine beautiful movements he divested himself of his coat and went to hang it up. How well Marta knew the sound of his movements, the quick light step! But she continued mechanically making crosses on the paper, her head bent forward between the candles, so that her hair made fine threads and mist of light, very beautiful. He saw this, and it touched him. But he could not afford to be touched any further.

'You have been waiting?' he said formally. The insulting futile question! She made no sign, as if she had not heard. He was absorbed in the tragedy of himself, and hardly heeded her.

He was a slim, good-looking youth, clear-cut and delicate in mould. His features now were pale, there was something evasive in his dilated, vibrating eyes. He was barely conscious of the girl, intoxicated with his own desperation, that held him mindless and distant.

To her, the atmosphere of the room was almost unbreathable, since he had come in. She felt terribly bound, walled up. She rose with a sudden movement that tore his nerves. She looked to him tall and bright and dangerous, as she faced round on him.

'Have you come back with a fortune?' she cried, in mockery, her eyes full of dangerous light.

He was unfastening his belt, to change his tunic. She watched him up and down, all the time. He could not answer, his lips seemed dumb. Besides, silence was his strength.

'Have you come back with a fortune?' she repeated, in her strong, clear voice of mockery.

'No,' he said, suddenly turning. 'Let it please you that – that I've come back at all.'

He spoke desperately, and tailed off into silence. He was a man doomed. She looked at him: he was insignificant in his doom. She turned in ridicule. And yet she was afraid; she loved him.

He had stood long enough exposed, in his helplessness. With difficulty he took a few steps, went and sat down at the writing-table. He looked to her like a dog with its tail between its legs.

He saw the paper, where her name was repeatedly written. She must find great satisfaction in her own name, he thought vaguely. Then he picked up the seal and kept twisting it round in his fingers, doing some little trick. And continually the seal fell on to the table with a sudden rattle that made Marta stiffen cruelly. He was quite oblivious of her.

She stood watching as he sat bent forward in his stupefaction. The fine cloth of his uniform showed the moulding of his back. And something tortured her as she saw him, till she could hardly bear it: the desire of his finely-shaped body, the stupefaction and the abjectness of him now, his immersion in the tragedy of himself, his being unaware of her. All her will seemed to grip him, to bruise some manly nonchalance and attention out of him.

'I suppose you're in a fury with me, for being late?' he said, with impotent irony in his voice. Her fury over trifles, when he was lost in calamity! How great was his real misery, how trivial her small offendedness!

Something in his tone burned her, and made her soul go cold.

'I'm not exactly pleased,' she said coldly, turning away to a window.

Still he sat bent over the table, twisting something with his fingers. She glanced round on him. How nervy he was! He had beautiful hands, and the big topaz signet-ring on his finger made yellow lights. Ah, if only his hands were really dare-devil and reckless! They always seemed so guilty, so cowardly.

'I'm done for now,' he said suddenly, as if to himself, tilting back his chair a little. In all his physical movement he was so fine and poised, so sensitive! Oh, and it attracted her so much!

'Why?' she said, carelessly.

An anger burned in him. She was so flippant. If he were going to be shot, she would not be moved more than about half a pound of sweets.

'Why?' he repeated laconically. 'The same unimportant reason as ever.'

'Debts?' she cried, in contempt.

'Exactly.'

Her soul burned in anger.

'What have you done now? – lost more money?'

'Three thousand marks.'

She was silent in deep wrath.

'More fool you!' she said. Then, in her anger, she was silent for some minutes. 'And so you're done for, for three thousand marks?' she exclaimed, jeering at him. 'You go pretty cheap.'

'Three thousand – and the rest,' he said, keeping up a manly *sang froid*.

'And the rest!' she repeated in contempt. 'And for three thousand – and the rest, your life is over!'

'My career,' he corrected her.

'Oh,' she mocked, 'only your career! I thought it was a matter of life and death. Only your career? Oh, only that!'

His eyes grew furious under her mockery.

'My career *is* my life,' he said.

'Oh, is it! – You're not a *man* then, you are only a career?'

'I am a gentleman.'

'Oh, are you! How amusing! How very amusing, to be a gentleman and not a man! – I suppose that's what it means, to be a gentleman, to have no guts outside your career?'

'Outside my honour – none.'

'And might I ask what *is* your honour?' She spoke in extreme irony.

'Yes, you may ask,' he replied coolly. 'But if you don't know without being told, I'm afraid I could never explain it.'

'Oh, you couldn't! No, I believe you – you are incapable of explaining it, it wouldn't bear explaining.' There was a long, tense pause. 'So you've made too many debts, and you're afraid they'll kick you out of the army, therefore your honour is gone, is it? – And what then – what after that?'

She spoke in extreme irony. He winced again at her phrase 'kick you out of the army'. But he tilted his chair back with assumed nonchalance.

'I've made too many debts, and I *know* they'll kick me out of the army,' he repeated, thrusting the thorn right home to the quick. 'After that – I can shoot myself. Or I might even be a waiter in a restaurant – or possibly a clerk, with twenty-five shillings a week.'

'Really! – All those alternatives! – Well, why not, why not be a waiter in the Germania? It might be awfully jolly.'

'Why not?' he repeated ironically. 'Because it wouldn't become me.'

She looked at him, at his aristocratic fineness of physique, his extreme physical sensitiveness. And all her German worship for his old, proud family rose up in her. No, he could not be a waiter in the Germania: she could not bear it. He was too refined and beautiful a thing.

'Ha!' she cried suddenly. 'It wouldn't come to that, either. If they kick you out of the army, you'll find somebody to get round – you're like a cat, you'll land on your feet.'

But this was just what he was not. He was not like a cat. His self-mistrust was too deep. Ultimately he had no belief in himself, as a separate isolated being. He knew he was sufficiently clever, an aristocrat, good-looking, the sensitive superior of most men. The trouble was, that apart from the social fabric he belonged to, he felt himself nothing, a cipher. He bitterly envied the common working-men for a certain manly aplomb, a grounded, almost stupid self-confidence he saw in them. Himself – he could lead such men through the gates of hell – for what did he care about danger or hurt to himself, while he was leading? But – cut him off from all this, and what was he? A palpitating rag of meaningless human life.

But she, coming from the people, could not fully understand. And it was best to leave her in the dark. The free indomitable self-sufficient being which a man must be in his relation to a woman who loves him – this he could pretend. But he knew he was not it. He knew that the world of man from which he took his value was his mistress beyond any woman. He wished, secretly, cravingly, almost cravenly, in his heart, it was not so. But so it was.

Therefore, he heard her phrase 'you're like a cat,' with some bitter envy.

'Whom shall I get round? – some woman, who will marry me?' he said.

This was a way out. And it was almost the inevitable thing, for him. But he felt it the last ruin of his manhood, even he.

The speech hurt her mortally, worse than death. She would rather he died, because then her own love would not turn to ash.

'Get married, then, if you want to,' she said, in a small broken voice.

'Naturally,' he said.

There was a long silence, a foretaste of barren hopelessness.

'Why is it so terrible to you,' she asked at length, 'to come out of the army and trust to your own resources? Other men are strong enough.'

'Other men are not me,' he said.

Why would she torture him? She seemed to enjoy torturing him. The thought of his expulsion from the army was an agony to him, really worse than death. He saw himself in the despicable civilian clothes, engaged in some menial occupation. And he could not bear it. It was too heavy a cross.

Who was she to talk? She was herself, an actress, daughter of a tradesman. He was himself. How should one of them speak for the other? It was impossible. He loved her. He loved her far better than men usually loved their mistresses. He really cared. – And he was strangely proud of his love for her, as if it were a distinction to him . . . But there was a limit to her understanding. There was a point beyond which she had nothing to do with him, and she had better leave him alone. Here in this crisis, which was *his* crisis, his downfall, she should not presume to talk, because she did not understand. – But she loved to torture him, that was the truth.

'Why should it hurt you to work?' she reiterated.

He lifted his face, white and tortured, his grey eyes flaring with fear and hate.

'Work!' he cried. 'What do you think I am worth? – Twenty-five shillings a week, if I am lucky.'

His evident anguish penetrated her. She sat dumb-founded, looking at him with wide eyes. He was white with misery and fear; his hand, that lay loose on the table, was abandoned in nervous ignominy. Her mind filled with wonder, and with deep, cold dread. Did he really care so much? But did it *really* matter so much to him? When he said he was worth twenty-five shillings a week, he was like a man whose soul is pierced. He sat there, annihilated. She looked for him, and he was nothing then. She looked for the man, the free being that loved her. And he was not, he was gone, this blank figure remained. Something with a blanched face sat there in the chair, staring at nothing.

His amazement deepened with intolerable dread. It was as if the world had fallen away into chaos. Nothing remained. She seemed to grasp the air for foothold.

He sat staring in front of him, a dull numbness settled on his brain. He was watching the flame of the candle. And, in his detachment, he realized the flame was a swiftly travelling flood, flowing swiftly from the source of the wick through a white surge and on into the darkness above. It was like a fountain suddenly foaming out, then running on dark and smooth. Could one dam the flood? He took a piece of paper, and cut off the flame for a second.

The girl in red started at the pulse of the light. She seemed to come to, from some trance. She saw his face, clear now, attentive, abstract, absolved. He was quite absolved from his temporal self.

'It isn't true,' she said, 'is it? It's not so tragic, really? – It's only your pride is hurt, your silly little pride?' She was rather pleading.

He looked at her with clear steady eyes.

'My pride!' he said. 'And isn't my pride *me?* What am I without my pride?'

'You are *yourself*,' she said. 'If they take your uniform off you, and turn you naked into the street, you are still *yourself*.'

His eyes grew hot. Then he cried:

'What does it mean, *myself!* It means I put on ready-made civilian clothes and do some dirty drudging else-where: that is what *myself* amounts to.'

She knitted her brows.

'But what you are *to me* – that naked self which you are to me – that is something, isn't it? – everything,' she said.

'What is it, if it means nothing?' he said: 'What is it, more than a pound of chocolate *dragées?* – It stands for nothing – unless as you say, a petty clerkship, at twenty-five shillings a week.'

These were all wounds to her, very deep. She looked in wonder for a few moments.

'And what does it stand for now?' she said. 'A magnifi-cent second-lieutenant!'

He made a gesture of dismissal with his hand.

She looked at him from under lowered brows.

'And our love!' she said. 'It means nothing to you, nothing at all?'

'To me as a menial clerk, what does it mean? What does love mean! Does it mean that a man shall be no more than a dirty rag in the world? – What worth do you think I have in love, if in life I am a wretched inky subordinate clerk?'

'What does it matter?'

'It matters everything.'

There was silence for a time, then the anger flashed up in her.

'It doesn't matter to you what *I* feel, whether *I* care or not,' she cried, her voice rising. 'They'll take his little uniform with buttons off him, and he'll have to be a common little civilian, so all he can do is to shoot himself! – It doesn't matter that I'm there –'

He sat stubborn and silent. He thought her vulgar. And her raving did not alter the situation in the least.

'Don't you see what value you put on *me*, you clever little man?' she cried in fury. 'I've loved you, loved you with all my soul, for two years – and you've lied, and said you loved me. And now, what do I get? He'll shoot himself, because his tuppenny vanity is wounded. – Ah, *fool* –!'

He lifted his head and looked at her. His face was fixed and superior.

'All of which,' he said, 'leaves the facts of the case quite untouched!'

She hated his cool little speeches.

'Then shoot yourself,' she cried, 'and you'll be worth *less* than twenty-five shillings a week!'

There was a fatal silence.

'*Then* there'll be no question of worth,' he said.

'Ha!' she ejaculated in scorn.

She had finished. She had no more to say. At length, after they had both sat motionless and silent, separate, for some time, she rose and went across to her hat and cloak.

He shrank in apprehension. Now, he could not bear her to go. He shrank as if he were being whipped. She put her hat on, roughly, then swung her warm plaid cloak over her shoulders. Her hat was of black glossy silk, with a sheeny heap of cocksfeathers, her plaid cloak was dark green and blue, it swing open above her clear harsh-red dress. How beautiful she was, like a fiery Madonna!

'Good-bye,' she said, in her voice of mockery. 'I'm going now.'

He sat motionless, as if loaded with fetters. She hesitated, then moved towards the door.

Suddenly, with a spring like a cat, he was confronting her, his back to the door. His eyes were full and dilated, like a cat's, his face seemed to gleam at her. She quivered, as some subtle fluid ran through her nerves.

'Let me go,' she said dumbly. 'I've had enough.' His eyes, with a wide, dark electric pupil, like a cat's, only watched her objectively. And again a wave of female submissiveness went over her.

'I want to go,' she pleaded. 'You know it's no good. – You know this is no good.'

She stood humbly before him. A flexible little grin quivered round his mouth.

'You know you don't want me,' she persisted. 'You know you don't really want me. – You only do this to show your power over me – which is a mean trick.'

But he did not answer, only his eyes narrowed in a sensual, cruel smile. She shrank, afraid, and yet she was fascinated.

'You won't go yet,' he said.

She tried in vain to rouse her real opposition.

'I shall call out,' she threatened. 'I shall shame you before people.'

His eyes narrowed again in the smile of vindictive, mocking indifference.

'Call then,' he said.

And at the sound of his still, cat-like voice, an intoxication ran over her veins.

'I *will*,' she said, looking defiantly into his eyes. But the smile in the dark, full, dilated pupils made her waver into submission again.

'Won't you let me go?' she pleaded sullenly.

Now the smile went openly over his face.

'Take your hat off,' he said.

And with quick, light fingers he reached up and drew out the pins of her hat, unfastened the clasp of her cloak, and laid her things aside.

She sat down in a chair. Then she rose again, and went to the window. In the street below, the tiny figures were moving just the same. She opened the window, and leaned out, and wept.

He looked round at her in irritation as she stood in her long, clear-red dress in the window-recess, leaning out. She was exasperating.

'You will be cold,' he said.

She paid no heed. He guessed, by some tension in her attitude, that she was crying. It irritated him exceedingly, like a madness. After a few minutes of suspense, he went across to her, and took her by the arm. His hand was subtle, soft in its touch, and yet rather cruel than gentle.

'Come away,' he said. 'Don't stand there in the air -- come away.'

He drew her slowly away to the bed, she sat down, and he beside her.

'What are you crying for?' he said in his strange, penetrating voice, that had a vibration of exultancy in it. But her tears only ran faster.

He kissed her face, that was soft, and fresh, and yet warm, wet with tears. He kissed her again, and again, in pleasure of the soft, wet saltness of her. She turned aside and wiped her face with her handkerchief, and blew her nose. He was disappointed – yet the way she blew her nose pleased him.

Suddenly she slid away to the floor, and hid her face in the side of the bed, weeping and crying loudly:

'You don't love me – Oh, you don't love me – I thought you did, and you let me go on thinking it – but you don't, no, you don't, and I can't bear it. – Oh, I can't bear it.'

He sat and listened to the strange, animal sound of her crying. His eyes flickered with exultancy, his body seemed full and surcharged with power. But his brows were knitted in tension. He laid his hand softly on her head, softly touched her face, which was buried against the bed.

She suddenly rubbed her face against the sheets, and looked up once more.

'You've deceived me,' she said, as she sat beside him.

'Have I? Then I've deceived myself.' His body felt so charged with male vigour, he was almost laughing in his strength.

'Yes,' she said enigmatically, fatally. She seemed absorbed in her thoughts. Then her face quivered again.

'And I loved you so much,' she faltered, the tears rising. There was a clangor of delight in his heart.

'I love *you*.' he said softly, softly touching her, softly kissing her, in a sort of subtle, restrained ecstasy.

She shook her head stubbornly. She tried to draw away. Then she did break away, and turned to look at him, in fear and doubt. The little, fascinating, fiendish lights were hovering in his eyes like laughter.

'Don't hurt me so much,' she faltered, in a last protest.

A faint smile came on his face. He took her face between his hands and covered it with soft, blinding kisses, like a soft, narcotic rain. He felt himself such an unbreakable fountain-head of powerful blood. He was trembling finely in all his limbs, with mastery.

When she lifted her face and opened her eyes, her face was wet, and her greenish-golden eyes were shining, it was like sudden sunshine in wet foliage. She smiled at him like a child of knowledge, through the tears, and softly, infinitely softly he dried her tears with his mouth and his soft young moustache.

'You'd never shoot yourself, because you're mine, aren't you!' she said, knowing the fine quivering of his body, in mastery.

'Yes,' he said.

'Quite mine?' she said, her voice rising in ecstasy.

'Yes.'

'Nobody else but mine – nothing at all –?'

'Nothing at all,' he re-echoed.

'But me?' came her last words of ecstasy.

'Yes.'

And she seemed to be released free into the infinite of ecstasy.

2

They slept in fulfilment through the long night. But then strange dreams began to fill them both, strange dreams that were neither waking nor sleeping; – only, in curious weariness, through her dreams, she heard at last a continual low rapping. She awoke with difficulty. The rapping began again – she started violently. It was at the door – it would be the orderly rapping for Friedeburg. Everything seemed wild and unearthly. She put her hand on the shoulder of the sleeping man, and pulled him roughly, waited a moment, then pushed him, almost violently, to awake him. He woke with a sense of resentment at her violent handling. Then he heard the knocking of the orderly. He gathered his senses.

'Yes, Heinrich!' he said.

Strange, the sound of a voice! It seemed a far-off tearing sound. Then came the muffled voice of the servant.

'Half past four, Sir.'

'Right!' said Friedeburg, and automatically he got up and made a light. She was suddenly as wide awake as if it were daylight. But it was a strange, false day, like a delirium. She saw him put down the match, she saw him moving about, rapidly dressing. And the movement in the room was a trouble to her. He himself was vague and unreal, a thing seen but not comprehended. She watched all the acts of his toilet, saw all the motions, but never saw him. There was only a disturbance about her, which fretted her, she was not aware of any presence. Her mind, in its strange, hectic clarity, wanted to consider things in absolute detachment. For instance, she wanted to consider the cactus plant. It was a curious object with pure scarlet blossoms. Now, how did these scarlet blossoms come to pass, upon that earthly-looking unliving creature? Scarlet blossoms! How wonderful they were! What were they, then, how could one lay hold on their being? Her mind turned to him. Him, too, how could one lay hold on him, to have him? Where was he, what was he? She seemed to grasp at the air.

He was dipping his face in the cold water – the slight shock was good for him. He felt as if someone had stolen away his being in the night, he was moving about a light, quick shell, with all his meaning absent. His body was quick and active, but all his deep understanding, his soul was gone. He tried to rub it back into his face. He was quite dim, as if his spirit had left his body.

'Come and kiss me,' sounded the voice from the bed. He went over to her automatically. She put her arms round him, and looked into his face with her clear brilliant, grey-green eyes, as if she too were looking for his soul.

'How are you?' came her meaningless words.

'All right.'

'Kiss me.'

He bent down and kissed her.

And still her clear, rather frightening eyes seemed to be searching for him inside himself. He was like a bird transfixed by her pellucid, grey-green, wonderful eyes. She put her hands into his soft, thick, fine hair, and gripped her hands full of his hair. He wondered with fear at her sudden painful clutching.

'I shall be late,' he said.

'Yes,' she answered. And she let him go.

As he fastened his tunic he glanced out of the window. It was still night: a night that must have lasted since eternity. There was a moon in the sky. In the streets below the yellow street-lamps burned small at intervals. This was the night of eternity.

There came a knock at the door, and the orderly's voice.

'Coffee, Sir.'

'Leave it there.'

They heard the faint jingle of the tray as it was set down outside.

Friedeburg sat down to put on his boots. Then, with a man's solid tread, he went and took in the tray. He felt properly heavy and secure now in his accoutrement. But he was always aware of her two wonderful, clear, unfolded eyes, looking on his heart, out of her uncanny silence.

There was a strong smell of coffee in the room.

'Have some coffee?' His eyes could not meet hers.

'No, thank you.'

'Just a drop?'

'No, thank you.'

Her voice sounded quite gay. She watched him dipping his bread in the coffee and eating quickly, absently. He did not know what he was doing, and yet the dipped bread and hot coffee gave him pleasure. He gulped down the remainder of his drink, and rose to his feet.

'I must go,' he said.

There was a curious, poignant smile in her eyes. Her eyes drew him to her. How beautiful she was, and dazzling, and frightening, with this look of brilliant tenderness seeming to glitter from her face. She drew his head down to her bosom, and held it fast prisoner there, murmuring with tender, triumphant delight: 'Dear! Dear!'

At last she let him lift his head, and he looked into her eyes, that seemed to concentrate in a dancing, golden point of vision in which he felt himself perish.

'Dear!' she murmured. 'You love me, don't you?'

'Yes,' he said mechanically.

The golden point of vision seemed to leap to him from her eyes, demanding something. He sat slackly, as if spell-bound. Her hand pushed him a little.

'Mustn't you go?' she said.

He rose. She watched him fastening the belt round his body, that seemed soft under the fine clothes. He pulled on his great-coat, and put on his peaked cap. He was again a young officer.

But he had forgotten his watch. It lay on the table near the bed. She watched him slinging it on his chain. He looked down at her. How beautiful she was, with her luminous face and her fine, stray hair! But he felt far away.

'Anything I can do for you?' he asked.

'No, thank you – I'll sleep,' she replied, smiling. And the strange golden spark danced on her eyes again, again he felt as if his heart were gone, destroyed out of him. There was a fine pathos too in her vivid, dangerous face.

He kissed her for the last time, saying:

'I'll blow the candles out, then?'

'Yes, my love – and I'll sleep.'

'Yes – sleep as long as you like.'

The golden spark of her eyes seemed to dance on him like a destruction, she was beautiful, and pathetic. He touched her tenderly with his finger-tips, then suddenly blew out the candles, and walked across in the faint moonlight to the door.

He was gone. She heard his boots click on the stone stairs – she heard the far below tread of his feet on the pavement. Then he was gone. She lay quite still, in a swoon of deathly peace. She never wanted to move any more. It was finished. She lay quite still, utterly, utterly abandoned.

But again she was disturbed. There was a little tap at the door, then Teresa's voice saying, with a shuddering sound because of the cold:

'Ugh! – I'm coming to you, Marta my dear. I can't stand being left alone.'

'I'll make a light,' said Marta, sitting up and reaching for the candle. 'Lock the door, will you, Resie, and then nobody can bother us.'

She saw Teresa, loosely wrapped in her cloak, two thick ropes of hair hanging untidily. Teresa looked voluptuously sleepy and easy, like a cat running home to the warmth.

'Ugh!' she said, 'it's cold!'

And she ran to the stove. Marta heard the chink of the little shovel, a stirring of coals, then a clink of the iron door. Then Teresa came running to the bed, with a shuddering little run, she puffed out the light and slid in beside her friend.

'So cold!' she said, with a delicious shudder at the warmth. Marta made place for her, and they settled down.

'Aren't you glad you're not them?' said Resie, with a little shudder at the thought. 'Ugh! – poor devils!'

'I am,' said Marta.

'Ah, sleep – sleep, how lovely!' said Teresa, with deep content. 'Ah, it's so good!'

'Yes,' said Marta.

'Good morning, good night, my dear,' said Teresa, already sleepily.

'Good night,' responded Marta.

Her mind flickered a little. Then she sank unconsciously to sleep. The room was silent.

Outside, the setting moon made peaked shadows of the high-roofed houses; from twin towers that stood like two dark, companion giants in the sky, the hour trembled out over the sleeping town. But the footsteps of hastening officers and cowering soldiers rang on the frozen pavements. Then a lantern appeared in the distance, accompanied by the rattle of a bullock wagon. By the light of the lantern on the wagon-pole could be seen the delicately moving feet and the pale, swinging dewlaps of the oxen. They drew slowly on, with a rattle of heavy wheels, the banded heads of the slow beasts swung rhythmically.

Ah, this was life! How sweet, sweet each tiny incident was! How sweet to Friedeburg, to give his orders ringingly on the frosty air, to see his men like bears shambling and shuffling into their places, with little dancing movements of uncouth playfulness and resentment, because of the pure cold.

Sweet, sweet it was to be marching beside his men, sweet to hear the great thresh-thresh of their heavy boots in the unblemished silence, sweet to feel the immense mass of living bodies co-ordinated into oneness near him, to catch the hot waft of their closeness, their breathing. Friedeburg was like a man condemned to die, catching at every impression as at an inestimable treasure.

Sweet it was to pass through the gates of the town, the scanty, loose suburb, into the open darkness and space of the country. This was almost best of all. It was like emerging in the open plains of eternal freedom.

They saw a dark figure hobbling along under the dark side of a shed. As they passed, through the open door of the shed, in the golden light were seen the low rafters, the pale, silken sides of the cows, evanescent. And a woman with a red kerchief bound round her head lifted her face from the flank of the beast she was milking, to look at the soldiers threshing like multitudes of heavy ghosts down the darkness. Some of the men called to her, cheerfully, impudently. Ah, the miraculous beauty and sweetness of the merest trifles like these!

They tramped on down a frozen, rutty road, under lines of bare trees. Beautiful trees! Beautiful frozen ruts in the road! Ah, even, in one of the ruts there was a silver of ice and of moon-glimpse. He heard ice tinkle as a passing soldier purposely put his toe in it. What a sweet noise!

But there was a vague uneasiness. He heard the men arguing as to whether dawn were coming. There was the silver moon, still riding on the high seas of the sky. A lovely thing she was, a jewel! But was there any blemish of day? He shrank a little from the rawness of the day to come. This night of morning was so rare and free.

Yes, he was sure. He saw a colourless paleness on the horizon. The earth began to look hard, like a great, concrete shadow. He shrank into himself. Glancing at the ranks of his men, he could see them like a company of rhythmic ghosts. The pallor was actually reflected on their livid faces. This was the coming day! It frightened him.

The dawn came. He saw the rosiness of it hang trembling with light, above the east. Then a strange glamour of scarlet passed over the land. At his feet, glints of ice flashed scarlet, even the hands of the men were red as they swung, sinister, heavy, reddened.

The sun surged up, her rim appeared, swimming with

fire, hesitating, surging up. Suddenly there were shadows from trees and ruts, and grass was hoar and ice was gold against the ebony shadow. The faces of the men were alight, kindled with life. Ah, it was magical, it was all too marvellous! If only it were always like this!

When they stopped at the inn for breakfast, at nine o'clock, the smell of the inn went raw and ugly to his heart: beer and yesterday's tobacco!

He went to the door to look at the men biting huge bites from their hunks of grey bread, or cutting off pieces with their clasp-knives. This made him still happy. Women were going to the fountain for water, the soldiers were chaffing them coarsely. He liked all this.

But the magic was going, inevitably, the crystal delight was thawing to desolation in his heart, his heart was cold, cold mud. Ah, it was awful. His face contracted, he almost wept with cold, stark despair.

Still he had the work, the day's hard activity with the men. While this lasted, he could live. But when this was over, and he had to face the horror of his own cold-thawing mud of despair: ah, it was not to be thought of. Still, he was happy at work with the men: the wild desolate place, the hard activity of mock warfare. Would to God it were real: war, with the prize of death!

By afternoon the sky had gone one dead, livid level of grey. It seemed low down, and oppressive. He was tired, the men were tired, and this let the heavy cold soak in to them like despair. Life could not keep it out.

And now, when his heart was so heavy it could sink no more, he must glance at his own situation again. He must remember what a fool he was, his new debts like half thawed mud in his heart. He knew, with the cold misery of hopelessness, that he would be turned out of the army. What then? – what then but death? After all, death was the solution for him. Let it be so.

They marched on and on, stumbling with fatigue under a great leaden sky, over a frozen dead country. The men were silent with weariness, the heavy motion of their marching was like an oppression. Friedeburg was tired too, and deadened, as his face was deadened by the cold air. He did not think any more; the misery of his soul was like a frost inside him.

He heard someone say it was going to snow. But the words had no meaning for him. He marched as a clock ticks, with the same monotony, everything numb and cold-soddened.

They were drawing near to the town. In the gloom of the afternoon he felt it ahead, as unbearable oppression on him. Ah the hideous suburb! What was his life, how did it come to pass that life was lived in a formless, hideous grey structure of hell! What did it all mean? Pale, sulphur-yellow lights spotted the livid air, and people, like soddened shadows, passed in front of the shops that were lit up ghastly in the early twilight. Out of the colourless space, crumbs of snow came and bounced animatedly off the breast of his coat.

At length he turned away home, to his room, to change and get warm and renewed, for he felt as cold-soddened as the grey, cold, heavy bread which felt hostile in the mouths of the soldiers. His life was to him like this dead, cold bread in his mouth.

As he neared his own house, the snow was peppering thinly down. He became aware of some unusual stir about the house-door. He looked – a strange, closed-in wagon, people, police. The sword of Damocles that had hung over his heart, fell. O God, a new shame, some new shame, some new torture! His body moved on. So it would move on through misery upon misery, as is our fate. There was no emergence, only this progress through misery unto misery, till the end. Strange, that human life was so tenacious! Strange, that men had made of life a long slow process of torture to the soul. Strange, that it was no other than this! Strange, that but for man, this misery would not exist. For it was not God's misery, but the misery of the world of man.

He saw two officials push something white and heavy into the cart, shut the doors behind with a bang, turn the silver handle, and run round to the front of the wagon. It moved off. But still most of the people lingered. Friedeburg drifted near in that inevitable motion which carries us through all our shame and torture. He knew the people talked about him. He went up the steps and into the square hall.

There stood a police-officer, with a note-book in his hand, talking to Herr Kapell, the housemaster. As Friedeburg entered through the swing door, the housemaster, whose brow was wrinkled in anxiety and perturbation, made a gesture with his hand, as if to point out a criminal.

'Ah! – the Herr Baron von Friedeburg!' he said, in self-exculpation.

The police officer turned, saluted politely, and said, with the polite, intolerable *suffisance* of officialdom:

'Good evening! Trouble here!'

'Yes?' said Friedeburg.

He was so frightened, his sensitive constitution was so lacerated, that something broke in him, he was a subservient, murmuring ruin.

'Two young ladies found dead in your room,' said the police-official, making an official statement. But under his cold impartiality of officialdom, what obscene unction! Ah, what obscene exposures now!

'Dead!' ejaculated Friedeburg, with the wide eyes of a child. He became quite child-like, the official had him completely in his power. He could torture him as much as he liked.

'Yes.' He referred to his note-book. 'Asphyxiated by fumes from the stove.'

Friedeburg could only stand wide-eyed and meaningless.

'Please – will you go upstairs?'

The police-official marshalled Friedeburg in front of himself. The youth slowly mounted the stairs, feeling as if transfixed through the base of the spine, as if he would lose the use of his legs. The official followed close on his heels.

They reached the bedroom. The policeman unlocked the door. The housekeeper followed with a lamp. Then the official examination began.

'A young lady slept here last night?'

'Yes.'

'Name, please?'

'Marta Hohenest.'

'H-o-h-e-n-e-s-t,' spelled the official. '– And address?'

Friedeburg continued to answer. This was the end of him. The quick of him was pierced and killed. The living dead answered the living dead in obscene antiphony. Question and answer continued, the note-book worked as the hand of the old dead wrote in it the replies of the young who was dead.

The room was unchanged from the night before. There was her heap of clothing, the lustrous, pure-red dress lying soft where she had carelessly dropped it. Even, on the edge of the chair-back, her crimson silk garters hung looped.

But do not look, do not see. It is the business of the dead to bury their dead. Let the young dead bury their own dead, as the old dead have buried theirs. How can the dead remember, they being dead? Only the living can remember, and are at peace with their living who have passed away.

FOR THE BEST IN PAPERBACKS, LOOK FOR THE 🐧

In every corner of the world, on every subject under the sun, Penguin represents quality and variety – the very best in publishing today.

For complete information about books available from Penguin – including Puffins, Penguin Classics and Arkana – and how to order them, write to us at the appropriate address below. Please note that for copyright reasons the selection of books varies from country to country.

In the United Kingdom: Please write to *Dept E.P., Penguin Books Ltd, Harmondsworth, Middlesex, UB7 0DA.*

If you have any difficulty in obtaining a title, please send your order with the correct money, plus ten per cent for postage and packaging, to *PO Box No 11, West Drayton, Middlesex*

In the United States: Please write to *Dept BA, Penguin, 299 Murray Hill Parkway, East Rutherford, New Jersey 07073*

In Canada: Please write to *Penguin Books Canada Ltd, 2801 John Street, Markham, Ontario L3R 1B4*

In Australia: Please write to the *Marketing Department, Penguin Books Australia Ltd, P.O. Box 257, Ringwood, Victoria 3134*

In New Zealand: Please write to the *Marketing Department, Penguin Books (NZ) Ltd, Private Bag, Takapuna, Auckland 9*

In India: Please write to *Penguin Overseas Ltd, 706 Eros Apartments, 56 Nehru Place, New Delhi, 110019*

In the Netherlands: Please write to *Penguin Books Netherlands B.V., Postbus 195, NL–1380AD Weesp*

In West Germany: Please write to *Penguin Books Ltd, Friedrichstrasse 10–12, D–6000 Frankfurt/Main 1*

In Spain: Please write to *Alhambra Longman S.A., Fernandez de la Hoz 9, E–28010 Madrid*

In Italy: Please write to *Penguin Italia s.r.l., Via Como 4, I-20096 Pioltello (Milano)*

In France: Please write to *Penguin Books Ltd, 39 Rue de Montmorency, F-75003 Paris*

In Japan: Please write to *Longman Penguin Japan Co Ltd, Yamaguchi Building, 2–12–9 Kanda Jimbocho, Chiyoda-Ku, Tokyo 101*